THE FAIRHAVEN
CHRONICLES
BOOK 1

A FRESH START IN
FAIRHAVEN

D0067143

THE FAIRHAVEN
CHRONICLES

BOOK 1

A FRESH START IN
FAIRHAVEN

SHARON DOWNING JARVIS

DESERET
BOOK

Library of Congress Cataloging-in-Publication Data

Jarvis, Sharon Downing, 1940-
   A fresh start in Fairhaven / Sharon Downing Jarvis.
      p.   cm. — (The Fairhaven chronicles)
   ISBN 1-57008-937-X (pbk.)
   1. Mormons—Fiction. 2. Bishops—Fiction. 3. Southern States—Fiction.
I. Title.
   PS3560.A64 F74 2003
   813'.54—dc21
                                     2002153747

Printed in the United States of America   54459-7063
Malloy Lithographing Incorporated, Ann Arbor, MI

10 9 8 7 6 5 4 3 2

Special thanks to Emily Watts,
Richard Peterson, and Dr. Bonnie Lyon

For my husband, Wayne, in appreciation for his love, advice, and encouragement—and in honor of all good bishops, everywhere

CHAPTER ONE

Y

" . . . THY SHEEP TO BLESS, THY LAMBS TO FEED"

It wasn't much of a hill, but weighed down as he was with the concerns of the day, James Shepherd, newly called but not-yet-sustained bishop of the Fairhaven Alabama Ward, felt he might as well have been carrying a week's supply of food and camping gear up Cheaha Mountain. He dropped to the grass, knowing and not caring that the heavy dew would soak the seat of his jeans, crossed his arms on his bent knees, and bowed his head against them. It was a relief to be alone for a little while; privacy was a rare commodity these days, and he suspected it was about to become even more rare and valuable.

Eyes closed, he found himself listening to the sounds of the April morning coming awake around him—grasses being lifted by a light breeze, songbirds and the squawk of a jay from a wooded area behind him, and from over the hill, the impatient voices of his cousin's milk cows lowing for relief. The ground he sat on had been his grandfather's and now belonged to his aunt's two sons, Rodney and Spurling Deal, though the farm still bore the name of Shepherd's Pass, in honor of his great-great-grandfather,

Micajah Shepherd, who had purchased and farmed it in the mid-1800s. Shepherd's Pass had always been a favorite retreat for this descendant, who, though he legally owned no part in it, still held title in his heart to its peace and solitude and green sweep of meadow in the foothills of the lower Appalachians as they stretched down from Tennessee and Georgia.

Bishop-to-be Jim Shepherd raised his eyes to the sky, pale green now in the early dawn, with a faint pink cast to a lone shred of cloud showing toward the north. The vista, the peace, and the freshness of the air relaxed him to the point that he wished he could stretch out and nap for an hour. There had been little enough sleep the last few nights.

"This probably isn't an important question, or even a needful one to have answered, Father," he prayed softly, "but why me? It's not that I mean to doubt President Walker's inspiration. He's a faithful man—always seems to be in tune with the Spirit. And I do confess I've had inklings lately that there was some change coming in my life, something I should prepare for, though being called as bishop never entered my mind. I'd have thought of Brother Warshaw for that—he has such a good knowledge of the scriptures—or Brother Tetton. With that degree in social psychology, seems like he'd have a good understanding of people and their needs and their motivations. But, Lord, I'm just a grocer! Thou knowest I'm willing, and I promise thee I'll do my best, but am I bishop material? I feel so inadequate, Heavenly Father!" He rubbed his forehead, which throbbed with the dull ache of sleeplessness.

"It's not that I mean to counsel thee," he added. "I'm just trying to understand what I have to offer. But I'll trust thee—and President Walker—until it's wisdom in thee for me to know more. Please, please help me, Father, to learn my duties quickly and to be responsive to the needs of the people. I know I'll need thee to be with me every minute, every hour. Please bless the ward members to accept me, and bless my wife and children to be strong and sustained through this because I realize this calling affects them deeply, too. I thank thee for the trust that has been placed in me. Now, please help me to get to my first meeting on time!"

He closed his prayer and stood up, blowing his nose and stuffing the handkerchief back into the pocket of his damp jeans as he headed toward his truck.

Y

"Jim, where've you been?" Trish Shepherd asked sleepily, leaning up on one elbow in their rumpled bed. "I got up an hour ago, and you were gone."

Her husband shucked off his jeans and sat down on the edge of the bed to remove his socks. "Oh, just felt like I needed to go for a little drive, clear my head this morning."

She reached over and rubbed his back. "You're worried, aren't you, hon?"

He drew a deep breath. "Why me, Trish? Why would the Lord want me?"

"Why not you? You're a faithful priesthood holder, a good family man. You know a lot of people, and everybody seems to like you. So why not you?"

He rubbed a hand over the graying blond stubble of his close-cropped hair. "Because I don't feel prepared. I mean, why not Brother Tetton, or Brother Warshaw, or even Dan McMillan? Somebody with some credentials, or experience, or whatever? I've never even served in a bishopric."

Trish smiled lazily. "I don't think the Lord requires references with his job applications, or credentials, or letters after your name. Maybe not even experience."

He grinned wryly. "Yeah, but I didn't even apply!"

"I don't know about that—you might have."

"What do you mean?"

"I mean, maybe in the premortal life, you agreed to this calling."

He stopped unbuttoning his shirt and looked at her. "Hadn't thought of that. You really think so?"

She shrugged, her cheeks still rosy from sleep. "Well, I don't know, of course, but I wouldn't be surprised. So maybe you're more prepared than you think you are."

He shook his head. "I surely hope so. How about you? Are you all geared up and excited to be the bishop's wife?"

Her nose wrinkled, and she gave a little flip of her head to clear a dark strand of hair from her eyes. He thought she looked about sixteen. Way too young to be the bishop's wife.

"I don't think *excited* is exactly the right word, though it's probably part of it. I'm also pleased, and honored, and scared, and kind of dreading not having you around as much as I'd like. But mostly just determined to be as supportive as I can."

"Well, you heard what President Walker said—they don't even consider a man to be bishop unless his wife is willing and able to support him, spiritually and emotionally. I sure couldn't do this without you, Trish—that's a given."

"I'm here for you, honey. But I suspect neither one of us really knows what all we're getting into."

He nodded ruefully. "And I suspect you're exactly right on that one."

Y

Standing in the congregation, facing President Walker at the pulpit, the new bishop remembered to raise his hand to sustain himself. His heart was pounding, and a trickle of sweat found its way down the small of his back. His two counselors, standing in other parts of the chapel, probably felt the same way, he comforted himself. At least they were in this together. It had been no problem selecting them. Their names had presented themselves to him as soon as he had begun to pray about the choice, with an unmistakable rightness that he had seldom felt about any decision, and that, in itself, was as reassuring as anything else about this experience so far.

He saw the sea of hands go up, was briefly aware of Trish and the three kids seated next to him, solemnly raising their hands to sustain him. Nine-year-old James Jr. elbowed four-year-old Mallory to remind her, and Mallory's little pipe stem arm went up into the air. Her daddy allowed himself a quick wink at her. There were no opposing hands raised, and he hoped that fact reflected honestly the ward's acceptance of him as their bishop.

He imagined his parents being there in the congregation. He knew his mother would be, if her health had permitted, but she was not well, having suffered the effects of a stroke and now undergoing a slow recuperation process at his older sister's home in Anniston. His father, who had never joined the Church, and who had passed away six years before, would have been there, too, he was sure, not knowing all the calling entailed but supporting his son in these new responsibilities, looking up at him with pride and confidence. Was it possible that he knew? Was it in any way possible that his dad *was* there?

"Now, brothers and sisters, change is never easy," President Walker remarked, after the new bishopric had taken their seats behind him. "And the changes we're making today go a little deeper than a simple change of bishopric. As you're well aware, we've made the difficult decision to combine the Fairhaven First and Second wards, because of the loss of so many fine members with the closing of Theodore Ruckman Field and the relocation of ChemSoft Industries. For twelve years, Fairhaven has supported two more or less fully staffed wards, but sadly, our numbers have dwindled, and we feel, with the approval of the Brethren in Salt Lake City, that it's in everyone's best interest to unite the two wards for the foreseeable future and to call an entirely new bishopric to serve you, rather than try to combine the two existing organizations.

"Bishop James Shepherd comes to you from the former Fairhaven First Ward, as does his second counselor, Brother Sam Wright. First counselor Robert Patrenko and ward clerk Joseph Perkins hail from what has been the Second Ward. Brothers and sisters, I testify to you that these men have been called of God to these positions. There is no doubt in my mind on that matter. The Lord has made it plain to me. They're going to have a lot of reorganizing to do, and I trust you'll put aside all former boundaries and regard yourselves as one body, one ward, as though there had never been a division."

He smiled. "You know, this is a bit like a marriage." He went on, "Maybe a second marriage, with children on both sides. Two separate entities unite, renouncing all former loyalties, except that which we owe to the Lord, and form a new family. And if you'll think about it, a ward *is* very much like an extended family, isn't it? We've got the parents and grandparents and the original children—those who have been in the area from way back. Then we've got some adopted children, who have joined the Church just recently, and some in-laws who have married into the family and taken up residence. And there will be more coming—those who will be converted or born or move in to join us in the days to come. But all are equal members of the family."

Bishop Shepherd continued to listen to the warm, familiar voice of his leader with half his attention, even as the other half ranged across the chapel, pausing briefly at one face and then another. He was acquainted with more than half of the members, either from church or the store or other associations, but it startled him to realize how little he actually knew of their personal lives and circumstances. That would have to change. As their bishop, he would have to know and be known. Cheery, casual greetings would no longer be enough.

His eyes rested on Richard Tetton, one of the men he would have expected to be called to this position. Yet he hadn't even felt impressed to call him, or Brother Levi Warshaw, for that matter, to be his counselors. A curious thing. He moved on to Sister Linda DeNeuve, a cheerful, patient young mother who had served well as Relief Society president in the First Ward. How would she feel if she were released at this time? Relieved? Or bereft, as if she had been let go for incompetence? And who was the Relief Society president of the Second Ward? He realized he didn't even know.

He noticed Tashia Jones on the right side of the chapel, five or six rows back. As usual, she was sitting by herself. An eleven-year-old black girl, she came to church regularly and promptly, her shining eyes and terrific smile testifying to her delight in being there, even though she came alone and as yet was not baptized. She was friendly and bright, but had a natural reticence that wouldn't allow her to gravitate toward any individual or family unless she was specifically invited to sit with them. He wondered what he might do to gather her in, and to facilitate her baptism.

He smiled to himself. He was already thinking like a bishop.

Y

"That was a beautiful blessing President Walker gave you, in your setting apart," Trish observed. The two of them were taking their traditional Sunday evening walk around their neighborhood, hand in hand. Sometimes the children came along; today they seemed to know that their parents needed a quiet time together, and each was occupied with pursuits of his or her own in the family room—reading, coloring, putting together jigsaw puzzles.

The bishop sighed. "Was, wasn't it? I wish we could have recorded it because I know I'm going to need to draw on all those promises for reassurance—probably on a regular basis."

"Even Tiff said it was awesome."

"Did she?" He chuckled. "I'm glad she was there. Of all the kids, she's old enough to know what's going on, and remember."

Tiffani, their eldest, at fifteen, had been uncharacteristically quiet about the advent of her dad's new position.

"I think she's just sort of digesting the whole thing," Trish said. "Probably trying to get a handle on exactly how it's going to affect her life—especially her social life."

"D'you think it will affect her social life?"

"I imagine so. Some, anyway. Maybe when she starts dating,

the boys will be a little more careful how they treat the bishop's daughter."

He grinned down at her. "Can't be all bad, then."

"Right. Unless she decides to head in the other direction, just to show she's no goody-goody, and no different from anybody else."

"Whoa! Mercy, mercy . . . you sure do know how to put fear in a daddy's heart."

She squeezed his hand. "I saw a book in the library once. It was called *The Truth about Preachers' Sons and Deacons' Daughters*. Now I kind of wish I'd read it."

"But in our church, everybody has a calling or two. I don't really see why it should be any harder to be the bishop's kid than the Gospel Doctrine teacher's kid or the Primary chorister's kid."

"Trust me, it is. If your dad's the bishop or the stake president, you feel this great obligation to be good all the time, and set an example—and yet, you still just want to be one of the guys—or gals."

"That's right, you've been there, haven't you? You were how old—seventeen or eighteen—when your dad was stake president in Arizona?"

"It was my senior year—I was just turning seventeen when he was called. I felt the weight of it to some degree, but I'd already made it through some of my teenage wim-wams, and before long, I was off to BYU. I think it'll be tougher for Tiff. She's younger, and not very sure of herself."

"We'll have to do what we can to ease the way. I guess it'll mostly be up to you, hon, but please advise me how I can help, okay?"

"Sure."

They strolled in companionable silence along the familiar, tree-lined streets. The sun had dipped below the horizon, and the evening chorus of crickets, tree frogs, and mockingbirds had begun. It was the bishop's favorite time of day, with lights just coming on behind the windows of the various homes they passed, families gathering for supper, children reluctantly going indoors for baths, homework-checks, and bedtime. At least, he hoped those were the scenarios for most of the households in Fairhaven. He especially hoped such peaceful pursuits were the norm for the one hundred thirty-four families that comprised the newly reorganized Fairhaven Ward of The Church of Jesus Christ of Latter-day Saints.

"You reckon there's ever been a more—uh—diversified ward than ours?" he asked.

Trish smiled. "Maybe. In some inner city wards in New York or Philadelphia, or some European cities. But I think we're right up there."

"Think about it. We've got black folks, white folks, Native Americans, Filipinos, Tongans, and Europeans. We've got college professors, miners, farmers, computer programmers, an attorney, a librarian, auto mechanics, teachers, retired military, and the unemployed."

"Even a grocer."

"Even a grocer," he agreed. "We've got country folk and city folk, new converts and descendants of the Mormon pioneers. Gospel scholars and the totally clueless. Willing to serve and willing only to be served."

"As my dad would say, those on their way into the Church, and those on their way out."

"That, too, I'm afraid."

"Sounds pretty normal to me."

"Sounds like an incredible challenge to me, to build a united ward with all that diversity. I don't think I can do it."

"To quote a famous general authority, 'You're right, you can't. But you and the Lord *can.*'"

"Who said that?"

"I imagine it's been said by more than one. But the one I know about was Elder Mark E. Petersen, when Dad was called to be stake president the first time, in California. I was just a little kid then, but I've heard him tell about it."

"Are you telling me your dad didn't think he could handle being stake president?"

She gave him a sideways look. "What—you think he was born with full-blown confidence and testimony and know-how?"

"Um—well, he does sort of project that image."

She laughed. "Trust me, he earned it. He paid his dues."

"Reckon he'll be real surprised to hear about our news—he and your mom, both."

"Oh, I don't know. Maybe not as surprised as you think. I'll call them soon as they're back from Mexico."

They had completed their usual route and were heading back down their block, stepping carefully on the buckled sections of sidewalk that resulted from the unremitting growth of the oak trees that stood like sentinels before the big old homes they guarded. The bishop's grandfather had built their house, having abandoned the farming life to his brothers, preferring instead to move to town and help distribute their produce in his market—the forerunner of the bishop's own present business. The grandfather's expressed desire had been to live in a substantial home on a tree-lined street, and two generations later, his descendants were still grateful for that preference. The house was sturdy and welcoming—a two-story brick with generous-sized rooms and a wide verandah across the front. The present occupants had been able to modernize the kitchen and add a family room just behind it, on the back of the house, and still retain a good-sized backyard for Trish's gardening adventures and the children's activities. The front yard was smaller, and this year she had dug up most of the lawn and planted a garden of English wild flowers behind the Victorian wrought-iron fence. The bishop had cringed when she did that, but he had to admit the effect had its charm. He didn't miss mowing that bit of lawn, either. It gave him pleasure to see his family home looking attractive and to know that Trish enjoyed caring for it and experimenting with its decor and landscaping.

Their neighbor on the west, Mrs. Hestelle Pierce, was out enjoying the evening in her yard, as well. Trish turned to her husband and mouthed the words, "Now, be good," as they approached. It was exactly the same wide-eyed, significant warning she often gave the children, when she anticipated some naughtiness. He smiled.

"Evenin', Miz Hestelle," he called out as they drew abreast of her.

"Well, good evenin', neighbors," she replied, smoothing back a wisp of gray hair. "How you folks doin'?"

"Well enough," the bishop replied, fanning himself with one hand. "Awfully warm, though, for April, don't you think?"

"Oh, idn' it hot? I declare, I suffer so from the heat I can't hardly stand to be outdoors."

She plucked at the front of her blouse to cool her neck.

"You better go get you a nice tall lemonade, with ice," the bishop offered.

"Iced tea with lemon, that's the thing. It's good to cool a body. I b'lieve I will."

Hestelle made her way up her front porch and into her home, and Trish pulled her husband unceremoniously toward theirs.

"You are so bad," she told him with mock sternness.

He showed her a face of injured innocence. "What?"

"Hot evening, indeed. It's perfectly pleasant, and you know it, Jim Shepherd. Cool for April, if anything."

"Well, weather's almost always a matter of opinion, don't you think? Miz Hestelle and I think it's warm."

They headed for the kitchen. "You just enjoy the power you have over that poor old lady's mind. You're naughty!"

"Why is Daddy naughty?" asked Mallory, strolling in with an armful of struggling Siamese kitten.

"Because he teases nice old Mrs. Pierce."

"Aw, Trish—she doesn't even know she's being teased!"

"That's what makes it naughty."

The kitten escaped and leaped for the counter and the top of the refrigerator, where she settled, safe from Mallory's over-affectionate grasp.

"Daddy's naughty, Daddy's naughty," Mallory sang.

The bishop hugged his wife's shoulders. "You reckon even a naughty old daddy could get a bowl of that pineapple tapioca?"

"Only if he promises to repent, and be nice."

"He'll promise just about anything."

"Ah, yes," said Trish with an exaggerated sigh. "That's a man for you. Even if he is a bishop."

Υ

He woke in the early dawn, with echoes of a voice resounding in his mind and heart.

"Fear not, James. You were called of Me. I needed a shepherd."

He lay perfectly still. The voice was peaceful but with a quality that burned its message forever in his consciousness. He recognized it; he had heard it a few times before. He never forgot information that came to him from that source.

"Dear Lord," he whispered, "thou hast a shepherd in name, and I promise thee, I'll do my best to become one in deed."

CHAPTER TWO

Y

" . . . GLORIOUS THINGS OF THEE ARE SPOKEN"

It didn't take long for Sister Helen Morley, the stake public affairs representative, to get an article in the *Fairhaven Lookout's* religion page about the new ward and bishopric. The bishop didn't even have to read it to know exactly when it appeared.

"Hey, congratulations, Reverend Jim," called Arthur Hackney, the produce manager at Shepherd's Quality Food Mart. "I read where you're the new preacher, or whatever, at your church."

"Oh, it's not quite that, Art. It's a temporary calling, for a few years. I just sort of run things, with the help of several other people. Actually, with the help of practically everybody in the congregation. We're a lay church, you know what I mean? Everybody does his part."

"That right? Well, whatever—I know you'll do a great job. You do, 'round here. 'Course, you don't have to preach to us, and save our souls." He chuckled.

The bishop laughed with him. "Preach to this bunch? I'm afraid that'd be beyond me."

"Well, I gotta say you set a dern good example, and I'm told that's even better'n a sermon."

The bishop thanked him, but immediately several scenarios flickered across the little movie screen he felt sure was installed somewhere in his brain. There was the time he had come to work on a Monday morning and found that the frozen food display that housed the fish sticks, popcorn shrimp, and Carolina crab cakes had been left unplugged, for who knew how long. A vile-smelling puddle had formed and snaked its way across the aisle and under the ice cream cabinet, requiring that both heavy containers be emptied and moved for the cleanup, and a good deal of stock had been lost. His language on that occasion, if memory served him, had been somewhat less than exemplary.

He also remembered thoroughly losing his temper with Mitzi Blaine, one of his checkers, when she kept calling in sick at the last minute every Friday afternoon—which just happened to be when her boyfriend got home from college for the weekend. He and Trish, had run into them on two of those Fridays— once in the movie theater and once over in New Hope at a little grill that served the best fried mullet and hushpuppies around. When he had confronted Mitzi about her bogus Friday illnesses, she had flown into a temper and accused him of sneaking around and following her. In actuality he had stayed late at work himself on two other Fridays to cover for her, so no one else would have to. But he wasn't exactly proud of the tongue-lashing he had administered. She, of course, had quit before he could fire her (which he really hadn't intended doing), her voice quavering with tearful indignation as she leveled him with, "And I thought you were a *nice* man!"

Trish had shaken her head, then consoled him by saying that it was a good wake-up call about methods of dealing with the impulses of young women—one that might stand him in good stead someday if his own daughter should show signs of rebellion. The image this possibility produced on his inner screen made him cringe. Daughters didn't tender their resignation to the family, if caught out in some flagrant bit of misbehavior, did they? Yet he knew they sometimes did.

"James Shepherd!" The imperious voice was unmistakable. It belonged to Mrs. Martha Ruckman, his fifth grade teacher. "James Shepherd, I need a word with you, if you can spare a moment!"

He turned from what he was doing with alacrity. "Yes, ma'am, Miz Ruckman. I always have a moment for you. How can I help you?"

The head of this small, fierce black woman didn't even reach his shoulder, but she commanded his attention—and that of half of his customers—as she peered into his face as if she suspected him of cheating on his spelling test.

"I want you to tell me," she said in measured tones, "exactly why I should allow my granddaughter to attend your church, instead of coming with me to Balm of Gilead to hear the sermons of Dr. Philemon Burshaw, a learned man and a mighty preacher of the word of God. His sermons are well thought out, articulate, and powerfully comforting to the soul! Now, why should Tashia not have the benefit of hearing him? What do you offer that's better, and how is it that you suddenly set yourself up as a preacher, when you and I both know you're a grocer and the son of a grocer, and never even been to divinity school?"

He wiped away the moisture on his forehead with the handkerchief Trish always insisted he carry. "Tashia's your granddaughter?"

"That's right. Tashia Jones."

"She's a wonderful little girl."

"She is, and I intend for her to stay wonderful. Now, answer my question, James. I am serious about this."

"Yes, ma'am, I can tell you are—and you should be. And goodness knows, if it came down to a contest between my preaching and Dr. Burshaw's, I'd have to say take her to hear him, every Sunday. I don't even speak to my congregation very often. We all take turns doing that. But there's more to it than who's delivering a message." He looked at the floor for a moment, searching his mind and heart, then back at his inquisitor. "Why does Tashia say she comes to our church?"

"She says she likes the feeling there. Says it's warm, and feels like home. Says nobody yells Jesus' name, but instead say it soft and reverent, and it feels right to her. Things like that."

The bishop nodded. "Well, I believe the good feeling that Tashia's responding to comes from the presence of the Holy Ghost, Miz Ruckman. Or maybe you'd call it the Holy Spirit. Same thing. We believe he testifies to us in our hearts, comforts and instructs us, helps us feel the love the Savior has for us."

"Now you're talking like a Christian, but some of my friends tell me your church *isn't* Christian. That's another thing you'd best tell me the truth about, right up front."

"Yes, ma'am, I will. The name of our church is The Church of Jesus Christ of Latter-day Saints, and like Paul said, we preach Christ, and him crucified. We also preach him resurrected and living and able to bless and help us, today—we preach him the same yesterday, today, and forever. Does that sound Christian to you?"

Mrs. Ruckman favored him with a smile in which he saw the antecedent of Tashia's, but then she grew serious again.

"Then what about that Joseph Smith, and Brigham Young—and a whole string of other men Tashia talks about? Why are they important?"

"We believe those men are prophets, like Moses and Elijah—men chosen by God to be his mouthpiece on earth to the people in our day, as the earlier prophets were in theirs. We honor and respect them, but we don't worship them, any more than we worship Noah or Peter."

"And so it was Joseph Smith that wrote that book Tashia brought home—the Book of Mormon?"

"Well, no ma'am, not exactly. Y'see, it was actually written by ancient men of God, and Joseph Smith was allowed to translate it into English, with God's help. What it amounts to, is another witness for Christ—the Bible, of course, being the first witness."

She considered his words for a long moment. "Well, I don't know if you're inspired or deceived, but you always were an honest boy, James. Honest and polite. I suppose, for now, I'll let Tashia keep worshipping with you."

"Thank you, Miz Ruckman, and why don't you come with her, sometime? We'd be honored to have you."

There was that smile again—hard to win but definitely worth it. "Personally, I quite enjoy the challenge of Dr. Burshaw's sermons," she said, with a lift of her head. "But you never know when I might come visiting. I thank you for your time, James. Good day, now."

She marched out of his store, straight-backed as a twenty-year-old, without buying anything or looking right or left. The bishop headed for the restroom and then took a can of soda pop to his office, where he stretched out on the old sofa he kept there. He sorely needed a break. In fifth grade, it had been called recess.

Those first couple of weeks, he and his counselors spent a good deal of time in deliberation and prayer, presenting to the Lord the names of those they felt might best fill the various callings needed to staff the ward and keep things running smoothly. But he had also tried to reserve some time for appointments with members who requested a visit with him.

He found an executive secretary in Brother Dan McMillan, who was a retired military supply officer and a very organized person. Brother Joseph Perkins became the ward clerk, a position he knew well and had held previously in the Second Ward. He also understood computers, with which neither the bishop nor either of his counselors had a great deal of experience. The bishop had Mary Lynn Connors to deal with the system at the store, and Trish, Tiffani, and Jamie at home, all perfectly comfortable with the one there. It was an area of expertise the bishop hoped to postpone delving into until retirement, when presumably there would be hours to fill. From the way Mary Lynn fussed at the store's computer, he wasn't sure he needed that kind of frustration in his life right now. He was especially grateful to have Brother Perkins on board.

A woman he didn't know, a former Second Warder, presented herself at his office on a Tuesday evening and introduced herself as Sister LaThea Winslow. He shook her hand and invited her to sit down across from him in one of the two church-issued chairs that faced his desk. She was a tall, rather severely elegant woman. He guessed her age to be somewhere in the late forties or early fifties.

"I'm real happy to have a chance to get acquainted with you, Sister Winslow," he said. "There's a good number of folks I don't know yet. What can I do for you this evening?"

"Bishop, I'm just here to offer my services to you in the ward and to let you know that I have some experience and background that will be useful to you."

"Well, that's wonderful. Could you tell me a little about your background?"

"I'd be glad to. You won't be aware, I suppose, that I'm a sixth-generation Latter-day Saint, and a descendant of several pioneer families who crossed the plains."

"Is that right!" He leaned forward and crossed his arms on the desk. "We don't have too many folks around here whose families have been in the Church that long."

"No, I suppose not. A few, I guess, may have moved in through the military, or what-have-you, as we did. My husband likes the climate, so we stayed here when he retired last year."

"I see. I s'pose you must've lived a number of different places then."

"Oh, yes—California, Arizona, Germany, Florida, here in Alabama—and Utah, of course."

"And I expect you've served in a lot of different Church callings."

"Here and there. Of course, it was somewhat difficult, while we were raising our family, and moving around so much. But now the children are grown, and we're settled, and I can take a more active part."

"Well, excellent. I'm sure we can find just the right calling for you. Let's see—do you happen to play the piano or organ?"

"I—well, yes—piano, that is. But I had something larger in mind, to be frank."

"Larger?" The bishop studied her face, trying to understand just what she was saying.

"Not to brag, but I do have some leadership capabilities, Bishop. I know how to conduct meetings, and I've had quite a lot of experience in entertaining groups. I'm well versed in the art of conversation and the rules of etiquette, and I'm told I'm an excellent cook."

"I see! That's terrific. Those are surely useful skills. Have you ever served in Relief Society?"

She smiled. "Bishop, may I just say that my mother and my two grandmothers served as Relief Society presidents in Salt Lake City, for a total of twenty-eight years between them? You might say Relief Society's in my blood!"

Light began to dawn. "Now, that's truly remarkable," he said. "And what experience have you had in Relief Society?"

"Oh—well, as I said, it was difficult in our position in the military to have much time to work in the Church. We'd no sooner get acquainted and begin to serve in callings, than Harville would be transferred. But I've been—let's see—a visiting teacher, and I've occasionally taught cooking classes— German cuisine, Southwestern specialties, and so forth."

"Sounds delicious. Well, you know, with your family background in Relief Society, it'd be nice to carry on that great tradition of service, wouldn't it?"

Her smile, which seemed to turn on and off with great suddenness, appeared again. "It certainly would," she agreed.

"And with the strength of good women like your mother and grandmother in your background, I expect you could handle all the different situations that present themselves to us here in this area. You strike me as a lady who could probably not only organize a wonderful dinner party for the sisters and their guests, but could also help a midwife at a birthing up in the hill country. Some of our sisters don't go to hospitals to have their babies. Too far, no insurance, too expensive—you know how it is, I'm sure. You Relief Society sisters, bless your hearts, seem to preside at the comings and goings of life. I imagine, with your background, you'd have no difficulty in dressing the dead, either."

"Excuse me?"

"Well, I'm sure you're aware that around here, we have no—um—funeral directors who are members of the Church, so when an endowed sister passes away, the Relief Society president has the privilege of dressing the body of the deceased in her temple clothing for burial. You'd know how to do that, I reckon."

"Well, but—of course, in Utah, all the mortuaries do have LDS people who . . ."

"What we ought to do, I expect, is send our missionaries around to all the undertakers in the area, see if they can't convert us one. Sure would come in handy!" He chuckled.

Sister Winslow looked stunned. "Yes—yes, that would be good."

He gazed at his desk for a long moment, then looked up. "Do you happen to know how to give shots, or change IV's?"

"Shots? You mean . . ." She shook her head, frowning.

"Hypodermic—pain shots? We have old Brother Bainbridge coming home from the hospital. He's got cancer, you know, and the doctors have said it's terminal. His wife wants him to have his last weeks at home with her, but the hospital will only release him if we can provide someone to be on hand to help him with his pain and keep his fluids up. They'll need somebody every few hours. Sister Bainbridge just isn't up to doing it. She doesn't see very well. Needs help, herself, as a matter of fact. And their insurance has already been stretched to the limit, with all his surgeries and treatments."

"I—see. No, I'm afraid I haven't had any training in nursing, or in delivering babies, either. Mine were born in military hospitals, and I was—medicated. Don't we have any nurses in the ward?"

"Well, let me think. Seems like Sister Frankie Talbot did some training in that direction before she married Gene. I'll have to check with her. Anyway, we really rely on the Relief Society to help out on all fronts. Tell you what—I'll talk things over with my counselors, sister, and we'll pray about it, and get back to you. Will that be all right?"

"Yes, Bishop, of course. You know—um—I believe I could be useful in other ways, too—not just Relief Society. Perhaps on the activities committee? I just love to plan parties!"

"Now, there's a thought. We're definitely looking for willing and talented folks to serve there. People with some experience in entertaining, and new ideas for ward activities. I feel the social aspect's going to play a real important part in unifying our two wards, don't you?"

"Absolutely, Bishop, I think you're right on the money. And I'd love to be of service in helping that happen."

He stood up and came around the desk to shake her hand

again and open the door. "Thank you so much, Sister Winslow. I'm just so grateful for the support people are showing for this new, green bishopric. It means a lot."

She hurried out to her car, and he wandered into the clerk's office, where his counselors and clerks were poring over the instructions to the Church's computerized membership program.

"How's it coming?" he asked, dropping onto a cushioned stenographer's chair.

"I think we're getting it," Robert Patrenko replied. "How's Sister Winslow? Everything okay with her?"

"I believe so. She was just—um—offering her support. Being willing to serve in the ward."

Brother Patrenko looked up and grinned. "Is that a nice way of saying she was doing a little aspiring to positions? Trying to get the jump on you, or the Lord, by suggesting exactly how and where she'd like to serve?"

"Well . . ." He didn't like to think of it just that way, but his counselor seemed to know the lady. He grinned back. "Something like that, I guess. I believe we came to an understanding."

"What'd she want—the Relief Society? I know her pretty well, you see—I was her home teacher for three years. I remember she was pretty indignant one time when Bishop Collins asked her to serve in the nursery. Wondered what he had against her, that he wanted her 'out of the loop,' I believe was how she put it."

"She seems to enjoy the social end of things, all right. I wondered about asking her to head up the activities committee."

"Perfect, I'd say," Brother Patrenko agreed, and Joseph Perkins turned from the computer screen and nodded.

"I see LaThea as a lady who needs to be noticed and praised and reassured that she's worthwhile," he said. "Harville's a good man, but I believe he takes all her efforts for granted, and he isn't one to shower praise and thanks on anybody."

"Well, put that down on our list of callings to pray about, all right? And now somebody, please tell me this—do any of our sisters who live away from town, up in the hills, have their babies at home, with a midwife?"

Sam Wright looked up. "I b'lieve Sister Nettie Birdwhistle does, don't she? Seems like I remember Frankie Talbot going up there a time or two to help out. Nettie's younguns come fast, I hear, and she don't even try to get down to town when things start rollin'. She's had nine or ten, hatn't she? She's got the process down real good, I reckon."

The bishop smiled in relief. "Good. Thanks." *And thank thee, Father,* he added silently. *I'm glad I didn't lie. I just didn't know where that truth came from!*

He had pondered who should be the new Relief Society president. Sister Linda DeNeuve had confided in him that she was expecting a baby and feeling especially tired, and Sister Rhonda Castleberry, who he learned had been president in the Second Ward, had been at it for nearly five years and in his opinion deserved a break, if not a medal. There were two names that kept coming to him. One was Frankie Talbot, who, it turned out, had indeed finished her nurse's training, though she wasn't presently working at it, being busy with her five children. Her husband commuted to work up at the Redstone Arsenal. Frankie was a small, vibrant, good-natured woman with red hair and seemingly boundless energy, but he worried that the weight of this calling might take too much from her and from her family.

The other name that kept coming to his mind was that of Ida Lou Reams. Ida Lou was an older sister who had lived in Fairhaven all her life. Her husband, Barker Reams, had never joined the Church, but had offered no objection to his family's participation. Ida Lou had little in the way of formal education, but she had a good knowledge of gospel basics and a warm, outgoing way that manifested itself in quiet acts of service to people, many of which, he was sure, were known only to the recipients. But Ida Lou had never been endowed in the temple, and he had reason to know that Barker drank, sometimes to excess. Would she have the support a woman needed to serve in this calling?

He put the matter to the Lord again and again, and still the two names were there. Finally he asked his counselors for their recommendations, without telling them the names he'd been considering. They knelt in prayer together, and then he asked each of them to write on a piece of paper the name that suggested itself. Brother Patrenko wrote his name quickly and handed the paper across to the bishop, who thanked him but didn't look at it right away. Brother Sam Wright seemed to be agonizing over his choice, and finally handed it over with a shake of his head.

"Tell you the truth, Bishop, I don't know why I wrote the name I did. My mind and good sense tells me that Sister Talbot oughta be the one, but—well, here's the name that just kept gnawin' at me. I'm prob'ly all wrong. I hatn't had much experience with this kind of a thing."

The bishop smiled. "Neither have I, Sam. Now, before I

look at these, I want to tell you the two names that have been, as Sam puts it, gnawin' at me these last few days. Sister Frankie Talbot is one, all right, and the other is Sister Ida Lou Reams."

He knew from the slight gasp Sam gave that he was on target. Bob Patrenko smiled. The bishop opened the slips of paper. The same name appeared on each. His throat threatened to close off, and he cleared it. "Well, brethren," he said, "if she accepts, we have our president." He stood up and went to open the door to the clerk's office. "Brother McMillan," he said with a note of triumph in his voice, "would you please ask Sister Ida Lou Reams to come in for an appointment, soon as possible? And invite her husband to come with her, if he will."

Y

He took the next afternoon off work and drove to his sister Paula's home in Anniston to visit with his mother and give her the news of his calling. Paula Trawick opened the door to her old-brick, ranch style home with its white wrought-iron "lace" around the front porch. She was as tall as he, and heavier by probably thirty or forty pounds. Her hair was fully gray, now, but still thick and wavy, and her skin looked younger than her years.

"Hey, there, Little Brother," she greeted, giving him a hug and patting his shoulder. "How's life treating you? All alone today—didn't bring the family?"

"Nope, just me, today. I just ran down for a quick visit to tell Mama something I think will please her."

"Don't tell me Trish's expecting again!"

"No, no—though we wouldn't mind at all if that was the case."

"I swear, ya'll are gluttons for punishment. Two were enough for me, I can tell you. Well, come on in. Mama'll be thrilled to see you. She worries if you don't show up pretty regular."

"Even now?" he asked, in a low voice. "She keeps track?"

"Oh, yeah. I know she can't communicate very good, but I'm certain as I can be that her mind's still plenty sharp and active. She still can't seem to say 'Jim,' but she says 'son,' and I know she means you. She has a few more words, since you were here last. The other day I fed her some soup, and I reckon I should've checked the temperature better, 'cause she yelled, 'Hot!' when she tasted it. First time she's said that. Bless her heart, she was real mad at me."

"It can't be easy, taking care of her full-time, Paula. You sure you're up to it, still?"

Paula regarded him steadily. "I don't reckon she'd care to be shipped back and forth between the three of us, in her condition," she said. "Even if you or Anne Marie was in a position to care for her, I don't think she'd do as well moving place-to-place, not to mention noise and children making her nervous. I reckon she needs stability and peace at this stage of life."

"Bless your heart, Sis, you'll be rewarded for this."

Paula shrugged. "I am rewarded. I have Mama's company. We were always close—even if I didn't join your church."

"I know. And I know she appreciates everything you do. Still, if you need a break—she could surely come to us for a while. Trish has even suggested it, and she'd be good to Mama."

His sister nodded. "Trish is a sweetie, and it's good to know ya'll are willing. I'm not real sure Anne Marie is, but that's another story. It's funny, but in most of the families I know, the care of the old folks seems to be left up to one of the kids—and in our family, I'm it. And you know what, Jimmie? I'm glad of it. It's company for me, just to know she's here. I reckon if Travis would ever retire, the house wouldn't seem so empty, but I swear that man is more married to his job than he is to me, and after the kids grew up and left, I purely hated being here all by my lonesome. So having Mama is a blessing. Come on in and see her, now—she'll wonder who in the world I'm talking to, in here." She turned, and he followed her to the family room behind the kitchen. "Mama? Surprise—your boy is here!"

His mother was propped in a recliner with pillows at her sides to keep her upright. There was bright sunlight spilling across the floor, and a whole indoor garden of potted plants gave a freshness to the air. She watched as he crossed the room to her and knelt at her side.

"Hi, Mama," he said, making himself smile, though he felt more like crying at the sight of her fragile condition and half-drooping face. Her right eye watered and gazed off to the side, while the left one peered anxiously at him. Half of her mouth turned up in a smile.

"Son?" she asked, her right hand reaching toward him. He took her hand and kissed it.

"Yep, it's me, Mama. How're you doing? You're lookin' better."

"Son. Good."

"Trish and the kids send their love, Mama, but I came down by myself today to tell you some news, okay? Guess what I've been called to be?"

"Son?"

"I've just been sustained as the new bishop in Fairhaven Ward," he told her and watched carefully to see if she comprehended. Her half-smile came again.

"Good," she said. "Good. Good son."

"Well, I hope I'm a good son—and I'm going to try real hard

to be a good bishop. You pray for me, okay, Mama? I know the Lord hears your prayers, even if they're silent ones. He always did, when you prayed for me."

Her left eye joined the right one in watering, and he knew these were real tears. She grasped his hand a little tighter and shook it gently.

"We have a hundred and thirty-four families in the Church in Fairhaven, now. Can you believe that, Mama? Remember when we first started going, and there were only a handful of us? Just a few members and investigators, and the missionaries. Now there's a stake in our area, and five wards. And a temple, right in Birmingham. We've sure been blessed, Mama."

"Good."

"It is good, isn't it? I'm glad to be a part of it. Glad you supported me—that we joined the Church together. That's a mighty sweet memory for me."

She shook his hand up and down again, and somehow he knew she meant, "For me, too."

He was silent for a moment, looking around the room. "This is a real pretty room," he commented. "I'm sure glad Paula takes such good care of you. And she was telling me how much she enjoys having you here."

"Good."

"She is good, isn't she? A real good daughter. Do you need anything, Mama? Is there anything I can do for you, get for you?"

His mother released his hand and patted the top of her head. He frowned.

"Does your head hurt?"

She didn't respond.

"Is it . . ." Suddenly the light dawned. "Do you want me to give you a blessing?"

She grabbed his hand again and pumped it up and down.

"Well, sure, Mama, I'd be happy to. Now, I didn't think to bring any oil, and I don't have any other priesthood holder with me, but I'll just do the best I can, okay?"

He stood and placed his hands on her head, silently praying for guidance. The words came, and he heard himself promising his mother that she would be comforted and sustained as her circumstances required, that she would gain in strength and mobility and the ability to communicate her thoughts, and that she would be helped to remember the many good and positive experiences of her life and feel great satisfaction and joy because of them. In the course of the prayer, he indirectly blessed his sister as well, asking that she be sustained and strengthened and experience continuing joy in her service to their mother. He closed the blessing, noting as he did so that there was a slight movement from the door to the kitchen. Paula hadn't stayed in the room with them for his visit with his mother, but he was pretty sure she had heard at least part of his blessing. He kissed his mother, and was surprised to hear her hoarse voice whisper a very clear, "Love you," as he did.

"I love you, too, Mama—very, very much. God bless you."

Paula saw him out, drying her hands on a kitchen towel. "By the way, Mama gets visitors from your church about once or twice a month. We let them come, 'cause it seems to make her happy. There's two men who come, and a couple of older ladies who seem real sweet. I reckon you sent 'em?"

"Not at all," he was pleased to tell her. "Mama's membership would have been transferred here to Anniston, and the bishop would have asked them to visit. Has he been to see her, too?"

"Well, I don't know who-all they are, but maybe so. There was a nice, older man one time, and he asked if she could have visitors."

"I expect that'd be the bishop."

"And so—that's what you are, now? I heard you telling Mama."

"Hard to believe, isn't it?"

His sister frowned. "I didn't say that, Jimmie. I reckon you'll do just fine. It's funny, but you always did have a knack for the spiritual side of things. More than me and Anne Marie put together."

He chuckled. "Well, I don't know about that, but thanks, Sis. And thanks again for your sweet care of Mama." He gave his sister a heartfelt hug and took his leave. He noticed that Paula stood in the doorway and watched him drive away.

CHAPTER THREE

" . . . BY HIM WE ARE KNOWN"

The next evening, the bishop parked his car and stood for a few minutes on the flagstone patio outside his kitchen door, enjoying the soft, perfumed air of the spring night. What was that fragrance, anyway? Trish would know; she was into flowers and gardening. He just appreciated the results. It seemed good, after the intensive meetings he had just endured, to have a few moments alone in the sweet, silent darkness of his own backyard. His briefcase and his brain were stuffed with more information than he had ever wanted to know about the families and individuals who made up his newly formed flock. He had met first with the outgoing bishop of his own ward, Tom Detweiler, who had filled him in on the situations and struggles, the strengths and weaknesses of people Jim had thought he knew rather well. Then former bishop Arnold Collins did the same for the folks of the erstwhile Second Ward. Jim felt his heart and brain were on overload, reeling under the knowledge that this couple were on the brink of divorce, another living separate lives under one roof—this family was on the verge of bankruptcy and the other one had already declared, these folks just had their car repossessed, that brother had been diagnosed with leukemia, this couple were childless and trying to adopt, that seriously handicapped young man wanted badly to serve a mission, a certain sister was losing her faith in God, and one family's newborn daughter had been diagnosed as profoundly deaf.

There were positive things, too—an excellent young lady had been accepted at BYU, another had chosen between two would-be suitors the one who would take her to the temple. An elderly couple were preparing to serve their second mission, and a good brother's diabetes finally seemed to be under control. Another man who had been out of work for months had found a suitable job, and a family with young children had decided to become active in the Church again. And a good many people were just steady, active, dependable sorts with reasonably happy lives.

The bishop took a deep breath. How, he wondered, even with infinite compassion and wisdom and love, did Heavenly Father bear the knowledge of his myriad children's trials and sorrows? Could exaltation—and godhood—really be the joyous thing it was reputed to be?

"Forgive me, Father," he whispered. "I'm just so . . . finite. Please help me to bear all of this knowledge without being bowed down by it. I know thy capacity is infinite. I just don't comprehend it."

He let himself into the kitchen, which was lighted only by the hood light on the range. It was late, a school night, and apparently everyone had gone to bed—except the Siamese kitten, who pretended to be alarmed at his presence and gave three sideways, stiff-legged hops before scampering under the table.

He chuckled. "I guess you're good for a little comic relief, if nothing else."

He picked up a note from the table: "Sorry, hon—had to go to bed. Dinner's in the fridge if you want to nuke it. Hope your meetings went well. Love, Me."

He lifted the plastic wrap on the plate in the refrigerator. Barbecued chicken, scalloped potatoes, green beans. A favorite meal, but not one he felt would sit well this late at night. He would have it for lunch tomorrow. He broke some bread into a bowl and poured milk over it, debated about adding a slice of cheese and a couple of radishes or a green onion, and decided against it. *Keep it simple, stupid,* he told himself.

Fatigue overtook him halfway through his meal, and his eyes closed. A drop of liquid on his hand startled him, and he woke to see the kitten, whom Mallory called Samantha, sitting by his bowl, daintily dipping her paw into the milk and licking it.

"Hey," he objected, and she sat, paw in midair, gazing at him with her slightly crossed blue eyes. He scooped her up and deposited her on the floor, where she immediately wrapped herself around his ankle. He stood up and walked to her dish, dragging her along, and poured some of the milk for her. The rest he emptied down the sink.

"You and I need to get something straight," he told the kitten, who purred loudly as she lapped. "I've never really liked cats. True, I've never had one before—always had a dog when I was a kid, but Trish doesn't cotton to dogs digging in her yard, and Mallory pestered us half to death for you. So here we are, and I'll do my best, but don't expect favors all the time. You're here on probation. Got that?"

The kitten didn't reply, being blissfully occupied, and the bishop went up to bed. Just before he fell asleep, the words of a hymn, one he couldn't even identify, floated into his mind: " . . . the weight of your calling he perfectly knows." It was remarkable, he thought sleepily, how the Holy Ghost can quote scripture and hymns, and bring them to remembrance as needed. Which, he supposed, was as good a reason as any for becoming familiar with such material. Then at least it was all there, in a person's subconscious, waiting to be plucked from the file and used when appropriate. He knew when it was the Holy Ghost, and not just the workings of his own mind, because of the clarity and power with which these messages came—and the way they stayed with him and taught or comforted him. Actually, as he recalled, the hymn had been talking about the adversary knowing the weight of one's calling, not the Lord— but both were true.

"Thank thee, Father," he whispered. "I know thou wilt help me bear the weight."

The bishop opened his office door and stepped out to shake hands with Sister Ida Lou Reams and her husband, Barker. It was Wednesday, but Sister Reams was dressed in her Sunday best, clutching her handbag and looking nervous. Barker, for the occasion, had put on a clean sports shirt and shaved, but looked none too happy about it. He gripped the tips of the bishop's fingers briefly and reluctantly, and with the air of a condemned man, followed his wife into the office.

Ida Lou Reams was a large woman, accustomed to hard work, cheerful, and uncomplaining. She was one of the first to arrive at any welfare or service project, and could be counted on to stay and clean up after ward dinners, whether she was on that committee or not. She and Barker had reared a family of five boys and one girl, plus two grandchildren for several years, until their widowed eldest son had remarried. She made a baby quilt for each new arrival in the ward, and could be counted on to sew roadshow or play costumes as needed. She taught the younger women to knit, crochet, or quilt, or even, Trish had informed the bishop with amazement, to make braided rugs out of plastic grocery or merchandise bags.

Ida Lou sat before him now, smiling bravely to cover her nervousness, her knuckles white on the handle of her purse.

"I'm real grateful you folks could come in, this evening," the bishop said, wondering how to put them at ease. "Barker, I'm sure you know you've got one of the finest wives a man could have."

Barker gave a curt nod. "We done okay together, I reckon."

"I'd say so. You've got a great family, and I've admired the way you keep your place up. The yard always looks neat, and it seems like your house gets painted every spring."

"Best to keep wood painted, so it don't rot nor warp."

"And most important, you've raised a fine bunch of kids—kind of people you'd like to have next door."

"Ida Lou's been a good mama."

"Well, but he supported me, Bishop. I couldn't have did it alone."

The bishop was glad that Ida Lou had finally found her tongue and dared to speak.

"It's a joint effort, isn't it—making a home and bringing up kids?"

She responded again, "Yessir, it is. I'm mighty thankful for ours. Oh, and you might not know, our Billy was just called to the bishopric down at Mobile."

"Is that right? Good for him! Wonder if he feels as new and green at it as I do!"

"Now, you're doin' just great. Don't you worry about a thing," she soothed. "And I expect Billy'll do all right, too, onc't he gits the hang of it, you might say."

"I'm sure of it. He's a real good man, as I recall." Feeling a knot of nervousness in his stomach, the bishop leaned forward. He cleared his throat. "Now, I imagine you folks are wondering why I asked you to stop by tonight." He smiled at them. She smiled back.

Barker frowned. "I'm wonderin' why you ast for the both of us," he said, "seein' as I ain't even one of your flock, so to speak."

The bishop nodded. "There's a good reason for that, Barker, and I appreciate your coming. You see, in our church, we never call a sister to a position of responsibility without making sure it's all right with her husband—to make sure that he feels okay about her accepting, that he'll support her in her calling."

"Oh, dear—I wonder what-all you have in mind for me?" Ida Lou fretted. "I hope it's something I can do."

"Well, I won't keep you in suspense. Ida Lou, the Lord wants you to serve as Relief Society president in our new ward."

She gasped, and her eyes immediately filled with tears. "Now, Bishop, you know I'm not an educated woman. I cain't stand up in front of people and say things right. Not like these young gals, who've been to school. It's hard for me to even get up and bear my testimony, you know that. You've heard me try."

"Sister Reams, the Lord knows your heart, and he knows your situation, and he must have confidence in your abilities.

I want you to know that this calling isn't coming *from* me—just through me. We all prayed about this decision, and came up with your name, independently, and when we prayed again, the Lord confirmed it to us. Knowing that, I'm as sure as I'm sitting here that he'll be with you and help you every step of the way. It's obvious that you have some experience and some talents and qualities that will be needful as we go about the business of uniting our two wards. There's some special way you can serve the sisters of Fairhaven, and set an example for them."

She cried quietly into a handkerchief, while her husband sat stoically, his only concession to her emotion being to rest his hand on the back of her chair.

"Barker, how do you feel about this?" the bishop asked quietly.

Barker shrugged. "Reckon I don't know what-all's involved," he admitted, "but Ida Lou's pretty much always done what she wanted, far as her church goes. Long as the house was kept up and the kids took care of and supper on the table, I ain't complained. So I reckon she can do this, iffen she wants. I won't stand in her way."

"Thank you, sir. Ida Lou, how do you feel?"

"I'm just not—good enough," she said.

Barker turned to frown at her. "Reckon you're good as anybody," he said.

"Amen, brother," agreed the bishop. "And better than most, in the ways that count. And you know, Ida Lou, you won't be doing it alone. You get to pick two good women to be your counselors."

Ida Lou looked up, eyes still streaming, and drew a shaky breath. "Oh, Bishop—could I have that little Frankie Talbot? She's the sweetest thing."

"Dear sister, you just confirmed again to me that your calling is inspired. Sister Talbot's name was another that I kept thinking of—almost as strongly as yours."

"I've been athinkin' about her a passel, lately, and I didn't know why. But it comes to me, now, that the Lord was tryin' to prepare me for this." She sat still a moment, as if listening. "What about Rosetta McIntyre, from the other ward? Have you already got her doin' something?"

"She's about to be released as a Primary teacher. She's a good choice, I believe. Any thoughts on who might be a good secretary?"

"Well, Bishop—could I just steal your sweet little wife for that?"

That surprised him. He realized he hadn't even thought about calling his own wife to a position in the ward! Of course she would need one—being bishop's wife wasn't an actual calling, even though he was sure at times it must feel like one—taking messages for him, being flexible about family activities, keeping things running smoothly in his absence. "I'll talk to her," he promised. "And to Sister Talbot and Sister McIntyre."

He went on to explain that she would be trained in her new calling by the stake Relief Society president, with help from the outgoing presidencies of both wards.

"I'll be working with you a lot, too—and I look forward to that. Thank you, Ida Lou, for accepting this calling. I believe it'll be a great experience for you."

By now she was smiling through her tears, but she shook her head. "I just can't fathom that Heavenly Father picked me—that he knows me and has confidence in me," she confessed. "I mean, I'm just me, not nobody special, like I think of Relief Society presidents being!"

"It's 'just you' he wants," the bishop assured her. "But I understand your feeling. I've felt a good bit that way myself, lately. Thank you, Barker, for being willing to share this good lady with us."

Barker grunted, but shook hands a little more warmly than he had, coming in. The bishop saw them out the door, then turned to see Sam Wright's head poking out of the clerk's office, a questioning look on his face. The bishop grinned and gave him a thumbs-up sign. Sam grinned back, nodding in satisfaction.

Jim had a few minutes before his next scheduled interview, and he took the opportunity to lean back in his chair, slip off his shoes, and prop his stockinged feet on his desk. It was nowhere near Christmas, but a line from a favorite carol kept running through his thoughts. "He knows our need, to our weakness is no stranger . . ."

"Thank thee, Father, for knowing us," he whispered. "our needs, our weaknesses, our strengths and possibilities. Thank thee for good people like Ida Lou Reams. Thank thee for preparing her. Bless her to both feel and be capable in her calling, and bless her husband for allowing her to serve. Help him to see his own possibilities, too."

A knock sounded from the door to the clerk's office. He swung his feet down. "Come in."

His executive secretary entered with such straight-backed military bearing that he almost expected him to salute.

"Yes sir, Brother Dan, what's on the agenda?"

"Brother Ralph Jernigan called, wants a few minutes with you, declined to say what about."

"All right. When did you tell him?"

"Said he could be here by seven-thirty. Does that work for you?"

The bishop sighed. Another dinnertime with the family missed. "Sure, I'll be here. Anything else coming up?"

"No sir, not from my end. Do you have any calls for me to make?"

"I do. Could you get me appointments with Sisters Frances Talbot and Rosetta McIntyre?"

"I'll get right on it. Then, I wonder—would there be anything else?"

"Why don't you go on home, Dan? I appreciate all you've done."

"If you need me . . ."

He shook his head. "Just those two sisters, if you can catch up to 'em."

"Thank you, Bishop. I'm sorry to rush out on you, but it's Susie's birthday, an' . . ."

"Then you take yourself home right now, my man, and let me make those calls myself. I've got a few minutes."

He made an appointment with Rosetta McIntyre and left a message for Frankie Talbot, asking her to call him at her earliest opportunity. Then he sat back and reviewed what he knew about Ralph Jernigan. It wasn't a great deal; the Jernigans had lived in Fairhaven for about three years and had been members of the Second Ward. Ralph had a broad face, usually sunburned, and narrow eyes under a black military haircut. The bishop recalled Sister Jernigan's face even better than her husband's—possibly because they were such a contrast. Hers was a pale oval with a pointed chin and a small mouth that always seemed to be forming an "O," and light-colored eyes that seemed perpetually surprised—or was it wary? She had a tendency to perch on the edge of her chair as if poised for flight. He couldn't recall what either of them did in the way of work, or if they had a family. He reached into his desk drawer and pulled out his working copy of the temporary ward list. No children were listed. Sister Jernigan's name was Linda.

He stood up and went to the clerk's office, knocking as he opened the door. It was dark; both Sam Wright and Dan McMillan had gone. Bob Patrenko was busy that evening, helping his wife cover their three teenagers' instructors at a parent-teacher conference at the high school, and Brother Perkins had to work. No help, there. He tried to remember what, if anything, Bishop Collins had confided in him about the Jernigans. He hadn't made any notations by their names, so he assumed there hadn't been anything too seriously amiss in their situation. He went back to his desk, said a prayer for guidance, and called home to say he'd be missing dinner.

"Mom's gone to my parent-teacher conference," Tiffani told him. "We already ate."

"Oh—sure, that's fine. If there's any left, just set it aside for me, okay? And what are you doing, Tiff?"

"I'm baby-sitting," she said, in a tone that let him know he should have realized the obvious.

"Well, thanks, hon. Mom and I both appreciate it. What are Jamie and Mallory up to?"

"Jamie's doing his homework, 'cause Mom let him play after school, and Mallory's trying to make the cat wear a doll's dress."

He chuckled. "That should be interesting."

"Dad, she's gonna get scratched, but will she listen to me? No."

"See if she'll talk to me for a minute."

"Okay, but when're you coming home? I can't read my book for English because Jamie keeps asking me for help, and Mallory's gonna need stitches any minute."

"Soon as I can, honey. I just have one more person to see, and then I'm outa here."

"Well, hurry, okay? I need to take a bath, too. Mallory! Come talk to Dad!"

"Daddy, you should see Samantha. She looks so pretty in her blue dress. It matches her eyes."

"Hey, Mallory. I'll bet she looks good, but how does she feel about wearing a dress?"

"Oh, she likes it. Be still, Samantha. I need to wrap you up in the baby blanket now."

"You know, honey, kitties have their own clothes. That's what her fur is for. She's probably way too hot in a dress and a blanket. How would you feel if you had to wear a dress, a blanket, and a fur coat tonight?"

"But she's my kitty. She's 'posed to play with me. Ow! Ow-ee, she scratched me! Ow, Daddee . . ." Her voice trailed off into tears, and he could hear Tiffani scolding her, full of agitated "I told you so's," and "Come on, let's go get you a Band-Aid."

"Hey, Dad," came Jamie's voice. "The cat just let Mallory have it. Can't blame the poor thing, it was stuffed into a dress."

"Hi, Jamie—good to talk to you. How bad was the scratch?"

"I dunno. Not too bad, I reckon. She's quit cryin'. It was on her hand. Hey, Dad? What's the Roman numeral for fifty-one look like?"

"Fifty-one? Wow, let's see if I can remember. What's fifty? Is it C?"

"No, that's a hundred."

"Does it say in your book what fifty is?"

"I don't know. I'm looking," Jamie said.

"Hang on, kiddo, there's somebody knocking, here." He

went to the door and admitted Ralph Jernigan, who glanced up and down the hall before entering the office.

Ralph gestured toward the door to the clerk's office. "Anybody else here?" he asked quietly.

"No, no—they've all gone. Let me just say goodbye to my son, here, and I'll be right with you. Jamie? Did you find what fifty is?"

"I think it's L. So do I just stick a one on the end?"

"I think so, Son. I'll double-check when I get home, but I'd better go, now. Hey, run and tell Tiff I said to be sure to wash Mallory's scratch, and put antibiotic ointment on it, okay? Thanks, buddy." He put down the phone and gave his attention to his visitor. He gestured to the chair in front of his desk.

"How are you, Brother Jernigan? It's good to have a chance to get to know you better."

Ralph Jernigan took a seat. He didn't smile. "Bishop, I'm here to ask what your plans are for emergency preparedness in our ward."

"Ah. Well, certainly that is a very important topic. I'm afraid we've been so busy organizing and staffing the ward that we haven't had time to do much planning in that direction, but I'm glad you brought it to my attention. I know the stake has a master plan, but—"

Ralph grunted and shook his head. "Way behind the times. It'd be too little, too late, if you take my meaning."

Bishop Shepherd wasn't sure he did. "Do you have some suggestions we might consider?"

"Bishop, do you mind if we close your window and the drapes? We're kind of exposed, sitting here, if you know what I mean."

"Well, it's a warm evening, but if you'll be more comfortable . . ."

In a moment the windows were shut and locked and the drapes drawn, shutting out the sweet smell of cut grass and the light of the setting sun. The bishop turned on a desk lamp, feeling stifled and slightly annoyed. He tried to ignore the discomfort.

"So what course do you propose we should take, Brother?"

Ralph Jernigan's narrow eyes narrowed even further, it seemed. "We can't be too careful," he said softly. "We have enemies, you know."

The bishop had been fanning himself with a copy of last Sunday's bulletin. He stopped.

"Enemies?" he asked. "What exactly do you mean?"

Ralph nodded knowingly. "They didn't all disappear with Carthage and Nauvoo."

"Enemies of the Church. Around here? Have you heard of any problems?"

Ralph gazed narrowly past him. "I have my sources. Have you had any work done on your office since you took over? Any new telephone lines, computer lines, and so forth?"

"Um—no, nothing. Why?"

"I wouldn't, if I were you. I think some of them work for the telephone company."

"Them?"

Ralph nodded. "The enemy. They want to destroy the Church. Inspired by Satan, of course. Rotten scoundrels. They hold meetings, to see how best they can get to us."

"Maybe, if you know anything specific, you should tell me, or the stake president."

"President Walker? He's a babe in the woods, when it comes

to this stuff. Good man. Too good, you know what I mean? Hard for him to comprehend evil. Got any protection, here? Gun?"

Bishop Shepherd shook his head. "You know, Ralph, the only protection I feel I need here is that of the Holy Ghost. There's no way I'd keep a gun around."

Ralph shrugged. "Your choice. Thought I'd warn you. But you'll need a plan of action. Evacuation routes. Safe houses. Food stashes, and weapons to protect them. Mobs'll try to take our food from us, you know. They'll kill for it. I'll tell you one thing: they're not gettin' mine."

The bishop drew a deep breath. "You have your year's supply, then?"

Ralph laughed. "Way more, Bishop. Way more'n a year. Me'n Linda, we got cans of wheat holding up the bed we sleep on, and cans of honey under our end tables in the living room." He lowered his voice even more. "I got a false back built into my clothes closet, hiding a stash of canned meats and stuff. We got powdered milk, and barrels of water. We could withstand a pretty good siege, I can tell you. And I've got guns and ammo aplenty. Let 'em come! They're not gonna get nothin' that's mine."

"Well, Ralph, I sincerely hope things'll never come to such a point that you'll have to defend your supplies."

"Oh, they will," Ralph said with certainty. "Prob'ly sooner than later, too. It's prophecy, Bishop—you know that."

"I'm aware that things could get pretty rough, all right. But I don't think we're there, yet. I really don't. Fairhaven is a remarkably peaceful place, and I don't know of any serious animosity toward the Church here, do you?"

Ralph gave him a knowing look. "Don't ask if you don't want to know," he said.

"I'm not sure I do," the bishop mused, half to himself. "Tell me, Ralph, are you a military man?"

"Had some training, here and there."

"I see. Well, maybe we can do this. Will you be on the lookout for trouble, and keep me posted? Just in case, you know . . ."

Ralph stood. "Be glad to do that for you, Bishop. Watch your back, now."

The bishop stood, too. "Will do, Ralph. Thanks for stopping by."

"I consider it my duty, sir."

The bishop watched as his visitor slipped quietly out of the building and circled his truck, checking his tires and who knew what else before he got in. He also appeared to be making a careful survey of the surrounding neighborhood as he drove slowly away.

The bishop shook away a chill from the back of his neck. He thought he knew, now, the reason behind Linda Jernigan's habitual resemblance to a startled rabbit.

CHAPTER FOUR

" . . . WHEN THERE'S LOVE AT HOME"

His two daughters lay asleep on the family room sofa, Mallory lying loosely in Tiffani's arms, her platinum hair gleaming against her older sister's antique gold, which lately was worn parted and twisted into interesting but tight shapes and braids that made her father wince. He set down his briefcase and picked up the library book that had fallen from Tiffani's hand.

"Tiff." He shook her gently. "Tiffi, you wanted a bath. I'll take Mal up to bed."

He lifted the unresisting Mallory into his arms as Tiffani stirred and opened her eyes.

"Oh, hey, Dad. Did I fall asleep? I was reading."

"Yep. Better get your bath, and when Mom gets home we'll have family prayer. I think Mallory's down for the count."

He carried his youngest up the stairs, shucked her out of her play clothes, and pulled a nightgown over her head. Samantha the kitten was curled up on Mallory's bed. With her claws hooked into the spread, she resisted his lifting her and unceremoniously dumping her onto the floor.

"Scat, you! You've caused enough trouble tonight."

"No, I want Samantha," Mallory protested sleepily, as he tucked her in.

"Even though she scratched you?"

"Yeah. I forgived her."

He allowed the kitten back into the room, where she jumped on the bed and settled beside Mallory, purring.

"Should we say a little prayer, Mal?"

"M-hmm," she agreed, but her breathing became deep and regular.

"I thank thee, Heavenly Father, for this beloved child," he whispered. "Bless her in every way and keep her from harm and evil." He dropped a kiss on her hair and pulled her door partially closed.

He heard Tiffani's bathwater running, and went across the landing to Jamie's room.

"Jamie, my man! Did you figure out Roman numeral fifty-one?"

Jamie was sitting up in his bed, reading a Harry Potter book. "Yeah, you were right. It was the L and a one." He yawned. "Is Mom home, yet?"

"Not yet. Want to come downstairs and have a treat while I grab a bite of dinner?"

"Sure. Dinner was just meat loaf, but dessert's that cold lemon stuff. Pie, I reckon."

"Lemon ice-box pie?"

"That's it."

"Hot dog! Climb on." He carried his son piggyback down the stairs to the kitchen, where they raided the refrigerator.

Jamie chose a nut-covered ice cream bar rather than the pie. His dad, knowing his likelihood of getting heartburn from eating a full dinner this late, took a couple of antacid capsules and threw caution to the wind. Trish's moist meat loaf with the sweet-sour topping, mashed potatoes and gravy, and cabbage-banana salad—who could resist?

"You know, I married your mom for her meat loaf," he confided to Jamie.

"Yeah? I didn't think it was *that* good."

"Oh, yeah, it is. I'm a meat loaf aficionado from way back."

"What's a—what you said?"

"Aficionado? It means—um—somebody who really likes something, or knows about it. Sort of an expert."

"Oh. Okay."

"So who d'you think's going to take Talladega this weekend?"

Jamie considered, looking at his ice cream as if it held the answer. "I reckon Dale Jr. will. It's about his turn."

"You think? I kinda think Jarrett is due."

Jamie shrugged. "Sure wish we could go see a Nascar race sometime. That'd be so cool."

"It would be. Wish they didn't usually race on Sundays. Oh, well—that's why VCRs were invented, don't you think?"

"Yeah, I reckon. Nascar and the Superbowl. And Monday night football."

"You may be right. But one of these days, Talladega'll hold one on a Saturday, and we're there, buddy!"

"Cool." Jamie gave him a wide, ice-creamy grin.

They ate in peaceable silence for a few minutes. The bishop sampled the tart smoothness of the lemon pie.

"Mmm," he said. "This is great. You know, I married your mom for her lemon ice-box pie."

"No way! You just said you married her for her meat loaf."

"And her pie. And her pineapple tapioca. And her chestnut dressing on Thanksgiving. And her enchiladas and clam chowder and—"

"And chocolate cake!" Jamie interrupted.

"That, too. *And* the fact that she was the sweetest, prettiest girl I'd ever met, and Heavenly Father agreed with me that she was my best choice. Between us, we somehow fooled her into thinking I was an okay choice, too."

Jamie chuckled.

The kitchen door opened, and the lady in question entered, laden with grocery sacks.

"Sorry to be so long," she said. "I stopped by the store for a few things and got talking to Muzzie. She was there getting stuff for her Brownie troop. Hi, honey—how long've you been home?"

"Just long enough to tuck Mallory in and tempt Jamie to a second dessert."

"So I see." She ruffled her son's hair.

"Mom—did you know Dad married you for your meat loaf and lemon ice-box pie?"

Trish's green eyes crinkled at the edges when she smiled, in a way her husband loved. "Is that right? That's funny, since he hadn't tasted my cooking at all before we got married."

"Dad?" Jamie's head swung toward his father, his grin echoing his mother's.

"Well, but you see, I could just tell, looking at her, that her meat loaf and lemon pie would be terrific."

"Uh-huh!"

Tiffani breezed in, wrapped in a robe, trailing flowery smells of scented shampoo and conditioner. "Hey, Mom. Did you remember to pick up my graph paper and pencils?"

"I did, and it's a good thing. When I talked to Mr. Warren, he said you were supposed to have had them with you Monday morning."

"I know. I kept forgetting about it. But I'll catch up. What else did you find out?"

"Well, parent-teacher conferences are always enlightening," Trish said, raising her eyebrows.

Tiffani sat down at the table and cut a sliver of pie, which she began eating with her fingers.

Trish frowned. "Use a fork, Tiff—and get a plate if you want some."

"That's all I want. I'm done. So, um—"

"So what do *you* think your Mom found out?" the bishop asked, regarding his daughter with a suspicious gleam in his eye. "What was there to find out?"

"Umm—I'm getting straight A's?"

Trish paused in putting away her purchases and took a small notebook from her shoulder bag. "Well, let's see. There is a possible A in P. E., but I can't be sure, because Miss Patman wasn't there to consult. Everything's pending in Algebra, because you're several assignments behind. Your book report was due yesterday in English, and you could stand to do some extra credit in that class, because your test score on A *Tale of Two Cities* was pretty low and is pulling your grade down. In World History you're doing pretty well, if you're satisfied with a C, which your mother is not, because—oh, no, how could this be—you haven't turned in your last two worksheets?"

Jamie groaned. "Oh, boy—you're in trouble, big time."

"Hush, Jamie. Mom, I'm almost caught up on all that stuff, honest I am. Did you—uh—was Mr. Pickard there?"

"Mr. Pickard. Oh, yes. Biology. What's this about refusing to dissect a frog?"

"He told you that?"

"Is it true?"

"Mom, it's way gross! I can't do that—I'd throw up!"

"Cool!" said Jamie.

Trish turned to her husband. "Did you ever dissect a frog in Biology?"

He well remembered the smell of the formaldehyde, the jokes and bravado of the guys in his group, the rubbery texture of the frog's underbelly as they sliced through it. "I sure did," he admitted.

"So did I," said Trish. "True, it was kind of disgusting, but it was interesting, too, to see how everything was placed, how the ligaments and muscles worked together. We did it, and you can, too, Tiff."

"Yeah, just think," Jamie put in, "the people who go to school to be doctors, they have to cut up dead *human* bodies!"

Tiffani turned on him. "They do not!" she cried. "That's not right, you don't know."

The bishop remembered a fishing trip with Tiffani when she was Mallory's age, when she had cried so hard over the "poor fishies" he caught that he'd had to release them, and they'd come home empty-handed. Later, when the realization had clicked in that tuna really was fish, she had refused to eat it for a year. His eldest was a girl for whom reality came hard.

"They do, too," Jamie was insisting. "I can prove it!"

His dad winked at him. "It's okay, Jamie. We don't need to

worry about that. This is just a frog problem. Now, Tiff—is there any alternative assignment you could do, instead of the frog?"

His wife and daughter both shook their heads. "I asked," they said, together. He had to laugh.

"Dad, it's not funny!"

"Right." His thoughts roamed back over the interview he had just conducted at the church. Fears needed to be faced, to be addressed, or they could overwhelm a person, cloud his judgment. He looked up. "Tell you what, Tiff—we'll pray about the frog problem, for you to be strengthened to be able to handle it. In fact, I'll give you a blessing before you have to do it. How's that?"

"A blessing about a *frog?*" His daughter looked skeptical. "Why would Heavenly Father care about that?"

"I believe he cares about all our needs and feelings. I think he'd want to help you overcome your fear and meet this challenge."

Tiffani looked miserable, but her green eyes flickered toward his in an appeal he recognized as hopeful.

"When do you have to do it?" he asked.

"Friday."

"All right, then. We'll start praying about it tonight, and Thursday night I'll give you the blessing."

"Okay," she agreed in a small voice.

"I wouldn't be scared of a dumb old dead frog if I was you," Jamie offered. "I can't wait till we get to chop one up!"

"That'll do, James, old friend. Trish, will you offer our prayer tonight?" he asked.

Y

The bishop was propped up in bed, reading from the book of Isaiah, while Trish creamed her as-yet wrinkle-free complexion. *Maybe that is why it stays so smooth*, he mused. Aloud, he said, "Honey, do you know Sister Jernigan?"

"Linda? Wispy blonde hair, big eyes?"

"That's the one."

"I know who she is. I served with her on a stake Primary committee one time. Why?"

"How does she strike you? Personality-wise, I mean. Attitude, and so forth."

"Um, she seemed sort of nervous. And anxious to get home, I remember that. I wondered if her husband was kind of impatient or something."

He nodded. "Something. Well, I just wondered. Oh, and— I'm not sure exactly how to go about this, but how would you feel about serving in Relief Society?"

She frowned. "I've been in Primary for eight years. I don't even get to go to Relief Society, except for Enrichment meeting. It'd be weird." She flashed a look at him in the mirror. "Are you just asking, or are you calling me to something?" She swung around on the vanity bench and faced him, her face half-creamed.

"Well, I reckon I'm calling you to be Relief Society secretary. Sister Ida Lou Reams asked for you."

"Ida Lou! Are you telling me she's going to be president?"

"It's looking that way. The Lord and her husband approved the choice, and she popped right out with the names of her counselors and secretary, so I think she must've had a little advance warning."

"Ida Lou—that's amazing! I never would have thought of her. But she's wonderful, of course. Totally kind and helpful and unassuming. You couldn't find anyone nicer. I don't think she's had a lot of experience with conducting meetings, and all. But she's sweet. Sure, I'd love to work with her. I guess I could use a change of pace."

"Thanks, hon."

"So who'd she choose for counselors?"

"Haven't talked to them yet, but if they accept, I'll tell you. Don't say anything to anybody, okay?"

"Okay, I know the drill. Just remember to find somebody really good for my little Primary class. I'll miss them."

The next afternoon he left the store early and drove across town to check on Brother and Sister Bainbridge. Parking outside their small white cottage with its colorful beds of zinnias and banks of hydrangea bushes, now grown a little wild, he sat for a minute trying to draw strength from heaven for the encounter. Brother Bainbridge had to know he'd been sent home to die, his cancer inoperable. What could he, their bishop, say in the face of such knowledge? What comfort and aid could he offer? He sent up a brief, fervent prayer and got out of his truck, carrying a basket of fruit Mary Lynn Connors had put together for him at the store.

Sister Hilda Bainbridge opened the door, squinting against the afternoon sunlight. "Who is it?" she asked.

"It's just me, Sister Bainbridge. Bishop Shepherd."

"Oh, Bishop! Come on in. I'm sorry—my eyes aren't so good, and the sunlight blinds me for a minute."

"How are you doing, Hilda? Did Roscoe get home all right?"

"Yes, he did, and I'll take you right in to see him. Now, what's this? For us? Why, thank you!"

"I hope you folks can eat fruit."

"Well, sure we can, and we can also offer it to all the good folks who come around to help us. Sister Talbot was here a little bit ago, and she's gone and organized some sisters to learn how to help Ross with the IV, so we don't have to pay somebody to come in so often. We do have a home health aide who'll come in once a day and help him bathe, but we couldn't afford anybody to do all the other things, day and night. I'm so grateful, because my eyes just won't let me do it, either."

The bishop was grateful, too. Frankie Talbot wasn't even called, yet, but she was already acting as a Relief Society leader would. The phrase "doing much good of her own free will and choice" came to mind.

He followed Hilda's slow progress toward a front bedroom, where a hospital bed had been installed, and where a much-emaciated Roscoe Bainbridge lay propped up with his eyes closed.

"Ross," said Hilda, "the bishop's here to see you."

Roscoe's head turned slowly on his pillows, and his eyes opened to half-mast.

"Hey there, Bishop. Congratulations. Heard you was called while I was away." His voice was hoarse and dry. He moved a hand toward the edge of the bed, and the bishop took it.

"Roscoe, it's good to see you. I'm glad you could come home."

"Reckon it's best. It was hard on Hildy, me being clear down to Birmingham. Now she can boss me around all she wants."

"That's right," Hilda agreed, her voice bright. "Gotta keep you in line." The bishop glanced at her. Her lips were pressed tightly together, and moisture had gathered in her eyes.

"I understand the good sisters of the ward are lining up to help keep you comfortable," he said to Roscoe.

"So I hear. Figure they're all anxious to take a poke at me with one of them needles. Prob'ly wish they could do that to their own husbands, but they'll take it out on me, 'cause I'm too lazy to run from 'em." He smiled weakly.

"I'm sure that's it," the bishop agreed with a chuckle.

"Hildy, why don't you get the bishop a drink of lemonade?"

"I'll just do that," she said and moved slowly from the room.

"Will you look after her, Bishop, when I'm gone?" Roscoe asked. "I don't reckon it'll be long, and I worry, you know. We don't have any younguns to watch out for her. Our one girl, Carolyn, passed away six years ago, you may recall."

The bishop swallowed. "Now there's no need to talk like that, Roscoe, but if it comes to that, I'll do my best. I promise you. And I know others will, too. She's a mighty sweet lady. We'll see she doesn't want for anything. Except I know she'll miss you an awful lot."

"Oh, I'll be around as much as the good Lord will allow," Roscoe said with certainty. "Hildy and me been together sixty-two years. Don't reckon a little detail like dyin' can keep us totally apart. Specially sinc't we got sealed, three years ago."

"Atlanta Temple, wasn't it?"

"Yessir. President Walker and his good wife taken us over with them. I bless 'em for it."

"And so do I. Now, Roscoe, is there anything else I can see to, for you? Anything you're worried about?"

For a minute he thought that Roscoe had drifted off to sleep, but then the sick man cleared his throat and spoke. "Done somethin' onc't that always troubled me," he said. "Don't rightly know what I can do about it, now, though."

"Want to talk about it?"

"Wadn't such a big thing, really. Kinda silly, in fact. But still, I stole somethin'. Defaced property, too."

"What'd you take, Roscoe?"

"Pitcher of Hildy."

"Come again?"

"Yep. I was goin' off to the army, and I didn't have no pitchers of her. Didn't neither of us have a camera. Couldn't afford such. Didn't reckon I could stand not havin' her sweet face to look at, so I went over to the library, where they kept a copy of the high school yearbook, and cut one out with my pocket knife. Her senior year. She graduated, and ever'thin'. I didn't, you know. Needed to work. Anyway, I cut it out real careful, so's it wouldn't mess up the book otherwise, and that pitcher was a real comfort to me while I was away. I still got it."

The bishop cleared his throat. He had no idea what to say.

"It's right in that there top bureau drawer," Roscoe said, gesturing weakly. "In my wallet, back of my driver's license. Hildy ain't never knowd about it, and I don't want her to know I stooped that low. If you'd just close the door for a minute, she won't come in."

The bishop closed the door gently. "You want me to get it for you?"

"Iffen you wouldn't mind."

He took the worn leather wallet from the drawer and found

the picture—a small, scuffed, black and white photo of a smiling girl with dark hair. The paper was worn soft by the years and much handling. He gave it to Roscoe, who looked at it briefly before his arm tired of holding it up.

"Been a comfort to me," he repeated. "But after I'm gone, Bishop, I wonder, could you do me the favor of puttin' it back where it goes?"

"Do you think that's necessary, Roscoe—after all these years? Does anybody even look at those old yearbooks in the library?"

"Don't matter, to my way o' thinkin'. Onliest way I can make res—res—what's that five-dollar word, Bishop? Means to make it right."

"Restitution?"

"That'd be it. Then I'd feel more like I'd borried that pitcher, and not stole it. I was young and dumb, you know? Didn't see that I was tainting my love for Hildy by doin' that. But now, I worry about it. It'd ease me considerable, Bishop, iffen you could do that for me. Private-like, you know?"

"I'll do it, Roscoe, and gladly. And I've got to say, that if that's the biggest sin you've got on your conscience, I'm not at all worried about your standing with the Lord."

"Ain't sayin' it's the worst I ever done, not by a long shot. I done took care of the others, though, far as I can remember. And I repented for this, but I just want it to go back where it belongs. I thank you, Bishop. You're a good friend. Just don't let on to Hildy, all right?"

"I won't," he promised. "Thank you for your trust." He slipped the small picture into his shirt pocket.

"You can open the door, now. And I'm so relieved I b'lieve I could sleep a little, after you take your lemonade."

"Good afternoon, then, Roscoe. I'll see you again, soon."

Roscoe nodded, his eyes closing. The bishop slipped out into the hall, where he intercepted Hilda walking carefully with a tall glass of homemade lemonade on a tray. He took it from her.

"Maybe we could visit in the living room while I drink this," he suggested. "Roscoe wants to nap for a while."

"I'm so glad he had a good visit with you, Bishop," Hilda said. "It wears him out to talk, but he seems to want to, with certain people."

"He's a really good man, Hilda. And he sure loves you."

She smiled, embarrassed. "I'm lucky we're sealed in the temple," she said.

"He mentioned that, too. And he's very concerned for you."

She nodded. "I know. I'll be fine, Bishop. I'll grieve when he goes, goodness knows—but I'll be fine. I have good neighbors who check on us, and lots of wonderful folks in the ward. So don't you be worrying about me."

"I won't worry," he promised. "But I'll keep a close watch, too—for Roscoe's sake."

"Well, thank you."

The bishop said his good-byes and went out to his truck, where again he sat for a long time with his head and arms resting on the steering wheel.

CHAPTER FIVE

"SHALL THE YOUTH OF ZION FALTER?"

He leaned back in his chair in the bishop's office and sighed in satisfaction. Frankie Talbot and Rosetta McIntyre had both accepted their callings as counselors to Ida Lou Reams in the Relief Society. Rosetta, a quiet, capable divorcee with two college-age children, seemed grateful that Ida Lou had thought of her, whereas Frankie's natural energy and enthusiasm for working with the women of the ward had practically catapulted her into acceptance.

"It seems to me you're already acting in this capacity," the bishop told her. "I'm real grateful to you for organizing the sisters to help Hilda Bainbridge get through these tough days. She's under a lot of strain, with Roscoe's care and her own limited vision."

"I know she is, and under the circumstances, I felt it was the least we could do. They're such sweethearts, both of them."

"They're the salt of the earth," the bishop agreed, thinking of the small, worn picture in his possession. "And I think the value of having the sisters go in is as much in the association it gives Hilda as in helping with the care. And you know, she's going to need a lot of continuing support after Roscoe passes away, too. I'm afraid the bottom's going to fall out for her. They've been everything to each other, especially since Carolyn died."

Frankie nodded soberly. "We'll be sure to stay close to her," she promised.

He expressed his pleasure and gratitude that she and the others had accepted this call, and promised that they would be sustained and set apart the following Sunday.

That done, he turned his attention to another of the responsibilities in the special bailiwick of the bishop—interviewing the youth of the ward. He looked at his appointment calendar. Two of the young people were scheduled for this evening—Thomas Rexford and Lisa Lou Pope. He knew both, to some extent. Lisa Lou was just a year or so older than Tiffani, and everybody in town knew Thomas Rexford, though they knew him by the inevitable nickname of "T-Rex."

T-Rex was a powerhouse on the high school football team— a bruising linebacker whose college costs were guaranteed to be paid if he could just stay healthy and keep his grades up. The bishop knew both of those needs were challenges for this particular young man, given his predilection for fast cars, motorcycles, pretty girls, and good times. He showed up at church once or twice a month, grinning and basking in the glory of the young people's adulation, and good-naturedly deigning to greet the adults as well, calling many of them by their first names, which had always made the bishop wince. His own children wouldn't have dreamed of doing so—they knew they were to refer to Church members by the respectful titles of Brother and Sister, other adults by Mr. or Mrs., and to say "Yes, ma'am" and

"No, sir" as occasion demanded. It was an established Southern tradition that had been drummed into him in childhood, and had served him well as an adult, for that matter. He was glad that Trish encouraged this little propriety as well, although she had informed him that "ma'am" and "sir" had pretty much gone the way of other such formalities in the Northern and Western states. He had a sneaking, possibly irrational, suspicion that this loss contributed to the lack of respect many youngsters seemed to have for all adults—and the general increase in juvenile crime. So it was that when T-Rex strolled into the bishop's office some twelve or so minutes late for his interview, his new bishop had to grit his teeth to hang on to his welcoming smile.

"A-ay, Bish!" T-Rex said, flashing his infectious 'aren't-you-glad-to- see-me?' grin. "Wass up?"

"How are you, Thomas?" the bishop responded, shaking the beefy hand and throwing one arm around the boy's massive shoulders. "Come and sit down."

T-Rex sprawled in one of the upholstered chairs, scrunch-ing down on his spine and crossing one sneakered foot over the other knee. "So how ya doin'? Is it cool, bein' bishop?"

"Well, it's a whole new experience, I can tell you that. It's pretty cool to get to spend a little one-on-one time with people, get to know them better. Which is why I asked you to come in this evening. How are things going for you, Thomas?"

"Goin' great, man!"

"Well, that's good to hear. But could you break that down a little? Be more specific?"

"Uh—like what?"

"Oh, you know—school, church, girls, sports, home-life."

"School's okay. Almost out for the summer, best thing about that."

"How're your grades coming?"

T-Rex shrugged, and his grin seemed to fade just a little. "Reckon I'll get by. I'm passin' everything."

"Will passing be good enough to get you get into whatever college you want?"

"I'll do okay. I think I'll be in pretty high demand."

"I know your football skills are legendary. I've enjoyed watching you a few times, myself."

"Oh, yeah?" The boy's face lit up again. "You actually go to the games?"

"When I can. I went with Tiffani and her girlfriends a couple of times this year, just to keep an eye on 'em, you know. You were pretty spectacular in that game against Redstone."

"Yeah, that was a great game. We knocked them suckers into next week, didn' we? Whoo-ee!"

"That you did. So how's the team look for next fall?"

"Not too bad. We're losing Rick Hatcher, and that's tough. He's been a real sweet quarterback. But we've got a couple of guys duking it out to replace him, and neither one's too shabby, so we'll be set. A lot of our line'll be back."

"Good. Glad to hear it. Got a girlfriend, Thomas?"

"Aw, you know—one and then another. Gotta spread the joy around a little." His grin returned, full-force.

"Keeping it light, are you?"

"Whatcha mean?"

"You know—staying morally clean. Treating the girls with respect. Honoring your priesthood. Not getting too physical, into petting and that."

The boy's eyes flickered. "Oh, sure. Keeping it light. I don't wanta get in girl trouble, no sir."

"Believe me when I tell you you'll be mighty glad in years

to come if you'll stay morally clean and save the important stuff for the girl you choose to marry."

"Marry! Man, that's a ways down the road. I'm only seventeen."

The bishop nodded. "Exactly. Keep that in mind, will you, Thomas? I'd reckon it can be really tempting when you're the popular man about campus—the football hero—and the young ladies are all admiring you and some of them are probably offering their favors. Don't you find that to be true?"

T-Rex's gaze slid toward the corner of the office. "Well, yeah, I reckon."

"Takes a lot of courage, I bet, to face what you have to, out on the field."

"Um—well, yeah, I guess, if you want to put it that way. A guy can't back down, that's for ever-lovin' sure!"

"There's another kind of courage, too. Do you know what I'm getting at, Thomas?"

"Why don't you go ahead and tell me?"

The bishop grinned. " 'Cause I'm going to anyway, right?"

Thomas's answering grin told him he was right.

"Well, I'm talking about moral courage. I think it's a real important kind of courage for a young man to develop. Obviously you've got what it takes, because you've already developed a lot of physical and mental courage. Moral courage is the kind that helps a guy be strong enough to do what's right, even when it's tough. Helps him be strong enough to say 'No' to a young woman's advances, when 'Yes' would be so much easier. And I know the girls these days don't just sit back and wait to be asked out, do they?"

Thomas shook his head.

"Same kind of courage helps him not cheat on an exam

even if he doesn't feel real confident in his preparation. Helps him have the strength to tell his bishop if there's something he needs to confess and repent of. That kind of courage. I think that's really important, don't you?"

Thomas nodded again, studying his hands. "I reckon." He glanced up. "Kinda hard to come by, though, Bishop."

"I know. But see, the thing is, you develop it same way you develop physical courage. Practice. You mess up, you get right back up and try again and do what you have to do to correct mistakes and strengthen yourself. You keep resisting temptations, and it gets easier to do. Scriptures say, 'Resist the devil and he will flee from you.' And a strong man is a praying man, because he's smart enough and strong enough to recognize his own weak spots, and to ask for special help to overcome them. It's sort of like asking the Lord to be your coach. Some people think a weak man is the one who prays, but I don't think so. Strongest guys I know are praying men."

Thomas's head jerked back just a little, as if the idea startled him. "Huh," he said.

"And, Thomas, I really want to see you grow up to be a strong man, inside and out. I admire what you've already achieved, and the Lord and I are both here to help you any way we can with developing that moral strength, just like your coach is there for you, helping you develop your physical strength and courage."

"Okay, Bishop. That's cool. That's good. I'll remember that. Well, I reckon I'd better get on home and finish up my homework and all."

"How are things at home?"

"Just fine," the boy said, but his eyes had grown wary, and he stood up, preparing to leave.

The bishop stayed seated. "Folks doing okay?"

"Sure."

"What's your dad doing these days?"

"Uh—he's just between jobs right now, but he'll get something soon. The base closure set him back a little, but he'll be okay."

"Mom working?"

"Uh—couple of afternoons a week, at K-Mart. But she has to spend a lot of time with my gramma. She's not doin' too hot. She's eighty-nine, and kinda like weak and confused."

"I see. You tell your folks I'll help any way I can, okay, Thomas? I'll be in touch with them. And thanks for coming to see me. We'll work on getting you advanced in the priesthood, too, all right? I see you're still a deacon. No shame there, but you'd make a fine priest."

"Oh, I don't know about that. I can't see me up there sayin' a sacrament prayer in front of ever'body. I mean, that's just not my style."

"Well, that's a ways down the road. One step at a time, right, Thomas? You took a big step today, coming in to see me. Thank you."

"Sure, Bishop. No problem."

The bishop stood, they shook hands, and the bishop opened the door to see him out. Lisa Lou was sitting on the sofa in the hall, waiting. Immediately Thomas's eyes brightened, and his grin returned.

"Hey there, Lisa Lou! How's my favorite girl today?"

Lisa Lou looked around. "Now, who would that be, T-Rex?" she asked, rising and coming forward with a self-conscious smile.

"Why, you, sugarfoot, who else?" Thomas waved and was

out the door. "See ya, Bish!" he called back over his shoulder. And a considerable shoulder it was.

"Come in, Lisa Lou. How are you?" the bishop invited. He left the door slightly ajar, for propriety's sake. Lisa Lou seated herself decorously.

"I'm just fine," she said shyly. "That T-Rex, he's a character."

"He is that," the bishop agreed. "I guess a lot of girls like him, huh?"

"Oh, yeah, I mean, yessir, they sure do. I used to, but not anymore. Not like that."

"Oh?"

She bent her head down a little, and her shiny light brown hair fell forward, hiding her face. "Yessir. I like somebody else, now."

"That right? Anybody I know?"

"Well—prob'ly you do. Ricky Smedley?"

"Oh, sure, I've known the Smedleys for a long time. Nice family. Let's see—Ricky's the second boy, isn't he?"

"Yessir. He's real sweet. In fact, I think I'm in love with him."

"Really. How old are you now, Lisa Lou?"

"Well, I'm sixteen, but—are you saying I'm too young to be in love, Bishop?"

The bishop sensed turbulence ahead. He tried to defuse the situation with a smile. "All depends," he hedged. He thought of his own great-grandmother, who, at fourteen, had married a man eleven years her senior and to all appearances had enjoyed a happy life with him. But those had been different times. Simpler times. "Depends, I guess, on your maturity level, and what you mean by 'in love.' Maybe you could define that for me."

Lisa Lou looked affronted. "Well—I mean, you know—it's like how you feel all jittery when you see somebody, how you think about them all the time, and want to write their name all over your notebooks, and get all flustered if they talk to you. How you feel like you'll just die if they don't ask you out, but you'll just die if they do? And you think they're just the cutest, sweetest thing in the world, and you can't stand it if somebody else is talking to them, instead of you? Like that . . ." she finished. "I mean, I expect you've felt that way before, haven't you?"

"I do seem to recall some of those feelings, sure enough," he agreed. "Now, answer me this: what do you want for Ricky?"

"Say what, Bishop?"

"What would you wish for him, if you had the power to do anything for him?"

"Oh, that's easy. I'd wish that he loved me back, and would be with me forever."

"Uh-huh. Doing what?"

She frowned. "I don't get what you mean."

"What would you be doing together? Oh, I know about the romantic side of things—I'm not asking that. I mean, what would you like to be doing with him, forever, other than that?"

"I don't know—whatever, I guess. I'd like to be his wife."

"And what would he be doing, while you were cooking and cleaning and taking care of his kids?"

She shrugged. "Working, I reckon. Is that what you mean?"

"What kind of work does Ricky want to do?"

"I don't know!"

"How much education does he plan to get?"

"College, I guess. He's never said. See, he doesn't—I don't think he knows—how I feel."

"Does he like you?"

Her cheeks reddened. "Well, like—I don't know! Sometimes I think he does. I mean, he smiles at me in the hall at school, and he asks me to dance, and stuff. One time he winked at me, and I took that to mean something."

"I see. More than it would mean if T-Rex winked at you, is that what you're saying?"

"Oh, way more. 'Cause, Ricky, he doesn't just go around flirting with everybody, like T-Rex."

"That's probably a good thing."

"Yeah, it is. T-Rex, he's cool and all, but he—you know—he gets around, and it never means anything, but Ricky, he's different. He's special."

"Okay, I understand. Now Lisa Lou, what are your ambitions? Let's talk about your goals and plans. How about your education—are you planning for college?"

"Well, you know—if I'm not married by then, I s'pose I'll go."

"And what would you like to study?"

She frowned. "Um, maybe like home-ec, or something. The truth is, Bishop, I just want to be a wife and mom."

"Not a thing wrong with that, either. Only problem is, things are more complicated these days than they used to be. So many young women find they need to work, to help put their husbands through college, or to supplement the income while he's getting started in a career, or they find themselves as single moms, for one reason or another. It's good to have some education, some kind of training to fall back on, when those times come along. And it's a lot easier to go to school before you're married than after. Even if you learn secretarial skills, or how to be a dental hygienist—short term courses rather than a four-year degree—you'll probably be mighty glad you did. Also, I've always thought that a girl with some education is so much more interesting to be with than one who doesn't know much. I know I'm glad my wife had the opportunity to get some college in before we married."

Lisa Lou looked at him speculatively. "Your wife's a real neat lady," she admitted, "I'd like to be like her."

He smiled. "Thanks. I have to say, you couldn't pick a better person to pattern after. Now, let's see. You're a Mia Maid, right?"

"Yessir."

"Great. And you're working on your Personal Progress goals?"

"Well—when I have time."

"All those goals are designed to help you become the best person—and the best wife and mother someday—that you can be. They're well worth the time they take to accomplish. Now, Lisa Lou, I'll tell you what: I'd like to meet with you again in a few weeks, and there are two special assignments I'd like you to do before we meet again."

"What would they be, Bishop?"

"First of all, I want you to think deeply about Ricky Smedley."

Her blush returned, and her smile. "Oh, I can do that, all right!"

"I want you to think about what I asked you before. What, if you love him, would you wish for him to have, if it were in your power to give it to him? Of course, I don't mean a cool car or anything like that. And I want you to find out, by talking to him, what he wants out of life. What his dreams are, at this point. What's important to him. Can you do that?"

"Sure!"

"Then I want you to think deeply about yourself. Get in

touch with the real Lisa Lou, who is an eternal spirit with gifts and talents and hopes and dreams of her own. Ask her what her real interests are—what she likes to do, what she thinks is important, how she wants her life to be in two years—in five years—in twenty years—and in eternity. Can you do that? And I want you to write all your thoughts down, and bring them back to discuss with me the next time we get together. All right?"

"Nobody ever asked me that stuff, before."

"Well, then—maybe that's why I feel impressed to ask you now. Maybe Heavenly Father wants you to think about these things."

"Wow." She looked at him solemnly. "I'll sure try."

"Good girl. Is there anything else you'd like to discuss?"

"I guess not."

"How's your family? Mom and Dad okay?"

She nodded. "Fine, I reckon, far's I can tell. I'm not home a whole lot, what with school and seminary and work and Young Women and hangin' with my friends."

"Where are you working?"

"Dairy Kreme, Wednesdays and Saturdays."

"Really? I'll stop in sometime, have you make me a malt."

"I'll make you a good one," she promised. "Thank you, Bishop. Um—don't tell Ricky, what I told you, okay?"

"My lips are sealed," he assured her, seeing her out.

He sank back down into his chair and wiped his forehead with his handkerchief, wondering if the air-conditioning in the building was as efficient as it needed to be.

Y

It was time, as he had come to think of it, for the "frog-blessing." After supper he and Tiffani and Trish went into Tiff's room and had her sit on her desk chair while Trish sat on the edge of the bed, and he placed his hands on his daughter's head and tried to open his mind and heart to the Spirit. The blessing, when it came, was less about the frog and more about the Lord's desire that his children improve themselves and learn all they can in this life, both temporally and spiritually. He blessed Tiffani that her fears would subside and her natural desire to learn would be enhanced, not only in biology, but in all her classes and with regard to the gospel as well. He assured her that she had an excellent mind and memory and that the Lord desired her to make good use of them, both for her own good and for the eventual blessing of the lives of others. After the blessing, he hugged her and told her how pleased he was with her as a daughter, and how much he loved her.

"I love you, too, Daddy," she whispered. "Thanks. I think that'll help."

"You just exercise your faith, sweetheart, and I think it will, too."

"Dad?"

"Yes?"

"When you give me a blessing, how much of what you say comes from what you want for me, and how much is really from Heavenly Father?"

He joined Trish on the edge of the bed. "Boy, that's a good question, Tiff. Sometimes it's hard to tell, and other times, I know I've found myself saying things I never had thought of myself. Things that just sort of came through me, you might say. But I like to think that the things I want for you and the things your Heavenly Father wants for you are not so different."

"But—did any of those surprise things come through, this time?"

"Well, I wasn't entirely sure what was meant by the part about you using your education to serve other people. I don't know if that means your own family someday, or if you'll be a teacher, or in the medical field, or whatever . . ."

"Ooh. Not the medical field. Too yucky."

Her dad smiled. "Don't limit yourself, baby, by your present squeamishness. That can be overcome. Besides, that was just an example. There are lots of ways to serve people."

"So, you didn't plan to say that part, huh?"

"I truly did not."

"Okay."

"You know, the best thing about doing well in school," Trish said, "is that then you're expanding your future options, instead of limiting them."

"What do you mean, Mom?"

"Well, if you take all easy classes, and only get so-so grades in them, you might not be able to get into the college or program or have the career you might one day want. But if you're prepared with good grades in important classes, then you'll have more choices down the road. And where you go to school, and what you study, will determine the people you meet and associate with, and since you'll choose a husband from among your associates, that could be a really important thing, too."

The bishop smiled to himself. Seemed like, with women, it all came down to marriage. How many guys did he know who considered that they needed good grades to get into a good program to meet the best girls?

"Besides," his wife continued, "the more you know, in all fields of study, the richer you'll be, inside. If you know about history and art and music and literature, your inner life—your mind and spirit—will be wealthy, whatever your circumstances. And if you learn about science and current events, you'll be more at home in the world around you, and better able to make good choices and decisions. And the more you know about the gospel, the stronger and happier you'll be, all lifelong."

All right, the bishop admitted. It wasn't all about romance. His wife was a wise woman. And he was a blessed man.

CHAPTER SIX

Y

" . . . FOR THE JOY OF HUMAN LOVE"

The cooler hours of early Saturday morning were generally heralded by a raucous chorus of lawn mowers
around the neighborhood, and Bishop Jim Shepherd
added the voice of his to the song. A few folks preferred to mow
on Sunday, or in the evening, but the consensus was still in
favor of Saturday morning. That way, the wives were happy to
see that chore, at least, out of the way, and more likely to agree
to whatever other activities their husbands or sons had in mind
for the rest of the day, whether it be a fishing trip, ball game,
golf at the club, or just lazing in the hammock, inhaling the
rising fragrance of new-mown Zoysia.

He mopped his face and happily steered his mower into its
corner of the garage, then stepped outside to admire his handi-
work. The shade was still deep, the corners of the yard bright
with Trish's caladiums and begonias. Surely, he thought, green
had to be his favorite color, and the Lord must love it, too, with
all the shades and tones of it he used in his creations.

"Your yard looks plumb lovely," offered Hestelle Pierce from her side of the fence. "I declare, your little wife has a way with flowers and such!"

"Does, doesn't she?" he agreed. "Left up to me, I'm afraid we'd just have grass and trees. But I sure enjoy her touches of color."

"So do I. How's ever'body at your house, Mr. Shepherd?"

"Doing well. I've had just a touch of allergies—a little sneezing and that, but nothing serious. How about yourself?"

"Oh, mercy—my allergies have been so bad this year! I declare, I've sneezed till I thought my head would like to pop off! And my eyes are so red and itchy I can't hardly see out of 'em. Reckon why we have such things—do you know? Why can't we just get along with God's creation, and not suffer from it?"

Hestelle's eyes looked perfectly clear to the bishop, but he didn't remark on it. "I'm not sure, Miz Hestelle. Maybe it has to do with all the weeds and things that were put on earth after the fall of Adam, you know, to 'afflict and torment man.' Allergies surely can afflict and torment a body, that's certain."

"Well, I sure wisht Adam hatn't of fallen! Reckon it must have been pure delight in the Garden of Eden—no allergies there, I'd wager. And we could all still be enjoyin' that, hatn't of been for the Fall. But I reckon Eve was just too much for him."

"I know what you mean, but then again, I don't suppose we'd even be here, would we, if it hadn't been for the Fall? They wouldn't have ever had children, in their innocent state, so it'd still just be Adam and Eve, all on their own."

Hestelle Pierce regarded him with surprise. "Well, I hatn't never looked at it like that," she said. "But I do b'lieve you're right! So you reckon weeds and allergies are what we've got to put up with, to be here?"

"That's how I see it. Like learning to work, and to choose between good and evil, and all that."

She nodded. "Earn our bread by the sweat of our brow, like the Good Book says."

"Exactly. And I think right now I'm going to go shower off some of this sweat and eat some of that bread. You have you a fine day now, Miz Hestelle."

"I thank you, Mr. Shepherd. Y'all do the same."

He wondered why, in all the years they had been neighbors, he had called her Miz Hestelle, while she, many years his senior, still insisted upon calling him Mr. Shepherd, instead of Jim. *Oh, well,* he thought. *If that's what she's comfortable with, I can go along.*

He took a hand towel from the branch of a chinaberry tree where he had left it, wiped his face and neck, and draped it across one shoulder. It was May, now, and the sun felt hot as soon as it was barely up. Nothing to what July and August would be, of course, but hot all the same.

"Jim, guess what!" Trish called happily from the range in the kitchen where she was turning hash browns. Most mornings she insisted they eat healthy cereals and fruit, but Saturday was their day for eggs, with pancakes, hash browns, or grits and bacon, ham, or sausage. On very special occasions, there would be Belgian waffles made with egg whites beaten to a fluff and topped with berries and real whipped cream.

"What, babe?" he asked, pausing to snitch a link sausage.

"Mom and Dad are coming, the first of June!"

"They are?" he asked weakly, then quickly revised it to

"They are! Terrific! Hey, Mal—Nana and Papa are coming to see us."

"I know," Mallory said, nodding wisely. "And Auntie Merrie, too."

"They're bringing Meredith?" Jim asked.

Meredith, Trish's younger sister, was the least favorite of his three sisters-in-law. It wasn't that he didn't like her, he told himself. It was just that he felt thoroughly patronized and barely tolerated by her. Of course, he hadn't seen her for three years. Maybe things had changed. Maybe they'd gotten worse.

"I know you dread it when my folks come," Trish was saying, throwing him an apologetic glance. "But they are my family, and I love them. Mom and Dad were thrilled when I told them you were bishop."

"Hey, I'm tickled pink they're coming. Aren't I, Mallory? See my ears? They're pink, aren't they?"

"They're real pink, Mommy. I think he's glad."

"I think he's hot."

"Well, thank you, my dear—I think you're pretty hot, too."

"Now, Jim . . ." she warned, unamused.

"Where're the rest of the troops?" he asked, feeling it best to change the direction of the conversation.

"Jamie'll be right down, but you can call Tiff if you want. Tell her I'm fixing her favorite breakfast, in honor of the successful frog experience."

"I take it I shouldn't shower before breakfast."

"Not if you want to eat with the family, which is a rare enough occurrence."

"Okay—be right back." He trudged up the stairs, admonishing himself as he went to be very careful of his wife's feelings, which apparently were running pretty high this morning, and maybe even about to overflow their banks. It was true he was a little disconcerted about the visit from his in-laws, but he had survived them before, and he would again. It was worth it, for Trish to have the opportunity to share her life with her family. He knocked lightly, then opened Tiffani's door a crack.

"Paging Miss Tiffani Shepherd, frog princess, victor of the biology lab, and favorite older daughter of her father," he intoned. "You are hereby advised that your favorite breakfast is about to be served in the south dining room."

A sleepy groan ensued from the direction of the bed. "I'm not hungry. I'm tired."

"I believe the menu includes savory link sausages, hash browns, fluffy scrambled eggs, and hot biscuits with pan gravy or strawberry jam."

"Mmm. Okay, I'll be down. In a couple of minutes."

Jamie bounded from his room. "Take your time, Tiff. I'll eat yours for you if you're too sleepy to get up," he offered with a grin, heading for the stairs.

"You will not! You'd better not touch mine!" Her dad heard her feet hit the floor.

"Ah—at last the princess arises to greet the dawn!"

"Dad, you're corny," Tiffani complained, but her voice held a giggle.

"Corn-fed from the cradle up. Never claimed otherwise. Oh—and Mom has a surprise announcement."

"What is it?"

"I wouldn't dream of stealing her thunder. See you downstairs."

He washed up quickly and joined the family at the table, grinning at Trish's pleasure in informing her two eldest of the forthcoming visit of their beloved Nana and Papa and Aunt

Merrie. They reacted with honest delight—and he wondered why he couldn't join them. Trish's parents were wonderful people—active and faithful in the Church, bright and happy and helpful in any way they could be. So what was his problem? He'd never been entirely sure, but whatever it was, he vowed to solve it—to clear it out of his life once and for all, so that his joy with his family on the occasion could be sincere and un-restrained. He had nearly a month to deal with the situation. He could prepare. He could repent. And he would do it, if it killed him.

After breakfast, while Tiffani took her turn clearing up the dishes, he played a computerized Nascar racing game with Jamie, and Trish worked on a talk she was preparing for the next day's sacrament meeting. She and the rest of the new Relief Society presidency had been asked to speak. Trish and the two counselors were old hands at speaking in church, but Ida Lou had been almost panic-stricken.

"Bishop, I don't have the words to say, like the others," she had told him, her eyes anxious. "I'm not educated, and smart about things like those young girls. All I know is how to work, and love people."

"Well now, see? I think that's exactly why the Lord called you," he had told her. "Those are wonderful qualities. Maybe you could talk about those things, since they're your strong points, and they also happen to be the two most important ele-ments of service. A fancy sermon's not what we need from you, anyway. Just a simple expression of your deepest feelings about the gospel and the Savior. Just be yourself, and your words'll come across just fine. You'll see."

"Oh dear. Will you pray for me?"

"Absolutely."

He would, too. And he sincerely hoped Ida Lou Reams would include him in her simple, heartfelt petitions to the Lord. If anyone could count on having prayers heard and answered, he believed it would be Ida Lou.

That afternoon Trish curled up on the sofa near where he was reading and said brightly, "Okay, I'm making my lists—one for things to do while they're here, and one for everything that needs to be done before they arrive. Help me think! I know the windows need washing, inside and out, and the carpets upstairs need a good cleaning. I'd love to get new wallpaper in the guest room, where we'll put my folks, and Merrie can have Mallory's room. Mal can bunk with Tiffani that week. We'll need to move her toys out of her room, but—"

"Why? Why can't Mal's toys just be neatly put on her shelves and in her toy box?"

"Jim, because she'll want to play with them! They'll need to be available to her. And besides, you just don't put a grown woman in a room filled with toys. It's . . . degrading, or something. Disrespectful. And I wonder if Samantha will follow Mallory to Tiff's room, or if she'll still want to sleep on Mallory's bed? Merrie might not enjoy sleeping with an active kitten."

"You're sure her—what's his name—Dirk? You're sure he's not coming, too?"

"He can't leave his work, Mom said, but Meredith needs a break. Besides, she hasn't been back here since Dad was transferred. She was what, then? Thirteen?"

He remembered that transfer. Brother and Sister Langham had been a presence in the small Alabama branch, as it had been, then—almost on the verge of becoming a ward—and it had been a loss to priesthood and auxiliary leadership to have them go. Worse than that, it had been a blow to the heart of a certain young brother in that branch, one eighteen-year-old James Dean Shepherd, when the Langhams left for Arizona, taking with them their sixteen-year-old daughter, Patricia, she of the shiny dark brown hair and lightly freckled nose that crinkled in the middle when she laughed, which she did delightfully and often. Life had seemed drab after the Langham station wagon headed west. It had been as though he had suddenly gone color-blind, seeing everything in shades of gray. Dances and activities had lost their appeal, and even the Sunday services didn't seem as meaningful as they had when Trish Langham had been sitting in the fourth row with her family, where he could surreptitiously check her reaction to touching or humorous things that were said from the pulpit. He hadn't told anyone of his feelings for Trish, so he suffered in silence when she was gone, preferring that to being questioned, teased, reassured that he'd get over it, or even showered with sympathy.

And then the letter came. Pale pink envelope with an embossed rose on the back, girlish script addressing it to Jim Shepherd Jr., in care of Shepherd's Quality Food Mart, handed to him by his father. He could still see his father's big, veined hand holding out the delicate missive, hear his voice saying, "Whoa, Son, if I didn't know better, I'd say this looks like a love letter. But who'd send you a love letter here at the store? In fact, who'd send you a love letter?"

Who, indeed? Jim had looked at the Arizona postmark and dared to hope.

"Oh," he'd said offhandedly, "it's not a love letter. It's just a friend from church. Her family moved away." He had stuffed the letter in his back pocket, to open when he was alone, and had gone back to mopping the produce aisle. But his heart had beat faster, and as soon as nobody was paying him any attention, he had sauntered into the rest room and sought privacy in a stall. It wasn't the most auspicious place to read a letter from Trish. He wished he were sitting on a split-rail fence up at Shepherd's Pass, with the sweet wind blowing through the grasses, and the cattle calling with their gentle voices. But this would have to do; he couldn't wait any longer. He slid a finger carefully under the flap of the envelope, trying not to tear it, and pulled out the single folded sheet.

Dear Jim,

How's everything going? How's everybody at church? I miss everybody. Tell Becky and Shellie hey for me. Out here they say hi, not hey, like there. It's real dry here, and cool and windy at night and in the early morning, but real hot in the afternoons. The school I go to is new and all on one floor, and a lot of the kids are like Indian or Spanish. Its ok, but I miss Fairhaven High. Do you ever see Muzzie at school? She was my best friend who wasn't LDS. If you see her, tell her hey for me and to write me. I've got letters from Shellie and from Sister Talbot and a cute note from little Brian Kent that I use to baby-sit.

So, how's work? And baseball? And are you going to race your truck on Saturday mornings this summer? If you do, I hope you win. The Church here is bigger than there, and there are more kids, but I don't know them much yet, and I feel kinda lonesome for some of the people there. Write me if you want.

Your friend,

Trish

P.S. I hope its okay to send this to your dad's store. My Mom doesn't know where she put the branch address list. Luff ya! T.

He read the letter over three times. Could it qualify, in any way, shape or form, as a love letter? How should he know? It was the first letter he could ever remember receiving in his whole life. When she said she missed some of the people in Fairhaven, did that include Jim Shepherd? When she put "Luff ya" in the postscript, could that be taken with any degree of meaning, or was it just girl talk? Did she really want him to write back? And how could he possibly say "hey" to Becky and Shellie and Muzzie for her? He was shy enough that he didn't even acknowledge the presence of those girls if he wasn't forced to. If he gave them Trish's message, they'd know she'd written him! Of course, that wasn't an altogether unpleasant prospect— maybe it would raise him a notch in their estimation—maybe like from nonexistent to a place in the land of the living. On the other hand, maybe they'd tease him about her. Or worse, maybe they'd write and tease her about him! Life had suddenly grown complicated.

"Jim? What're you grinning about?"

"Hmm? Oh, yeah, I think Merrie must've been about thir-teen when you moved away, because you were sixteen, weren't you?"

"Yes, but you're avoiding my question. Why the big grin?"

He felt himself blushing, an acutely embarrassing thing after all these years. "Thinking about getting that first letter from you," he admitted. "I was such a dope—such a rube. No sense at all about girls. Scared to death to write back, but too crazy about you not to."

Trish came and sat on his lap, pressing her cool cheek against his flaming one. "I still have that answer you sent me," she said softly. "I practically wore it out reading it over and over."

He chuckled. "Huh! Must mean you couldn't decipher it, 'cause it can't have been that good."

"It wasn't. It was very stiff and noncommittal and polite. Not very personal at all."

"Well, heck, I guess not—I was afraid your dad would read it!"

"He wouldn't have. Nor Mom. Merrie would've, though, if she'd found it. I kept it hidden in my scripture tote, with tithing receipts and my patriarchal blessing."

"Wow—I was in good company."

"That's right—and that letter was almost as inspiring to me as the other things."

"Come on, Trish. You just said it was stiff and—"

"Yes, but it was from you. In your very own not-so-great handwriting. See, even then, I think I loved your spirit first. I loved that you were a convert, and took the gospel seriously. And you were so nice. Not phony-nice, and not namby-pamby, goody-goody nice, but genuinely nice. Kind to people. And unassuming. No big-head, swaggering jock. Just a down-home, solid, good person."

He shrugged. "Didn't have anything to be big-headed about. Just an ordinary kid."

She shook her head. "Huh-uh. Not ordinary at all. Pretty rare, in fact. And I didn't want to lose touch with that—with you."

He tightened his arms around her. "Good thing you kept writing."

"Sure is—what was the ratio? Ten of my letters to one of yours?"

He winced. "Sorry, babe. I'm not much of a letter writer, even now."

"Oh, you improved."

"I did?"

"Over time, you actually began to answer my questions, and to share your thoughts. That was so cool, you can't imagine."

"I had thoughts?"

"And a sense of humor about things that tickled my funny bone. And a growing testimony, that shone through more and more as you grew up."

"Well, you know how it is with converts. The Church and the gospel were pretty meaningful to me, even as a young guy."

"You see? I picked up on that, and it seemed . . . priceless. Sometimes you'd tell me about your conversations with Mac, how you'd debate over scriptures and things. Most of the guys I knew didn't talk much about the gospel, except maybe right after they came home from their missions, and then they'd taper off on that, and I think sometimes it was because they sensed that the girls got bored with hearing about it. But I never got bored, reading about things that meant a lot to you. I was sorry when you didn't get to serve a full-time mission. I knew you wanted to."

"It was a dream I had, but it didn't work out."

"It's too bad. I know your dad's illness complicated things."

"Yeah, well—I felt torn, knowing I should go, but knowing that Dad needed me, too. Reckon I just wasn't strong enough in the faith, yet, to stand up for what I believed. I've often thought it's likely Dad would've been blessed with better health, if I'd have just gone."

"Maybe so, and maybe not. But I think you did okay. It was a sacrifice you made, to be there for him and your mom, and to keep the business going through his illness. I believe Heavenly Father understands. He knows your heart."

The bishop sighed. "Well, then he knows that I still wrestle with myself over that decision. I expect I'd be a better bishop and a better husband and father now if I'd served a mission. I'd have had experiences I just couldn't get working in the store. But . . . I made my choice, and I live with it."

"I don't see how you could be a better husband or father, honey. And it seems to me you're off to a great start as bishop, too."

He kissed his wife—once and then again. "I appreciate your vote of confidence, babe," he told her. "You have no idea how much."

Mallory came into the room, her eyes alight at the sight of her mommy sitting on her daddy's lap. "Me, too—me, too," she cried, climbing on Trish's knees. "Big hug, just like the Teletubbies!"

CHAPTER SEVEN

" . . . ON THIS, THE SABBATH DAY"

Bishopric meetings were a comfort to him. There, more than anytime or anywhere else, he felt that the responsibility of caring for the more than one hundred families who comprised the Fairhaven Ward was not wholly his. He and his counselors and clerks had fallen into a trusting, companionable relationship, which was a bit of a surprise to him, considering how different they all were. First counselor Bob Patrenko, fortyish with receding straight black hair, was an educated man with a keen eye for propriety and a good understanding of the *Church Handbook of Instructions*. Sam Wright, chubby-faced and about as down-home as they come, could read human nature as accurately as Brother Patrenko read the handbook, and his good-old-boy manner belied his sharp intellect and caused this second counselor to be underestimated by some who didn't know him well. Joseph Perkins, a brown-haired young man with wire-rimmed glasses, was a fine ward clerk, good with the computer and conscientious about keeping the records up-to-date. He had a kindly, forgiving way about him. Executive secretary

Dan McMillan had already made himself invaluable by keeping the bishop organized and his appointments reasonably spaced and the people reminded of the times. Just because the bishop kept expecting him to salute, click his heels, and reply "Aye, aye, sir" was no reason to complain. Dan was a good man.

Early on this Sabbath morning, grateful beyond measure that the Lord had blessed him with their faithful help, the bishop looked fondly at this collection of men. He glanced down at the agenda Dan had prepared for their discussion. "Special needs" was the next category, with several members' names listed underneath.

"Roscoe and Hilda Bainbridge," he read. "How is Ross doing? I haven't seen him for over a week."

"I was over there yesterday," said Sam Wright. "Seems to me he's 'bout the same, and Hildy's holdin' up, so far. Said they hatn't had to increase his pain medication, so I reckon that's good. But he don't eat much, and it's gettin' so danged hot in that little house. They ain't got nothin' but a little bitty table fan that they keep where he is, but the kitchen and livin' room catches the afternoon sun, and I reckon pore old Hildy about wilts in there."

The bishop thought of his air-conditioned store and home and truck. He well remembered how hot it could be in a small house with no cooling system, especially on nights with no breeze when the temperature barely dipped a few degrees just before dawn. As boys, he and his buddy, Mac—Peter MacDonald—had once spread an old sheet out on the lawn at Mac's house and doused it with water, then lay down nearly naked on it to cool their overheated bodies enough to allow them to fall asleep. This year's weather wasn't quite to that misery point, but it was unthinkable to let Ross and Hilda suffer unnecessarily from the heat in their already precarious condition.

"Wonder how they'd feel about a room air-conditioner? I'm sure we could get them one," he suggested.

"Sometimes, older folks who aren't accustomed to them find them too cold," Brother Patrenko offered. "They might prefer something like a window fan, to draw the hot air out of the house and let the cooler evening air come in. When it is cooler, that is," he added with a shrug.

"I'll check with them," the bishop said. "Do we have any other older folks who might suffer from the heat?"

"Well, Junious and Nita Mobley are getting up in years, but they have all them shade trees around their place, and they sit up on a hill, so if there's any breeze to be had, they'll get some. I don't know if they've got any kind of cooling, though."

The bishop made a note. "Thanks, Sam. I'll check with them, too. How about the Minshews?"

"They've got a couple of air-conditioners," Brother Perkins said. "I home teach them, and it's always cool in the living room, at least."

"Good. Now, I see the Rexfords listed here. What's the concern with them?"

Bob Patrenko spoke. "I put their names on the list, Bishop, because Brother Rexford's out of work still, and I'm not sure they have everything they need. Reason I think that is that my wife sat beside Sister Rexford at Relief Society last week, when they were passing around a sign-up sheet to help with desserts for Enrichment night, and Sally said Lula Rexford passed the list right on, whispering something about how she couldn't even afford to make dessert for her own family these days."

"Believe I'll have Sister Reams check that one out. Lula

might open up to her. Thomas mentioned to me that his dad was looking for work, but he seemed to think they were doing okay still."

"Well, Bishop," Sam Wright put in, "if they was down to their last crust, they'd give it to T-Rex, they're that proud of him, and never say a word about needing more. They plumb dote on that boy and his football career, and I reckon they'd mortgage the farm, if they had one, to meet his fees and all."

"Does T-Rex have a summer job lined up, I wonder?"

"Nothin' but football practice, I'd wager. Do him good to earn a few bucks, though. That young'un's had his way greased for him a bit too much for his own good, I'm afraid."

"I could probably use him at the store a few hours a day, if he's willing."

"Be careful how you approach him or his family about that," Bob Patrenko advised. "They're pretty independent folks."

"Okay, thanks for the tip. I'll be careful. By the way, the name's not on our list, but I keep thinking about the Jernigans. How are Ralph and Linda doing?"

"I hatn't seen 'em out of late, have you?" Sam asked the group. No one had.

"Who're the home teachers there?" asked the bishop.

"Um—that'd be Brother Smedley and young Leland Exum," Brother Patrenko advised, and the bishop knew the appellation "young" was to differentiate Leland the deacon from his uncle, Leland Exum the high priest.

"Would you give Brother Smedley a call, Bob, and see what he knows about those folks? I keep having an uncomfortable sort of feeling about Ralph's state of mind. He seems to be a little—I don't know . . ."

"Paranoid?" supplied Bob. "You know what the kids in the ward call him? 'Brother Hunker in a Bunker.'"

The bishop couldn't suppress a smile, but it quickly faded. "I got the impression the man's dealing with a load of anxiety— why, I don't know, but it looks like he's transferring it into fears for the Church. He warned me about our enemies."

"He'll warn anyone who'll listen with a straight face," Joseph Perkins said. "I think he's got his poor little wife scared half out of her wits. She jumps if you say hello to her."

The bishop nodded. "Have Brother Smedley call me directly, would you, Bob? I wonder what we can do to help those folks."

"Maybe some counseling?" suggested Bob.

"Don't reckon Ralph'd take kindly to that suggestion," Sam put in. "He's convinced he's right and gets real offended when folks don't take him serious."

"Let's all make that a matter of prayer, brethren," the bishop suggested. He looked down at the last two names on the list. "How're things with Brother Dolan, Bob? You're their home teacher, aren't you?"

"Doing better. His leukemia appears to be in remission, at least for now, and he's back working half-days."

"That's great. How're they doing, financially?"

"They insist they're fine. He has good insurance, and they had some money and some food storage put away. Cassie's working part time, too. They're quite a remarkable young couple."

"Be a good thing if we were all as prepared as they are, wouldn't it? But keep tabs on the situation, Bob, if you will. Those medical bills can be overwhelming, even with good insurance. Now, I see Melody Padgett's name here. What's happening with Melody?"

"I added her name, Bishop," said Dan McMillan. "She and my wife are friends, and Joanie said something the other day that kind of bothered me. I'm sorry if I shouldn't be butting in, being just the executive secretary—"

"No, no," interrupted the bishop. "I want your input on things right along with my counselors' and clerks'. You're a part of this bishopric. What did Joanie say?"

"Well, sir, she hinted that she thought Melody was being physically abused by her husband. She had just seen her at some kitchenware party."

The bishop had a sickening feeling, even contemplating the idea of slender, suntanned Melody Padgett being slapped around by her husband, Jack, who was three times her size. "Did Melody say that had happened?" he asked.

"No, sir. Apparently she just hemmed and hawed when Joanie asked about some bruises on her face and arms. Made up a story about getting hit with a softball. Acted nervous, left the party early without buying anything or having any dessert. Said she shouldn't have come."

"I see. Would you go ahead and make an appointment for Melody to come in and see me, Dan, whenever's convenient for her? Needless to say, this has to be kept between us, brethren. Jack may be perfectly innocent. I, for one, surely hope so."

"Yes, sir," echoed Dan. "So do I."

The bishop glanced around the group. They were each frowning or looking sober, not meeting each other's eyes. He knew they must all be assessing what they knew of Jack Padgett's character, asking themselves if he seemed like a wife-batterer. He didn't know Jack well, himself, the Padgetts having moved into the Second Ward area a couple of years before. They were attractive, in their early thirties, with one small daughter, and attended meetings on a fairly regular basis. Jack was an elder and a former Marine, who now managed several in a chain of automotive supply stores and seemed to do well at it. Melody was quiet in mixed company but seemed to mingle well with the sisters and to have a ready laugh when she felt at ease. He hoped beyond hope that things had not come to the point between them that Jack would lose control and hit his wife. What could prompt a man—a member of the Church and a priesthood holder—to do that? He could understand anger and frustration, jealousy, arguments, and harsh words between couples who were at odds with each other, unfortunate and regrettable though those things might be. But he had real difficulty imagining the kind of rage that would prompt a man to raise his hand against the woman he had married. He tried to imagine hitting Trish and couldn't do it, but somehow he could imagine the heartsickness and sorrow and self-loathing he would feel if he ever deliberately hurt her or one of their children.

He shook the images away and continued with the business of the meeting. It would soon be time for the priesthood and auxiliary leaders to join them for ward council meeting.

Y

Bishop Shepherd sat on the stand, listening to the soft prelude music from the organ, watching the congregation as it gathered for sacrament meeting. Those participating in the meeting were already seated on the stand, and it was his practice to have everything as much in order ahead of time as possible, so that the members could observe a tranquil, reverent example in their bishopric and clerks, and hopefully allow themselves to be soothed by the gentle music into a similar state, ready to worship. It wasn't easy. People were friendly, wanting to greet each other, to take care of last-minute bits of ward business before the meetings started—even to ask him questions or turn in tithing envelopes. He, himself, had been as guilty as anyone in times past, but now it was as if his sensitivity had been heightened by sitting up front for the past seven or so Sundays, observing the situation. Periodically, he knew, the full-time missionaries complained that when they brought investigators to church, the newcomers were appalled by the lack of reverence and quiet in the chapel, so unlike the services they were accustomed to attending in other denominations. He knew the problem was not peculiar to his ward—but, of course, his ward was the only one in which he had the opportunity to solve it. But how?

Trish had given him a suggestion, which he had passed along to Sister Margaret Tullis, the ward organist. Whenever the congregation seemed especially noisy coming in, she was to finish the phrase of the music she was playing and then switch to the Primary song "The Chapel Doors." Anyone, Trish had reasoned, who had ever been a Primary student or worker, would recognize that song and its message: " . . . We gather here on the Sabbath day to learn of Jesus, to sing and pray. So when we come through the chapel doors, 'Sh, be still.'" It had seemed a suggestion worth implementing, and he had watched with some amusement as certain people would suddenly recognize the song and its import and settle down, quieting their children as best they could. Others remained oblivious and continued to chat, and after three Sundays he had made mention of the reverence effort from the pulpit, asking the people to listen for the "reminder song" and conduct themselves accordingly. Then a group of Primary children had sung the song twice through, the congregation joining in the second time. Now it was the children who noticed when the song was being played and hushed their parents. He smiled to himself. *A little child shall lead them,* he thought.

He was pleased with the way the sacrament meeting talks came together on that particular Sunday. Ida Lou started hers, reading stiffly from cards held in her trembling hands, but she soon gave that up and just talked, allowing her humility and love to shine through her simple words. Sister Talbot was her usual enthusiastic self, bubbling about projects and events that were being planned for the sisters, and Rosetta McIntyre's talk was, like herself, quiet, meaningful, and thoughtfully organized. He smiled throughout Trish's remarks, as she used her sense of humor and her experience in the Church to give examples of how the sisters could make a real difference in the lives of those they served. It was evident that the four women complemented each other and worked together well.

Thank thee, Father, for choosing these sisters for this time, he prayed. *What a strength they are to us all—and especially to me.*

Y

Ida Lou Reams lost no time in speaking with Lula Rexford and reported back to the bishop that Lula admitted they were having some lean times, but that her husband was totally opposed to accepting any help from anyone.

"So, basically, I reckon they're living out of their garden, and she says they've got plenty of squash and beans and tomaters, but she reckons she's going to have to sell off her mama's silverware pretty soon if her husband don't find work.

But she won't tell him about that, 'cause he wouldn't let her. I don't know, Bishop—I'd be glad to share my bottled beets and carrots and apples, and some meat from our freezer, but she says no, thanks, that Brother Rexford would know it wasn't hers and ask where it come from. I reckon they hatn't never done much about food storage, and that. What should we do?"

"Well, I'll talk to young Thomas, and see if he'll accept some summer work at my store, and I'll talk to his dad, too, and check with the stake employment specialist to see if there's anything going that Brother Rexford'd be willing or able to do. For the short term, I don't know. For one thing, try to coax Lula out to Enrichment meeting this Tuesday, will you?"

Ida Lou cocked her head and looked at him like a bright-eyed sparrow. "You have an idea for that?"

He regarded her with a tired smile. "At the moment, to tell the truth, I don't have a clue why I even said that. But it can't hurt—and maybe by Tuesday, I'll be able to come up with something."

"The Lord'll bless you, Bishop. I'll pray for the Rexfords, too."

"I'm sure you already do—and for all the other folks who are struggling as well. Thanks, Ida Lou."

Y

He caught up to T-Rex that very evening, pulling up in front of the Rexford home just as the boy was backing out of the drive. The bishop honked and beckoned with a large motion to let T-Rex know he was the object—or one of them—of the bishop's visit. The boy left his truck running and sauntered over to the bishop's vehicle, sporting his hail-fellow-well-met grin that was so effective in winning him friends among both genders and all ages.

"Well, hey there, Bish—what brings you around? Checkin' up on me? I was at church t'day!"

"I saw you were, Thomas, and it did my heart good. No, I'm not checking up on you, not at all. I just wanted to catch you before things get crazy again on Monday. I don't normally talk business matters on Sunday, but I've been wondering if you might be interested in helping us out at the store this summer, bagging and stocking? I sure could use a strong guy like you around."

"Love to help you out, Bishop, but no can do. Coach won't let us work."

"Not even part-time?"

"Nope. We have two-a-days for all of June, then one-a-days through July, and back to two-a-days about the second week of August. Plus, he expects us to lift weights in our spare time. He says jobs are too demanding, take too much of our energy."

"Is that right? Well. Sounds like he has plans for you, all right. But heck, Thomas—I really am disappointed! And I was hoping you could use the money."

"The money'd be cool, but Coach is pretty tough on us, all right. He don't even want us going camping or on vacation trips, and I'm not supposed to ride my motorcycle till after football season, either. Sure, like I'm giving that up, on these summer nights—*not!*" Thomas laughed, and slapped the door of the bishop's truck. "But, hey, I'm sure sorry, Bish. Tell you what— why don't you ask Rick Smedley or Jason Ezell? Reckon they could use something to fill up their summers."

"Hmm. Well, thanks anyway, Thomas. Say, is your dad home?"

"How come? You gonna offer him a job baggin' groceries?" Thomas hooted with laughter again. "I don't reckon he's that desperate, yet!"

Little do you know, my boy! He just may be, the bishop thought wryly.

Aloud, he said, "Nope, just want to hand him a list of positions that's circulating in the stake, see if there's anything up his alley."

"Okay, cool. I think he's out back, if you want to just walk around the house. Mom's not home. See ya, Bish!"

The bishop waved to the boy, got out of his truck, and headed around the corner of the one-story frame house. It was well kept, and the yard was groomed to a fare-thee-well— nothing overgrown or weedy or languishing from neglect. He found Brother Tom Rexford relaxing in the deep shade of a huge old pecan tree, apparently amused by the antics of a pair of squirrels that raced in fits and starts around the limbs of the tree.

"Well, howdy-do, Bishop! Come and set," he invited, sitting up straight in surprise.

The bishop reached to shake Tom's hand, then plunked himself into a white lawn chair. "How are you, Brother Rexford?" he asked. "This is sure a pleasant scene. Wonderful old tree."

"We like it out here, of an evenin'. What can I do for you? Lula's gone over to her mama's place. The old lady ain't doin' too good. Needs a lot of help anymore. Wears Lula out, but her one sister lives down in Pensacola, and the other one that's in Birmingham ain't worth a damn. Pardon my French, Bishop, but she don't take hold at all, where her mama's concerned."

"Quite a burden for Lula, then," the bishop observed. "Does her mother live alone?"

"Does, and won't budge. She could come here, we got a room for her, but no, she's gotta stay in her own place that she's used to. I dunno—maybe it's best. Sometimes you hear of old folks wanderin' off, when they're put somewheres they're not used to."

"That's true. Is there any help from the county or state available—home health people, and that?"

"A nurse checks in twice a week. Old lady's got real minimal Social Security, is all, and long as she's in her own home, that's all she can get. And don't even want that! Thinks they're gonna steal her blind."

"Well, now. That is rough. I know she's not LDS, but does she have a church that could have folks check in on her, sit with her, or whatever's needed?"

"Nah. Never did affliliate with any church that I know of. Pitched a fit when Lula got baptized a Mormon, but hatn't never taught her any other way, so I don't see where she had cause to interfere."

"I see. Well. How're things going for you, Tom? I know you were affected, like a lot of other folks, by the base closure. Any prospects in sight for work in your field?"

"Nah. Don't reckon I'll find the same kind of work I was doin' there. There just ain't any call for it, other places. But I'm lookin' around. Somethin'll turn up, sooner or later."

The bishop unfolded a paper from his pocket. "I brought along a list of available jobs put out by our stake employment specialist, in case there's anything you're interested in. It's a recent update—I just received it yesterday, so I assume the jobs are all still open—but if there's anything that interests you, I'd suggest you call about it first thing in the morning. Lots of folks are looking for work."

Tom Rexford quickly perused the list. "Nah—don't reckon there's any of these I'd want to do. 'Preciate it, though, Bishop. I'll come up with something pretty soon, I'm sure."

"No offense, Tom, but I want you to know that help is available, especially with groceries and commodities, while you're going through hard times. It must take a lot of food to keep a young man like Thomas filled up. I imagine he'd need considerable protein, with all his muscle building and football practice. Let us help out with that, if you're willing."

"Boy eats a grundle, I'll admit that. But so far, we're doin' okay. Got a good garden, that helps out, and Lula, she's workin' a few hours a week."

"I just spoke to T-Rex. I was sure hoping he could help me out at the store this summer. I could use a strong young fellow like him. But he said Coach won't let him work."

"That's right. The kids have to sacrifice a lot to play football for him, but you gotta admit he's whipped them into a pretty good team. It's important to Tommy, and we'll see that he has whatever he needs. We're a pretty self-sufficient family, Bishop, no offense."

"All right. No offense taken. But remember help's available. We take our turns giving and receiving, you know? Help each other out in this church. That's how the Lord designed it. All private and confidential, of course."

"Don't reckon your family'd ever go hungry, would they, what with you bein' a grocer?"

"Not if I can help it. And I feel the same about every family in the ward, Tom, including yours. So if things get too tough, don't hesitate a minute to let me know. It's no disgrace. Other times, you'll be the one contributing, and someone else will benefit. That's the program."

Tom Rexford stood, and held out his hand, indicating that as far as he was concerned, the visit was over. "I'll let you know, if we ever get to that point, Bishop. 'Til you hear otherwise, though, the Rexfords are just fine."

The bishop walked back around the house to his truck, his step a little less springy than it had been a few minutes before. "Somehow," he muttered ruefully, "that didn't go as well as I had hoped. Doggone it, self-reliance is all well and good, but seems like it ought to start with putting aside food and money for tough times, not with being stubborn and proud when your family's in need!" He hit his steering wheel a resounding thump. "Lord, help me to be patient," he prayed. "I'm not nearly as good at it as I thought I was!"

CHAPTER EIGHT

Y

" . . . MY UNSEEN WOUNDS"

Sister LaThea Winslow stopped by his office at the church early on Tuesday evening with a glowing report on plans for the first social activity planned for the newly combined Fairhaven Ward. Apparently in her element, she described her committee's ideas for a multicultural affair, featuring food and displays and entertainment from various ethnic groups represented in the ward—Polynesian dances and food from the Tuapetagi family, Southwestern dishes and music from Paulo and Ramona Cisneros, a display of paintings and miniature stilt-houses from the Lipa family of the Philippines, and a pot of spicy seafood gumbo from the Arnauds, a black family who hailed from New Orleans. The bishop told her he thought it sounded fine—but privately he wondered if the ward should hand out small packs of antacid medication for party favors.

After her visit, he paged through his scriptures, trying to settle his thoughts in anticipation of his scheduled meeting with Melody Padgett. The situation was a delicate one, and he wondered how to broach the subject of her husband's treatment of her without offending her or giving away the name of the people who had tipped him off that there might be a problem. He had prayed several times about the matter since Sunday, and he had to trust that the Lord would put words in his mouth when the moment came—and that He would give Melody courage to confide in this new bishop whom she didn't really know.

Dan McMillan tapped on the door from the clerk's office and put his head around the corner. "The Padgetts are here," he said.

The bishop winced. "Both of them?" he asked softly.

"Yes, sir. I made the appointment with Melody only, but Jack's here with her."

The bishop nodded. He had a sinking feeling that this was not a good sign. He breathed another silent prayer and went to invite them in.

"It's good of you folks to come," he began, as he shook first Melody's cool, slim hand and then felt his own fingers crushed in Jack's vise-like grip. He had never considered himself a wimp when it came to good, firm handshakes, but he had to steel himself not to react negatively to the crunch of this ex-Marine's powerful hand. Could such a handshake, he wondered, possibly be construed as a warning to a religious leader who had been cheeky enough to ask for a one-on-one interview with his wife?

The Padgetts sat down across the desk from him. Both were smiling genially, and Jack was chewing gum. His face, under his blond crew cut, was a sunburned red, and Melody's tanned complexion revealed only a slight yellowing under her makeup to indicate a fading bruise on her left cheek. The bishop smiled back at them, surreptitiously massaging his own bruised hand under the desk, prepared to concede that this man could probably caress his wife's face and leave a mark.

"So what have you got on us, Bishop?" Jack asked, cracking his gum. "Heard about our tax evasion, or our moonshining operation, or is it the drugs we peddle you're concerned about?"

The bishop managed a chuckle. "Oh, none of the above, I assure you. I'm pleased to have the chance to get to know you folks." He improvised wildly. "I wanted to check with you, Sister Padgett, about your Primary calling. How long have you served in Primary?"

Melody was still smiling. "It's been nearly five years, I believe, but I enjoy it. They're a challenge, but they're sweet little kids. I have two more in my class since the wards were combined, but one of them hardly ever comes, so I usually just have five or six."

"I see. I was thinking that five years is a long time to serve in an auxiliary, and have to miss Sunday School and Relief Society. How do you feel about that?"

"Oh, well, you know—sometimes you do tend to feel kind of out of things in Relief Society when you don't get to go for a long time—but I don't mind, really. I'm used to it."

Her husband glanced at her. "Primary's a good place for Mel," he stated. "She always wanted a bunch of kids, but we've only got the one, so this way, she feels fulfilled, don't you, hon?"

"Hon" nodded and kept smiling.

The bishop regarded her steadily, trying to read something—anything—in her eyes that would give him a clue as to her real situation and her true feelings.

"My wife has always enjoyed teaching Primary, too," he said, just for something to say.

Melody nodded. "She seems nice, your wife." Her eyes

flickered toward Jack. "Of course, I don't really know her very well. Just from hearing her talk in church last Sunday."

"Well, thank you. I sure think she's nice. I believe she's kind of glad to have a little change from the same old routine, though, and I wondered if you might be ready for one, too."

"Um, what did you—"

"I think Primary's Mel's natural habitat," Jack said. "She flourishes there, works really hard on the lessons she gives those kids. I definitely think you ought to keep her there, where she's a real asset to the ward."

"I understand she does a terrific job," Bishop Shepherd agreed. "Is that what you would prefer, Sister Padgett—to stay put for a while?"

Her smile never wavered. "Yes, that'd be lovely."

He turned his attention to Jack. "And let's see, what do we have you doing, Brother Padgett?"

Jack's smile was confident, even smug. "I'm a home teacher, Bishop. These days, I'm pretty busy with my stores. As you may know, we just added another one, in Anniston. Right now it'd be hard to hold another calling and do it justice. Maybe when I get things a little better organized I can take on more church work."

The bishop nodded. *That's okay, buddy,* he thought. *There isn't a calling in this Church that I'd trust you with right now.* Aloud, he said, "Who are your home teaching families?"

"Um—let's see. Don't you have a record of that here?"

"Not right in front of me." It was in his top right drawer.

"Well, it's—oh, of course, it's the Rivenbarks and the Dempseys. I go with the elders quorum president—what's his name—Hank."

"Oh, Hank Ezell—great. Okay. And you folks, as you say, have the one little daughter, Andrea?"

"Andi, yeah. She's six."

"Starting first grade in the fall?"

Jack answered. "No, I don't like the school system around here. Melody's going to homeschool her, aren't you, hon?"

"Yes." Melody was still smiling. "I had a couple of years of elementary ed before we were married. I'm looking forward to teaching Andi."

"I see. Where are you from originally, Sister Padgett?"

"Florida. I grew up in Ft. Walton Beach."

"And where did you go to college?"

"University of West Florida, in Pensacola. That's where I met Jack. He was stationed there, with the Marines."

"Okay, sure. And Jack, where do you hail from?"

"Delaware. Wilmington."

"How'd you folks end up here in Fairhaven?"

"We were sent here to manage a couple of Auto-Tec stores, and we've built it up to five now."

"Doing well, then, financially? Enjoy your work?"

"Very much. And I don't think Mel complains about the bacon I bring home, do you, hon?"

"Not at all," agreed Melody, smiling.

"And I expect the ward doesn't complain about our tithing checks, either. Isn't that right, Bishop?"

"Well, I confess I'm not conversant with how much anybody's contributions are, at this point. But if you're paying tithing, that's great. You'll be blessed for it. And let's see, now—have you folks been sealed in the temple?"

Melody looked at Jack. His grin subsided briefly, then returned. "Haven't got to that, yet, Bishop, but we will in due time, don't you worry. Now, is there anything else? We don't like to leave Andi with a young sitter for too long."

"I don't believe there is," the bishop said mildly. "Thank you both for coming in. It's quite a challenge getting acquainted with everyone as quickly as I'd like to. But I want you to know I'm always available to you folks, at any time, if I can be of service in any way. Sister Padgett, I believe Enrichment meeting's about to start, and if you'd like to stay on for that, I know Trish or one of the other sisters would be glad to give you a ride home."

"Oh. Um, no, I can't make it tonight. We have other plans."

"All right. Ya'll have a good evening now." He stood and saw them out. Jack took Melody's arm, just above the elbow, and the bishop saw her flinch slightly. *Probably pinching old bruises*, he thought, with a sudden desire to swing his fist at Jack's firm, manly chin. He didn't even feel guilty for the impulse, though it was a decidedly un-bishop-like response.

He walked out into the fragrant warmth of the May evening to get some things from the back of his truck. The Padgetts had parked toward the back of the building, and as he lifted a cooler from the truck bed, they drove past him. He couldn't see Jack, but Melody turned her face toward him as they passed. Their eyes met. She wasn't smiling.

Huffing with the effort, he carried two heavy coolers to the kitchen of the church and caught Sister Reams's eye.

"Here you go, ladies," he said, as she and Frankie Talbot came forward. "I understand you're having a bread-baking demonstration tonight, so I guess it's the loaves and the fishes.

These fish were brought to me this afternoon by a fellow I know who works for the Fish and Game division. They were caught this morning, for a routine check for problems and diseases. They were all found to be healthy, so he went ahead and cleaned them, and they've been on ice ever since. I brought some plastic bags, so at the end of your meeting, whoever wants some can help herself. Please encourage everybody who likes fish to take some. I know not everyone will, so those who do should take enough for two or three meals. They'll freeze just fine."

Ida Lou Reams twinkled at him. "The Lord did come through, didn't he?" she whispered. "And the sister we talked about is here, too. That's something of a miracle in itself, 'cause she don't usually make it to this meeting."

He grinned back at her. "Hope she likes fish."

"Well, you just watch—she will, or He'd have provided something else."

He returned to his office and put through a call to Hank Ezell, elders quorum president and home teaching partner of Jack Padgett.

"Brother Hank, I'm concerned about something. This is all confidential, of course. Are you alone?"

"Laura's at Enrichment meeting, and the kids are playing out back."

"Give me your impressions of Jack Padgett—as a home teacher, a quorum member, a husband and father—whatever you know."

He heard Hank whistle softly. "Well, as a home teacher, I

frankly haven't seen much of Jack. He's been my assigned partner for nearly a year, and I believe he's only gone out with me
twice. I guess he's really busy building his business, because he
sure doesn't seem to have much free time. When he did go with
me, he was pleasant enough—jolly, I s'pose you'd say—but he
seemed a little uncomfortable, too. Maybe edgy would be the
word. Like he'd rather be somewhere else."

"I see. And how about in other settings?"

"Um—he comes to quorum meeting a couple of times a
month. Generally sits in the back, by the window. Once in a
while, he'll make a comment or answer a question, but—well,
some of his comments seem kind of unusual."

"How's that?"

"Let's see. It's kind of hard to pinpoint exactly what I mean,
and I don't know that I remember any examples, offhand, but
he seems sort of cynical, and off in left field a tad, I guess. Just a
bit off the beaten track. And I don't know if it's his military
training, or what, but I have the notion that he feels just a little
bit superior to the rest of us. Like I remember one time when
Brother Ross had borne his testimony about the truthfulness of
the Book of Mormon, I happened to glance at Jack, and he was
smiling, but in a sneering kind of way, and shaking his head. So
it wasn't anything he said, that time, but the look on his face
just sticks in my memory. Does that make sense? I hate to fault
a man for the look on his face—doesn't seem fair, does it? But I
had to wonder what it meant."

"Thanks, Hank. I think I understand exactly what you
mean. Have you had any opportunity to observe Jack with his
family?"

"Oh, just in church, you know. His wife's a real quiet sort,
isn't she? So's the little girl, for that matter. Very well behaved

in meetings, the child is. I don't know much about them, but he seems affectionate—often has his arm around his wife. Does that help any, Bishop?"

"I believe so. I appreciate it. If you notice or think of anything unusual about Jack or the family that you feel I should know, would you let me know, very privately? I just feel a little uneasy about them, somehow."

"Well, Bishop—that'd probably be your spirit of discernment speaking to you, wouldn't it? Sure, if I notice anything amiss, I'll let you know. And by the way, I want you to know we appreciate all you're doing and feel like you're off to a great start."

"Thank you, brother. That means a lot."

He put down the phone and sat quietly, thinking of Hank's remark about judging people by their facial expressions. He thought of the two expressions he had seen on Melody Padgett's face—the contrast between that perpetual smile and the haunted look she had thrown in his direction as she was being driven away by her husband. Of the two expressions, he feared the latter was the more honest.

The phone rang, and he let Dan McMillan take it in the clerk's office. It was only a moment until Dan knocked discreetly on his door.

"It's Brother Smedley, Bishop," Dan said. "Are you available to take his call?"

"I sure am. Thanks, Dan. Hello, Brother Smedley, thanks for calling back."

"Bishop? I understand you wanted to talk to me about the Jernigans."

"I sure did. How are those folks doing, from your point of view as their home teacher?"

"Well, okay, I think, but it's hard to tell—they're kind of stiff, or something. And very serious. It's hard to get either of them to crack a smile."

Unlike those who smile all the time, as a guise, thought the bishop. "Do you ever get the impression they're frightened of something, or stressed out?" he asked.

"I sure do, though I couldn't tell you what it would be."

"Has Brother Jernigan talked to you about his feelings about preparing for emergencies?"

"Oh, always. That's a favorite topic with him. He seems pretty knowledgeable about food storage and that—but the thing is, he tends to dwell on the idea of somebody trying to take it all away from him. Prepared to defend it with his life, if necessary, and all that."

"Uh-huh. Has he mentioned enemies of the Church to you?"

"Hinted at it—like he knows something he isn't telling."

"I see. Do you know Linda very well?"

"Not really. I mean, she's always there, but she hardly ever puts in a word. Just listens to everybody else. Sometimes I've taken Avolyn with me when my partner couldn't make it, and she tries to get Linda to talk, but mostly you just get nods or one-word answers. She looks to Ralph to do the talking, it seems."

"So what do you think, Brother Smedley—is Ralph okay, or do you think he's dealing with some irrational fears?"

"To tell you the truth, I get the feeling the man's purely

plagued by fears, and I suspect Linda's caught the same outlook from him. I find I'm always giving them messages of comfort and faith and trust in the Lord, but I'm not real sure any of it sinks in."

"Wonder what brought Ralph to that point, and what, if anything, we can do to help him."

"I wonder, too. If they could just once relax and be at ease, somehow—but I don't know how to bring that about."

The bishop sighed. "Neither do I, Brother. But let's pray for them, and keep working with them the best we can, okay? I'd sure hate to see Ralph lose it one day and whip out a gun to protect his wheat and honey against all comers."

"Amen to that, Bishop. And he does have quite an arsenal."

"Are you comfortable continuing to visit them?"

"Yes, sir, pretty much. I've learned how to approach Ralph and to take his concerns seriously. I do believe his heart's in the right place, you know? But his paranoia, or whatever, gets in his way."

"Do you happen to know if they've ever had any children?"

"Well, there's a photograph of a little blonde girl in their living room, but I don't know who she is. She looks something like Linda, but she might be a niece or something. It's funny I've never asked, come to think of it, but somehow Ralph always seems to drive the conversation down his own roads."

"I hear you. Okay, thanks, Brother Smedley. I appreciate all you're doing."

The conversation over, the bishop rose to stretch his legs and get some air. He wandered toward the kitchen of the meetinghouse, from which emanated the unmistakable fragrance of baking bread. Sisters were gathered in a corner of the cultural hall, watching dark-haired Magda Warshaw demonstrate kneading the dough and then rolling three strips of it to braid into a round pan. Magda and her husband, Levi, were Polish Jews who had emigrated to the United States after joining the Church in Germany. The bishop smiled, listening to the instructions she gave in her pronounced accent. Trish always said she loved to listen to Magda's lessons or talks because her accent made her comments easier to remember. He suspected that was because the listener had to pay closer attention to understand the remarks, to begin with.

He walked around the building and strolled outside, enjoying the approaching twilight and the care with which the grounds were maintained. The Fairhaven meetinghouse was located in a nice neighborhood and did nothing to detract from it. He was grateful that the Church maintained quality, well-designed, and well-kept buildings, both for the sake of the members and for the good impression they gave to the general public.

He could recall going to his first meetings of the Church, which were held in the social hall of a local business and charity brotherhood. The missionaries who picked him and his mother up for the meetings explained that they needed to go a little early to have time to sweep up the cigarette butts and other debris from the Saturday night parties and to set up chairs for the meeting. It had grown to be a natural thing for him to help them throw open the windows to dispel the tobacco and stale-beer odors and to push the broom or set up the rows of folding chairs. He was glad he had been around in those early days of the Church in Fairhaven, glad that he had those memories—but even more glad that now they had their own building, dedicated to the purposes of worship and learning, that they could fill it every Sunday, and that it never had to reek of offensive odors from substances the Saints didn't even use.

Still, he remembered, the Spirit had managed to distill upon those small gatherings in that musty hall. Hadn't he felt it there, and his mother, too? How brave those young missionaries had been, inviting visitors and investigators to such simple meetings under such un-church-like circumstances—many of them people who were accustomed to robed choirs and professionally prepared sermons! Surely it was a testimony of the truthfulness of the restored gospel that hearts had been touched and testimonies engendered under those conditions. It had been better when they had outgrown the social hall, and they had, while their own meetinghouse was under construction, been kindly invited by the Seventh-day Adventists to share their building. It had seemed only right and natural, years later, when the Adventists' church had gone up in flames, to offer them a home for their services in this chapel, and to help them to rebuild. Though they differed in many points of theology, there was still a friendly relationship between the two congregations.

He went back inside, passing by the kitchen just as the sisters were slicing the golden loaves they had taken from the oven, and they called out to him to sample the product. Sister Warshaw handed him a thick slice on a napkin and gestured to the dishes of butter and jam just ready to be taken out to the cultural hall.

"Have some," she invited. "Is good."

"Thank you," he said warmly. "There are perks for being here on Tuesday evenings after all!"

"At least, once a month there might be," agreed Joanie McMillan with a smile. "The other Tuesdays, you brethren might just have to order in pizza. Have a glass of cold milk, Bishop."

"Ve should send food on Tuesdays, why not?" said Magda brightly. "Ve could take turns, it should not be hard. Is too far for all to go home and come back. Your Dan does not, does he?" she asked Joanie.

"No, we live too far out, so he comes right from work, and stays as long as needed, and I'll bet you do the same, don't you, Bishop?"

"Well—yes, usually I have interviews that start shortly after I leave the store. I've run home in-between a couple of times, but usually I just grab something quick from the store and head straight over here."

"And who else is here on Tuesdays—both counselors, and Brother Perkins?"

"Not always all of us, but usually one of the counselors or the clerk—depending upon what needs doing. There are generally three of us here."

"No reason why ve should not bring dem food," Magda persisted. "Will that be acceptable, Bishop?"

He grinned. "It's not necessary, but you bet it will. It needn't be fancy, full-course meals, though, ladies. Just a simple bite of something—whatever's on hand. You could take it to the clerk's office—maybe in disposable containers, so we don't have to worry about getting dishes back to people, would that be good?"

"That would be simpler, wouldn't it?" Joanie agreed, wiping her hands on a towel.

"And no pressure on anyone to participate, okay? Just those who would really like to."

"Ve will tell Sister Reams and send around a list to sign, before we leave tonight." Magda's no-nonsense voice settled the matter, and she went to push in the cart of bread and jam and milk and to consult with Ida Lou.

The bishop ate his bread contentedly, then watched from the hallway as the coolers of fish were emptied. He was gratified to see that, among others, Lula Rexford went home with two heavy, icy bags in her hands.

"I thank thee, Father, for the kindness of near-strangers," he whispered as he headed back to his office, thinking of the man, a mere acquaintance, who had brought the fish to him at his store, saying, "I just figured you could find someone who could use them, if you don't want them all yourself." The donor was a man he had met at a community planning meeting months earlier, and they had struck up a conversation about the fish population in the local waterways and lakes. They had discussed the care that had to be taken in purchasing fish from fisheries around the country for sale in his store and the problems certain areas had with pollution from industry. The man had remembered his interest.

"Bless that man for his generosity," he continued his prayer. "Bless him and his family to always have what they require."

CHAPTER NINE

Y

" . . . SEASONS OF DISTRESS AND GRIEF"

On Wednesday afternoon he arrived home to find Trish on a ladder in the guest bedroom, applying water to the wallpaper with a dripping sponge. From this activity he read that preparations for the advent of her family were in full swing, and he knew that there would be certain expectations of him along the way.

"Hey, babe—how can I help?" he asked cheerfully.

"Oh, Jim, you're home. Good. Check the paper in the corner there by the door—see if it's ready to strip yet."

He whistled. "We're stripping, are we? Sounds interesting."

His wife didn't rise to the bait. "It's interesting to me because I can't wait to get this old paper out of here. I've wanted to for years, and this is the perfect excuse. I tried to steam it off, but that was too slow."

He regarded the paper, which was a pale pink with an occasional sprinkle of small white flowers. He rather liked it, but this was obviously not the time to say so.

"What's the new paper like?"

"Sage green with tiny beige stripes, and I'm putting up a coordinated border with several kinds of birdhouses on it."

"Birdhouses."

"You'll love it; it's really cute. And I'll group three birdhouses on one end of the dresser to continue the theme. I have that little barnwood one with the silk flowers twining around it, and I'm sure I can find a couple of others to go with it."

He nodded. He was sure she could, too.

"Then I'll have to decide what goes on the bed. Obviously that ruffly thing has got to go. And I'll want coordinated towels and rugs in the bath, there."

Briefly, he wondered how much his in-laws' visit was going to cost him—and why. Did coordinating towels and rugs and sage-green wallpaper somehow say to them that their daughter was in good hands—that she was happy and cherished and well cared for, while the pale pink walls and ruffly thing would scream of neglect and penury? He had to trust her instincts; his own were apparently comatose from disuse in such matters.

"Is that piece ready to come off?"

"Let's see. Yep, I do believe it is."

"Just let it fall onto the drop cloth. If it sticks anywhere, I'll throw you the sponge."

"Okay. Just don't throw in the sponge—whatever that means." The strip of paper came off, a wet, curling, unwieldy thing that tried to flop in all directions at once. He made a face. Wallpapering—or unwallpapering—was one of his least favorite occupations.

"How're the kids?" he asked.

"Good. Mallory's playing at Kirsten's house, Jamie's at Cub Scouts, and Tiffani is supposed to be starting dinner."

"She all caught up with her assignments at school?"

"Far as I can tell she is, and I think we'll finish the year in pretty good shape. She did some extra credit work in English to help balance out that test grade—and, of course, you helped her with the frog." She threw him a smile.

"Well. The Lord helped, actually."

"True. How are things with the ward—any appointments tonight?"

"Um—no appointments, but I can always visit people. I don't think there'll ever be a time when I shouldn't be doing more than I am." He sighed.

"You don't want to burn out, though, almost before you get started."

"I know. 'Take an even strain,' my dad used to say. He never explained exactly what he meant, but I think I'm beginning to get it. Just a slow, steady pull—no jerks and stops and rushing headlong downhill with the load."

"Makes sense. Check that next panel, okay?"

The panel came off, except for a section in the middle that clung to the wall and began to rip. "Sponge," he called, holding up one hand. "Scalpel. Whatever works."

She tossed him the sponge, which he used to saturate the sticky portion of paper until he could coax it off the wall.

"I'm sure glad this is strippable paper," Trish remarked, as her husband stepped around the mess on the floor and the covered bed to return the sponge. "Everything okay at the store? Any good melons showing up yet?"

"Yes and yes. I'll bring one home tomorrow. Hey, Trish, what do you know about Melody Padgett?"

"Not much, except she's gorgeous, with that tan and that beautiful hair of hers. I've never had occasion to get to know her. Don't think I've ever seen her in Relief Society—has she been serving in Primary or Young Women?"

"Primary. Seems to enjoy it—been there five years."

"Ah—a woman after my own heart."

"The funny thing is—and I hope I'm not telling tales out of school here, so please don't mention this—but her husband seems to want her to stay in Primary, in the worst way. Totally stonewalled my suggestion that she might enjoy a change."

"Huh. Why is that—just taking her side in the matter?"

"I don't know. Wondered if you had any insight."

"Well, maybe he likes the idea of her serving in the auxiliary where their little girl is."

"That's a thought. You know, I haven't visited Primary much, except to slip in the back and watch our kids give their talks and that—but it seems to me that the teachers don't have a whole lot of time to visit and talk with each other."

Trish smiled. "There's generally not much free time. It usually took about all I could do to keep track of my own little class and help them settle down and be reverent. If I even said hello to the other teachers, I was doing good."

"M-hmm. So not a whole lot of interaction between the teachers that hour. And, of course, the next hour, they're in their classrooms."

"Right. About the only socializing we had as Primary workers was at the leadership meetings. Sometimes we'd combine those with potluck suppers or Saturday brunches just to have time to visit."

"I see."

"So, what are you thinking—that Brother Padgett doesn't want Melody to be where she can visit with other people?"

He looked at his wife. "The thought occurred to me."

She stood still, the dripping sponge in her hand. "Wow," she said softly. "That's scary."

He nodded. "It sure is."

"Is he the type to be abusive or something?"

"Is there a type?"

"I guess you can't always tell, can you?"

"I do think he's pretty controlling."

She made a face. "I couldn't tolerate that. I'm grateful you're not that way."

He grinned at her. "Maybe I'm just so subtle about it that you don't recognize my strategy."

"Maybe you're not that subtle about anything, Mr. Guileless, Open-faced Bishop."

"Aw, you really know how to hurt a guy."

"I'll make it up to you. But seriously, Jim—what do you think he's doing to her?"

The bishop shook his head. "Don't really know anything. Possibly hitting her, definitely controlling her—I don't know what else. I'm hoping she'll tell me—or somebody in authority."

Trish dropped her sponge into a bucket and leaned back against the ladder. "I imagine it'd be hard for her to talk about stuff like that. It'd be really embarrassing."

"Yeah. Ironic, isn't it? If he's the abuser, then he's the one who should be embarrassed. Yet we both realize that she's the one who would be."

"I guess it'd be tough to admit you've been putting up with abuse. You might be afraid people would wonder what you'd done to deserve it, or why you hadn't got out of the situation."

He sighed. "I sure hope I'm wrong about the whole thing."

"What are you supposed to do if you're not?"

"Well, anytime you suspect abuse, or child endangerment,

anything like that—you're duty bound to report it to the authorities. But—I feel like I should be a little more certain than I am before I do that. After all, she didn't tell me anything—didn't ask for help. Didn't tell anyone else that I know of, either. I thought I saw an old bruise on her face, but it could've been an accident. And I am Jack Padgett's bishop as well as Melody's. Oh, boy. I believe I'm going to talk to President Walker—just in general terms at this point."

"Good idea. He might already know something about the family, for that matter."

"Could be. Bishop Collins didn't mention anything about them, though—at least, not anything that I remember or wrote down."

"Do your counselors know what you suspect?"

He nodded. "It came up in bishopric meeting, but I think they're all like me—just hoping it ain't so."

"Do you want me to discreetly check around among the sisters?"

He smiled. "No, babe, but thanks. I want you to be the perfect bishop's wife and see, hear, and say no evil."

"Okay, I'll be a good little monkey. But, tell you what—Ida Lou's busy trying to revamp the visiting teaching list so that people from the two wards can get acquainted. I could easily get Melody added to my list. Then, if I *happen* to learn anything, I promise I'll mention it only to you."

"I can't think of any objection to that," he agreed, grateful once again that he'd had the amazing good fortune to marry that shiny-haired girl. She had never been a gossip, but she was actively interested in people's welfare. It was a good combination.

He was relaxing after dinner in a lounge chair in the shade of the backyard, nearly asleep, when his son called him to the phone.

"It's that preacher friend of yours, I think," Jamie said. "The guy with the really low voice."

"Mac?" He pushed himself up from his seat, physically reluctant to move but delighted to hear from Peter MacDonald, which was a rare occurrence. Mac was a busy pastor to a large so-called nondenominational Christian flock in Atlanta. It was a tribute to the strength of their lifelong friendship that it had survived and flourished despite their many doctrinal discussions and disagreements over the years. He took the call in his and Trish's bedroom.

"Big Mac! How's it going, man?"

"Hey, Brother," came Mac's voice, still deep, but with a weary note to it as well. "How are things in your world?"

"Good, good. It's a treat to hear from you. What's up?"

"I just needed a voice of sanity from the sanest guy in the sanest town I know. Is Fairhaven still the same town you and I grew up in?"

"Well, it's growing, like most places, in spite of the base closing and ChemSoft pulling out—and no place seems as quiet and simple as I seem to remember Fairhaven being when we were kids—but yeah, it's still pretty sane. Why? Is Atlanta crazy?"

"Any city this size goes a little nuts from time to time. All these people with so many different life-styles and economic levels and ethnic backgrounds, all packed together like the proverbial sardines in a can, sweltering in the heat—I'll tell you,

Jim, it gets pretty wild. There was a bomb scare at Ruthie's middle school today, for example. They had to send everybody home, which wasn't the greatest because of so many working parents, but somebody had built something that looked like a bona fide bomb and put it in the boys bathroom. Turned out to be a fake, but the note that alerted the office that it was there was written in Spanish, so now everybody's down on the Hispanic kids, although *they* say the Spanish in the note is written wrong and misspelled and couldn't have come from them, but was just an attempt to make them look bad."

"All of which just tends to make them band together more closely, right? So that now there's more of an 'us and them' mentality than before?"

"Exactly." Jim heard a heavy sigh from his friend. "And that's just one example. Every day we hear of gang violence and drive-by shootings and car thefts and stabbings and rapes and what have you. I confess, Jim, that I don't know exactly what Isaiah saw when he wrote, 'woe to them that join house to house,' but sometimes I wonder if he didn't see Atlanta—and all these other huge cities we're so proud of."

"I've wondered about that myself. I guess I'm just a small-town boy—well, make that a small-city boy—I don't know if Fairhaven really qualifies as a small town anymore. But I've never had any great desire to live in a New York or Chicago or even Dallas or Atlanta, nice though they are to visit. I like to know my neighbors and a good portion of the townspeople. I like to walk down the street and recognize at least some of the folks I see."

"Well, I've lived here for nine years, and if I got out of our neighborhood, I'll bet I could walk around town for a couple of weeks and not run into anybody I know. Of course, some folks like it that way—they enjoy the anonymity and privacy, you know?"

"I reckon so. Shy folks, introverts maybe."

"Ha! And you know me, Jim—I don't qualify as one of those!"

"Never have, Mac, that's for sure. So are you thinking of leaving the city, finding a kinder, gentler place?"

"Oh, I don't know. There're so many good, positive things here, too. I mean, Atlanta's vital and progressive and parts of it are absolutely gorgeous. There are plenty of interesting things going on. I love my work, and we have a nice house in a good neighborhood, but even here, the kids get pulled into stuff I'm not comfortable with. Petey's a lot like me—he wants to be out there in the middle of everything, but he doesn't have the maturity and judgment yet to know what might not be safe or good for him."

"I hear you. So are you serious about making a change? What does Ruthanne say?"

"She loves Atlanta. The shopping is great, and she can be as busy as she wants with Christian women's groups and Bible study and garden clubs and such. She does a lot of good, you know? I hate to uproot her from all the friends she's made and the things that are important to her. Petey would object, too, I think—he's going on sixteen and very partisan about his high school and his friends. Our Ruthie, though, might be glad enough to try a smaller community. She doesn't make friends as readily as her mom and brother, so she's not quite so entrenched. As a seventh grader, she's kind of overwhelmed right now with life in general. That's a scary age. You remember?"

"It sure is. It was hard for Tiff, even here in Fairhaven, and I remember how I felt at twelve and thirteen, for that matter. For a while, I was actually glad that I had to go sweep floors at the store after school. It gave me an excuse not to have to hang out with some of the guys we'd grown up with who suddenly seemed to be different people."

Peter MacDonald chuckled. "Like Jakey Forelaw?"

"Man! You ever see anybody change like Jakey? One day he was an ordinary, skinny little kid, playing baseball and riding his bike out to the river to fish, and next thing I knew, he'd put on about forty or fifty pounds, grown six inches, and started cussin' and sneakin' beer from his dad's cooler. It was downright spooky."

"It was. I had a major growth spurt about then, too, but I stayed skinny for a long time. Now I wish I could take a few pounds off without some major life-style renovation! But the most interesting changes, I thought, were in the girls."

"Isn't that the truth? I got embarrassed just looking at some of them. All of a sudden they needed bras and were wearing lipstick."

"Lisa French."

"Oh, mercy—I thought Lisa had skipped ten years over the summer between sixth and seventh grades."

"She had, no doubt about it. Poor kid. She was twelve going on twenty-one, and not a shred of good judgment to go with that body. But how could she have? Makes you wonder how much negative behavior comes from kids whose bodies just plain outgrow their minds and their upbringings!"

"That's a thought, all right. Don't know about you, Mac, but I wouldn't care to go through it again—all that growing-up business."

"At least we made it fairly well intact, my friend. No drugs or gang wars or alcoholism or legal problems or pregnant girl-friends. Just a few speeding tickets."

"For which I'm forever grateful," the bishop agreed. "And we've both been blessed with wonderful wives and good kids."

"Right. A lot to be grateful for." Mac's sigh was deep, and Jim could hear the weariness in it. "Now if we can just pull those good kids over Fool's Hill, we'll have it made in the shade, huh, buddy?"

"Reckon that's the next challenge. One of them, anyway."

"Right. So what else is going on in Fairhaven? What're you doing in your church these days?"

"Well—I've just been called to be bishop."

"Bishop! Sounds heavy."

"Exactly. But don't go visualizing fancy robes and tall hats. The bishop just sort of oversees the ward—the congregation—and keeps things running."

"Well, good for you, Jim! Sounds like a lot of responsibility, but you've never been afraid of that, so I'm sure they've got the right man for the job."

"At least I don't have to preach every Sunday," the bishop said with a light laugh. "I'm afraid that'd be way beyond me."

"Actually, I don't have to anymore, either," Mac replied. "I've got an assistant pastor—a woman, as a matter of fact—and a youth pastor and a minister of music. So I can spend more time ministering to people and their needs, which is what I enjoy most."

"Sounds like a fine situation. You must have a good-sized church."

"We have almost two thousand members, give or take a few. And a beautiful new sanctuary that we're working hard to pay for. The stained glass window above our pulpit is incredible—

it's worth coming to see, all by itself. You and Trish ought to make the trip soon, Jim, and visit with us. We'd love to have you. Don't see enough of old friends anymore."

"I know. Everybody's busy. But hey—it sounds beautiful. I know Trish'd love to see it. She's crazy about stained glass. Maybe we can get away some weekend. Right now we're preparing for a visit from her parents and her sister—the one who doesn't approve of me."

"Bless you, my son." Mac's deep voice held a smile. "May you have the strength of twenty."

"Oh, I'm just planning to stay out of sight for the duration and let 'em have at it."

Mac laughed. "Now that sounds like a plan, but I'll bet it won't get by Trish! Seriously, though, Jim—sneak away when you can and come visit. Come while we're still here, because between you and me, my friend, that may not be for much longer."

"I'll see what I can do, Mac. Hey, thanks for calling."

"My pleasure."

He left the phone and went back to his shady reverie, but he couldn't quite recapture the blissful half-asleep state he had achieved earlier. For one thing, the cat Samantha insisted on leaping up on his chest and kneading him with her surprisingly forceful little paws. He removed her once, but she came right back, settling down and purring aggressively.

"Pushing your luck, kitty," he told her, and she narrowed her half-crossed blue eyes at him in what was very nearly a grin and purred louder. It was ridiculous. He chuckled in spite of himself.

"So what d'you think, Samantha? How'm I going to make my peace with my sister-in-law Meredith and keep Trish and everybody happy, if Meredith comes on with her usual attitude—'Why did my beautiful sister settle for this ignorant country bumpkin when so many BYU-graduate professional types were courting her?' How am I going to handle that?"

The kitten gazed at his mouth, stretched one paw forward and placed it firmly on his lips.

He turned his head to one side before she could deploy her claws.

"Yeah, you're probably right," he told her. "Just say nothing, huh? Mum's the word." He stroked the kitten's warm back. "After all, if Trish is happy, and she claims to be, why should I worry about what Miss Highhat thinks? On the other hand, if Trish truly is happy, why this frenzy of cleaning and decorating and scheduling and menu planning? Isn't our ordinary daily life good enough to display to the family? Is she trying too hard to prove something?"

Jamie's voice interrupted his conversation with the cat. "Dad, there's a message on the phone you'd better listen to."

He came to his feet with a rush of guilt. There had been that annoying chirp on the line when he was talking to the Reverend Peter MacDonald, and he had chosen to ignore it, intending to check when they finished talking to see if there was a message. He had forgotten.

Jamie punched in the code as he approached and handed him the phone. He heard Ida Lou Reams's voice, soft at first, saying, "Oh, dang it, I hate talkin' to these message things." Then louder, as if she had to bridge the gap with her own volume, "Bishop? Bishop, if you get this here message, I need to let you know that Brother Roscoe Bainbridge is dyin'. Hilda called and said she don't think it'll be long now, so I'm goin' over there to be with her, but I thought you should know. Um—well, okay, thank you. Goodbye. Uh—this is Ida Lou."

He put the phone down, deleting the message.

"Thanks, Jamie," he said softly. "Reckon I'd better get going. Where's Mom?"

"Washing down the walls in the guest room, getting ready to put the paper up."

"Okay."

"Daddy!" Mallory launched herself at him. "Come and play Candyland with me. Please?"

"No can do right now, sweetie. Daddy has to go somewhere. If I get home in time, maybe I can play later. Sorry, though."

"Dad? Brother Bainbridge is old, isn't he?" Jamie's face was solemn.

"He's pretty old, Son, and he's been very sick. He's ready to go. It'll be a good thing."

Jamie frowned. "But, I thought dying was the worst thing that could happen to a person. How can it be good?"

The bishop put his arms around his son and held him tight for a moment, breathing in his good, honest, boy-smell of sweat and bubble gum and fresh air. "Trust me on this, Jamie. We'll talk more about it later, but for now—no, dying is definitely not the worst thing that can happen. Especially not in this case. Gotta go now."

He took the stairs in twos, poking his head in at the door of the spare room. "Trish, Brother Bainbridge is apparently dying, and I need to go over there. I'm sorry, babe, I'd planned to help you paper tonight."

"You go ahead. You have to. Do you need me to do anything?"

"Ida Lou's already gone over. You might want to alert Frankie and Rosetta, in case she hasn't called them. I'll call back if there's anything needed tonight."

"All right, sweetheart. My love and sympathy to Hilda."

He nodded. "Be back when I can."

CHAPTER TEN

" . . . THE PASSAGEWAY
INTO ETERNITY"

As his truck jounced through the back streets leading to the Bainbridge home, the bishop reflected that he had only been present at one death in his life—that of his own father. It had been a difficult passing, painful to watch— his dad propped straight up on pillows, eyes wildly turning from side to side, mouth gasping for air, and face turning blue as his lungs filled with fluid. Remembering that, the bishop didn't know whether to hope that Roscoe would still be breathing when he arrived or not. He did hope that Ida Lou had made it in time so that Hilda would not have been alone in that moment.

"But she wouldn't have been alone," something whispered to his heart. "I would have been there."

"That's true, Lord," he murmured. "I thank thee for that."

He parked his truck behind Ida Lou's car and hurried to the porch. Ida Lou opened the door to him, her eyes red, but her face composed.

"Is it over?" he whispered, and she nodded.

"It was a sweet time, Bishop. A precious moment."

"I see. I'm sorry I was late. I just got your message. How's Hilda?"

"I'm fine, Bishop. I'm right here. Come on in," Hilda called from her rocking chair. She held a lace-edged handkerchief to swimming eyes, but miraculously, she was smiling.

"Sister Hilda," he said, going forward to kneel beside her. "I'm so sorry. Roscoe was a wonderful man."

"Thank you, Bishop. And don't you feel a bit bad. Everything's just like it oughta be."

"You have a wonderful attitude, dear sister."

"She's just a rock," Ida Lou said, pulling a chair over for him. "She's been real strong."

Sister Bainbridge leaned forward and patted the bishop's knee. "I'm just so proud," she confided. He felt a little taken aback. *Proud?*

"How do you mean, Hilda?" he asked.

"When the time come, Ross opened his eyes and said, 'Carolyn!' It was our girl, Bishop. She come for him, you see, to meet him and take him home to Heavenly Father. Then he just give a big sigh and was gone. Isn't that right, Sister Ida Lou?"

"That's exactly how it was, all right."

"I'm just so proud it happened that way. That it was Carolyn who come."

Proud, he realized, in this case meant glad and grateful.

"I'm thankful it happened that way, too," he agreed. "Roscoe certainly endured to the end in righteousness, and his passing was sweet because of it. And the two of you and Carolyn will surely be a forever family."

"Oh yes, Bishop, that's what I want. And can I tell you something else?"

"Of course you can."

"Right after Ross give that big sigh, somehow I just felt like him and Carolyn both threw their arms around me and give me the biggest hug! I never felt so loved in all my life. What do you make of that, Bishop? It's like I'm just still baskin' in the sunshine of that feelin'."

Bishop Shepherd found himself unable to speak. He reached for Hilda's hand and squeezed it a couple of times, then cleared his throat. "Sister Hilda, I pondered on the way over here what I could say to give comfort and to help you understand the reality of the continuation of life after death. And you just preached me the best sermon I ever heard on the subject."

"So you really think Ross and Carolyn could have hugged me? It's not exactly like I felt it physical, you know? More spiritual."

"Other than greeting each other, what would they have been more concerned about in that moment than comforting you and letting you know of their love? Yes, I think that experience was real, Hilda—and I think it was done through the power of the Holy Ghost, who surely allowed you to feel the Lord's love for you, too. After all, one of his big assignments is to comfort us."

"Well, I'm comforted, I truly am. And I'm just so proud."

"So am I, Hilda. So am I. Now may I have a moment with Brother Roscoe?"

"Of course, Bishop. You go right on in."

Ida Lou bustled by with an armload of soiled sheets. "I've cleaned him up a bit, Bishop, and called the doctor and the funeral home. Somebody should be here directly."

"Thanks, Ida Lou. I'll only be a moment."

There lingered a faint smell of sickness on the air, but a

window was open, the curtains stirring gently. Roscoe, emaciated and ancient-looking, appeared composed and relaxed. The
IV bottle hung idly—its drip no longer needed.

"Well done, my friend," the bishop whispered. "May we all
do as well. And I won't forget my promises to you, brother. Now
go in peace into eternity." He bowed his head in a silent prayer,
ignoring the tears that gathered and fell. They were tears of
gratitude. He was just so proud.

Y

The funeral was set for Saturday morning, and he was to
conduct and speak. There would be a viewing for an hour before
the service, but none on Friday evening. Sister Bainbridge had
insisted that the ward social, long scheduled for that date, be
held as planned.

"I won't attend the party, Bishop—I reckon you understand
about that—but I want everyone else to go and to have a good
time. Ross wouldn't have wanted to interfere with things."

The bishop conferred with his counselors and with the
activities committee. Much of the food had already been purchased, he learned, and some of the participants might not be
available on the next Friday. It was agreed that the party go on.

He wasn't in much of a party mood, given the sobering
effect of Roscoe's passing. But he drove his family to the
meetinghouse, arriving just a little early so that Trish could help
with serving, as she had agreed to do. The sight of the cultural
hall assured him that Sister Winslow and her committee had
outdone themselves. Several decorated booths stood around
the perimeter of the hall, and the long banquet tables in the
middle were covered with white paper and adorned down

the middle with trails of ivy interspersed with colorful, fresh-cut flowers and small American flags. A banner above the dessert table, blue with silver lettering, proclaimed: "Unity Amid Diversity," which he knew was the theme of the party. It was a noble aim, for the country and for the Fairhaven Ward, one which he hoped both could achieve.

Trish headed for the kitchen, and Tiffani and Jamie gravitated toward friends their age. He took Mallory by the hand and wandered over to the nearest booth, decorated to look like a Polynesian grass hut, with some kind of red tropical flower blooming around the front. He had to touch a blossom to determine that it was silk and not real.

"Talofa, Bishop," greeted Brother Tuapetagi, smiling as he deposited a platter of shredded pork next to a tray of something that smelled fragrant but didn't quite resemble anything the bishop was accustomed to eating.

"Evening, brother," the bishop responded. "Things are smelling mighty tempting around here. What are those?"

"Fried banana pieces. And we've got Kalua pig, pineapple chicken, and rice."

"Oh, boy! I'm going to need three stomachs tonight because I know I'm going to have to try everything."

"Not me," piped up Mallory. "I'm not eating a pig! I'm having cake and ice cream."

Her father chuckled. "Doubt if I'll even make it to the desserts tonight. Your booth is looking mighty pretty, Sister Lani," he added, as one of the Tuapetagi daughters placed a large container of rice on the table. She smiled shyly.

"She's dancing tonight," her father said proudly. "She and Hika and their mother. The boys, too, unless they chicken out. Ruth will help me sing."

"We'll look forward to that," the bishop promised, as he moved toward the Cisneros's booth, which had been built to resemble the rounded-corner, adobe structures typical of the American Southwest and Mexico.

"Wow," he murmured, peeking under the foil cover of a large pan of enchiladas. "I'm in trouble, for sure."

The Arnauds's booth suggested a white frame house with lacy wrought-iron grillwork across an upper balcony.

"Evening, Bishop, and little Mallory," said Camelia Arnaud, as they paused. "You folks hungry for gumbo tonight?"

"Sounds good to me. Only problem is, Camelia, so does everything else. What'm I going to do?"

She chuckled. "Well, you just eat a little, rest a little. Eat something else, rest a little. They tell me we're keeping the food out for the whole evenin', so folks can try this and that."

"A feast, for sure. Who made the booths?"

"Well, Sister Winslow, she designed them, and her husband figured how to make them stand up, and we all helped work on our own. I did that railing up there, with black poster board and an Exacto knife, and I tell you true, Bishop, it plumb took forever!"

"I just bet it did, but you did a wonderful job—it looks like the real thing. I sure hope somebody's taking pictures of all this."

"Reckon they will. We brought our video camera, too. Joe wants to record this for posterity, he says. Although right now, I don't reckon posterity cares about much except running around and causing mischief!" So saying, she grabbed her five-year-old son, Currie, as he raced by. "Where are your sisters, boy?"

"They're tendin' the nursery babies," Currie said, struggling to escape his mother's grasp.

"Well, do I have to put you down there with them? Or are you old enough to stay out here and act like a big boy?"

"I ain't no baby!"

"Well, then—you stop that running around, or I'm going to have to tie you up here like a puppy dog. Maybe somebody'll throw you a bone, if you get lucky."

"No way, Mama! I want gumbo, and a praline!"

"Then you stay right here by me, 'cause I'm the one handing out those goodies."

The bishop grinned at Currie and moved toward the last booth, the only one that didn't feature food. The Lipa family was into art, and their booth included a display of watercolors and oils of scenes from their native Philippine Islands, as well as a table-top village of small native-style huts cleverly built of sticks and twigs, which enchanted Mallory.

"They're so little!" she said. "I could play with them, couldn't I, Daddy?"

"I don't think they're to play with, are they, Fabiana?" he asked the Lipa's graceful, fourteen-year-old daughter.

She shook her head regretfully at Mallory. "I'm afraid not. I used to want to, when I was little, too, but I wasn't allowed. So I tried to build my own to play with. They weren't as neat as these, but they were better than nothing."

Mallory looked up at her dad. "I could do that, couldn't I, Daddy?"

"Well, sure, we'll have to try. Get your brother to look at these—maybe he'll help you make one."

Mallory pouted. "He'll make it a fort and smash it with rock bombs."

"Well, maybe he could make one for each of you, and I'll tell him yours is off-limits," he soothed. He glanced around the hall, in which the decibel level was rising by the minute as families arrived and children found each other. He saw the Jernigans sidle in and stand at one end of the room, looking around apprehensively. He made a beeline for them and shook their hands.

"How are you folks this fine evening?" he asked.

They didn't reply, as if his inquiry didn't signify, but Linda looked shyly at Mallory.

"Pretty little girl you've got," she said softly.

"Yeah, this is Mallory, and we kinda like her," he replied, giving his daughter a squeeze.

"Keep her with you at all times," Ralph said. "Always in sight. Can't be too careful, you know."

"That's true," the bishop agreed, remembering what Brother Smedley had said about a picture in their living room of a little blonde girl. Should he ask? Maybe not now—not if she turned out to be a sad memory for them. This was a happy occasion, and he wanted them to relax and enjoy it.

"Smells great in here, doesn't it? I can't wait to try some of everything."

Ralph nodded, and Linda ventured, "Looks pretty, too. Real colorful."

"Bishop," Ralph asked, leaning in close, "you got anybody patrolling outside? I'd be glad to take that on, if you don't. Just to keep watch on things—make sure nobody's car gets messed with, or nobody who doesn't belong is hanging around."

"Oh, I don't know, Ralph—I'm not real sure that's necessary. I'd rather see you in here relaxing and enjoying yourself."

"Tell you the truth, I'd rather be out doing that, than sitting in here wondering if everything was all right. I could take a plate out with me, and eat as I walk around and observe. It'd be no bother."

"Well, bless your heart, if you'd really like to do that for us, I suppose it'd be fine."

"Yessir, thank you, Bishop. I'll just go out now, and Linda can run me out a plate when everything's ready."

"Now, Linda," said the bishop, "if Ralph's going to be outside, then I'd like you to come and sit with our family. Will you do that?"

Linda's large pale blue eyes darted a look at his face, and her small mouth relaxed briefly into a smile. "I'd like that, thanks," she said, whereupon Ralph turned and marched out the door.

The bishop looked around the hall, where families were gathering at the long tables. It came as no surprise that the north end of the hall seemed to be attracting members of the former Fairhaven First Ward, whereas Second Ward members gravitated toward each other at the south end. He and his counselors, as well as the Relief Society presidency, began to execute their plan. The Shepherd family, being former First Warders, would elect to sit among Second Ward families, while Sam and Dixie Wright and their children, for instance, would invade First Ward territory. The bishop watched Bob Patrenko as he uprooted his ten-year-old son, Reynolds, from the spot he occupied beside his good friend Joey Thomas and settled his family in the other end of the room. He caught Bob's eye and gave him a thumbs-up sign. Then he found space for his own family plus Linda Jernigan, across from two families he didn't really know very well, and leaned over to greet each person with a smile and a cordial handshake. "Operation Unity," as he had come to think of it, was underway.

When the hall was full and the food was all displayed, Sister

LaThea Winslow stepped to a microphone and asked for quiet, then welcomed all to this first social of the new ward and thanked the committee and many others who had worked so hard to make it a memorable occasion. She was flushed and beaming with pleasure as she invited Bishop Shepherd to offer the invocation and say a few words.

Bishop Shepherd hadn't known that invitation was forthcoming, but he offered a brief and sincere prayer of thanks and a blessing on the food, then stood silently for a moment, gathering his thoughts.

"Brothers and sisters, most of you are aware that Brother Roscoe Bainbridge passed away yesterday after a long bout with cancer. We considered postponing this event, but Sister Hilda Bainbridge urged us to go on with it as planned, and we felt it was the right thing to do. Please be aware that Brother Bainbridge's funeral will be here in this building tomorrow at eleven, with a one-hour viewing prior to the service—and we extend our sympathy and love to Hilda in this difficult time. She is a wonderful lady—one whom I've come to respect deeply.

"Now, you know, folks, it does my heart good to see all of you here together, sitting mixed together as former First Warders and Second Warders, reaching out in friendship and love to one another, looking for new and rewarding associations as well as enjoying the associations we had with one another in our former situations. I'm grateful for the way you're pulling together to make our ward a cohesive unit, a true extended family, as President Walker advised us to do. I'm grateful for the opportunity I have to get acquainted with the folks I haven't known before, and an occasion like this is so valuable because it gives us the opportunity to visit with one another—and I happen to know that Sister Winslow and her committee have a couple of activities planned for us tonight that should help us with that getting-acquainted process. Now let's remember that we are no longer 'strangers and foreigners,' but fellowcitizens of the Fairhaven Ward of The Church of Jesus Christ of Latter-day Saints. That said, I've got to admit I can't wait much longer to begin sampling the delicious foods prepared by members of our ward and so attractively displayed for our enjoyment! Sister Winslow, where do we begin?"

He sat down amid scattered applause, as Sister Winslow began to describe the various culinary offerings and how best to access them in an orderly manner.

He enjoyed the food and probably ate too much of it, he admitted to himself, as he tried to live in the moment and be warm and accessible and friendly, and as he listened and watched and admired the dancing and singing, and as he participated in the games and activities. One activity included listing all the countries and cultures represented in the ancestry of those present.

"Tonight we're celebrating and enjoying four of the cultures represented in our ward," Sister Winslow explained. "But you can see from the list we just compiled that we have folks who have either lived in or descended from a total of forty-eight different countries. The ones most frequently represented are those of the British Isles and Scandinavia, but you can see all the others listed here, from Poland to Japan to Nigeria and Canada and France. Perhaps another time we can enjoy contributions from these places."

"Just don't ask me to prepare haggis," called out Dan McMillan. "I'm not that Scottish!"

"What's haggis?" whispered Tiffani, amid the general laughter.

Trish looked about to explain, then thought better of it. "Trust me," she whispered back, "you don't want to know."

Tiffani frowned, but knowing his daughter's sensibilities, her father thought his wife's discretion was wise.

As much as he enjoyed the festivities, it came as a relief to slip into his office for a few minutes of private contemplation while the cleanup committee did their thing, with the help of Trish and the kids. He wanted to reread the remarks he had outlined for Roscoe's funeral the next day. It was to be his first funeral—the first he had conducted—and, he realized, except for his father's, the only LDS funeral he had ever attended. His mother had asked the Church to conduct the services for his nonmember dad, but he remembered the procedures only vaguely. The fact was, nobody in the Fairhaven First Ward had died for years. A lady in the Second Ward had passed away a couple of years before, but he hadn't known her and hadn't attended the funeral. There had been Brother Lodger, of course, but he had gone to live in a rest home in Florida, close to his daughter, and his funeral had been held there.

It had been a new and humbling experience earlier that afternoon to go to the Humboldt Funeral Home with Sam Wright and Brother Arnold Collins, the high priest group leader, to dress Brother Bainbridge's body in the temple burial clothing. Sister Hilda had lovingly laundered and ironed the same clothing Roscoe had worn when they were sealed in the Atlanta Temple, and given the articles to the priesthood brethren with a tremulous smile.

"I thank ya'll, brethren, for doin' this for Ross—and I know he 'preciates it, too," she had said. "I like to remember him wearin' these in the temple when we was sealed. It was the handsomest I ever saw him look. Better even than when we was married." She chuckled. "I know what Ross would say to that. He'd say that's just 'cause of my eyesight goin' bad. But it wadn't. It was because of him gettin' better and better through the years. Don't you think that when folks do better, they look better?"

Bishop Shepherd smiled, remembering that. There was truth to her statement, too, he thought, although the ravages of disease had left Roscoe wasted and wrinkled since that happy day in the temple. In spite of this, it struck the bishop with some surprise how heavy the emaciated body still felt as they turned and dressed it—how firm and cold the flesh. Death became very real in those moments. Once they were finished, he asked the other two to go ahead, saying, "I just want a moment alone with Brother Roscoe, if you don't mind." When they had gone, he took out his wallet and removed the worn little picture of the young Hilda.

"I tried, Roscoe, to return this as you wanted me to," he whispered to the still form. "But the lady at the library told me that those old yearbooks had long been stored in the basement of the old library, where they were burned up in a fire about twelve years ago. I'd forgotten all about that fire, and I reckon you had, too. So, since this has been precious to you all these years, why don't you keep it, my friend?" He slipped his hand under the pleated robe and put the picture into the pocket of Roscoe's white shirt. "God be with you, brother," he said, and went to tell the funeral director that the body was dressed, except for the cap, which would be put on just before the funeral.

Y

Lying beside Trish on Friday night, his mind reviewed the events of the ward social.

"Good turnout, don't you think?" he asked.

"I thought so. Best of all, lots of interaction between First and Second Warders."

"Yeah—even if we had to be sneaky and engineer some of it. I was glad the Jernigans came—wasn't sure they would."

"Linda was sweet, I thought, sitting by Mallory and listening so seriously to all her prattle. What was Ralph doing?"

"Patrolling the perimeter."

"Really?"

"Well, I don't think he sits down and relaxes easily, and he's not much for small talk. So he was probably happier walking around outside and munching Polynesian chicken, protecting our cars and our property from . . . whatever."

Trish giggled. "Maybe from the zucchini elf—although it's a little early for him."

"Zucchini elf? That's a new one for me."

"Haven't you heard the old joke—'Why do Mormons always lock their cars while they're at church?'"

"No, why?"

"So nobody'll fill them with zucchini."

"I'm not sure that's funny," he replied, chuckling in spite of himself. "We didn't plant any this year, did we?"

"Goodness, no! Hestelle keeps us supplied. I grate and freeze it for zucchini bread, I pickle it and put it in soups and stir-fry it and stuff it and—"

"Maybe you should write a cookbook. Call it, 'How to Stuff a Wild Zucchini.'"

"Funny man. Um . . . Jim?"

"M-hmm."

"I didn't see the Padgetts at the party, did you?"

"Nope. I hoped they'd come, but I wasn't too surprised they didn't."

"It's all fixed up with Ida Lou. Starting in June, I'll be Melody's visiting teacher."

"That's great. I love you, Sister Bishop."

"Love you, too, Brother Bishop."

CHAPTER ELEVEN

Y

" . . . EVERY DAY SOME BURDEN LIFTED"

All in all, it had been a very satisfying funeral, Bishop Shepherd reflected, as he pulled his truck into its accustomed spot behind the market on Saturday afternoon. President Walker had given a comforting talk on the spirit world and the resurrection, Roscoe's younger brother had traveled from Tennessee to give the life sketch (which Hilda had helped to write), and the chapel had been full of people, Church members and others, who had known and loved Roscoe Bainbridge. Hilda seemed to have withstood it all very well, for which her bishop was abundantly grateful, and the Relief Society sisters had swept her along in a cloud of love and warmth and service, staying by her side as much as possible through the whole experience, somehow trying to do anything daughter Carolyn might have done, including preparing a delicious luncheon for relatives and out-of-town participants.

The only thing was, he admitted to himself, his upper lip was just going to have to stiffen up. It wouldn't do to have a bishop breaking down in tears at such services, which he had nearly done at several points, such as when he had first escorted Hilda in to see her husband in his casket, then about an hour later when that casket had been closed for the last time. He'd had to clench his teeth when he had slipped into the chapel at the beginning of the service and asked the congregation to please rise, in honor of Roscoe and his family. Then there had been that one spot in the life sketch, when Roscoe's brother had departed from his written text and said, "I don't reckon Hildy ever even knew about this, but I remember when Ross was gettin' ready to go off to war, and he went over to the liberry and cut him out a pitcher of Hildy from the school yearbook— figgered he needed it worse than that old liberry did, I reckon— and he kept it with him for the duration. Reckon it were a comfort to him. He shore loved his Hildy."

The bishop had dared a glance at Hilda in that moment and saw her turn to her sister-in-law and mouth the words, "I knew."

Whoa, Roscoe! he had thought. *We thought we were being so secretive about that picture, and here she knew it all the time.* He felt his throat choke off, and then, unaccountably, the urge to chuckle at the same time. *And if she hadn't known, she would now, with your tale-telling brother here!* He had had to cough to cover the strange, explosive sound that resulted from this mix of feelings.

"Man, I'm drained," he muttered to himself, heading into the store from the stockroom. "I never knew that funerals were more exhausting than a day's work." Having missed some of Thursday and Friday due to Roscoe's death and the demands of the ward social, he felt obligated to show up for at least part of Saturday. He looked around. Business was pretty brisk for a gorgeous, near-summer Saturday afternoon. He spied Lula Rexford moving slowly down an aisle, picking up one item after another, considering each carefully, and rejecting most. He watched to see which direction she turned at the end of the aisle, then raced down another and into his office.

"Hey, Mary Lynn," he greeted his office girl, startling her with his abrupt entrance. "Where do we keep those buy-one-get-one-free labels?"

"Right here," she responded, handing him a box. "Are we having a sale?"

"A short one," he said, rushing out with the labels and a pad of paper. He literally ran to the aisle ahead of Lula Rexford and affixed a label on a good brand of canned vegetables and soups, then headed for the dry beans and rice area, slapped a couple on pudding and cake mixes, and made a beeline for the refrigerated foods. Beef roasts and cut-up chicken parts received labels, as did milk, cottage cheese, and frozen juices. He looped back around to the produce and baked goods areas and added a few signs there, then quickly penned an announcement and handed it to Mary Lynn, indicating that she was to get on the speaker. Giving him a strange look, she complied.

"Good afternoon, shoppers, this is your lucky day! We are having a special, one-hour, buy-one-get-one-free sale on selected items. Look for the stickers, and take one labeled and one identical unlabeled item of the same or lesser value to the checkout line before 3:45 to receive your discount. And thank you for shopping at Shepherd's!"

He grinned, gave her a thumbs-up, and hurried back out, being sure to avoid Lula, and made a list of all the items he had tagged. He ran three copies of the list and had Mary Lynn take one to each of the checkers for verification.

"I don't get it," Mary Lynn said bluntly, as she returned from this errand. "What gives, Jim?"

He grinned. "I guess we do. Won't hurt us, and if word spreads that such things happen here, maybe it'll even be good for business. In the meantime, we're being good Scouts—just doing our daily good turn."

"But—when did you think of this? You just buzzed in here, and I didn't even expect—I mean, I thought you were at a funeral today!"

"I was. It's over. Let's just say I'm so glad to be alive that I wanted to help out a few people."

"Just for an hour, huh?"

"Well, frankly, if we did it for much longer, we'd run out of some of the marked items because of not planning ahead. You've heard of impulse buying? Well, this is impulse selling."

"Okayyy, you're the boss." She bent toward her computer keyboard again, her long brown hair falling forward to hide her expression. He smiled and went about his business, his funeral-fatigue forgotten.

Y

He enjoyed his afternoon; it was good to get back to simple daily pursuits after dealing with weightier matters. It was almost time to go home when Muzzie Winston hailed him from the produce aisle.

"Hey, Jim, I hear your in-laws are coming!" she caroled, tossing her mane of streaked blondish-brown hair in a way that had always unnerved him. And it had been such a good day.

"That they are," he agreed, smiling. "Been talking to Trish, have you?"

"Uh-huh, she called me about a little decorative birdhouse I have. Wanted to know where I found it. Said she was fixing the place up because her folks were coming. And Merrie."

"Yep—and Meredith. Kids are over the moon 'cause Aunt Merrie's coming."

"You okay with it?" Muzzie asked, cocking her head to one side like a sympathetic bird.

"Sure, why wouldn't I be?" Muzzie was altogether too perceptive for his comfort—or too well informed, he wasn't sure which.

"Well, I'm just remembering that she wasn't too thrilled when you guys got married. Not that it was her business, mind you, I'm not saying that. Or that she was right. Just wondered how things have shaken down since then."

"Oh, I think we're probably all a little more mature by now. Hopefully," he added, with a grin. "I know a small-time grocer didn't fit her ideal of the perfect husband for Trish, but she's got her own big-time businessman now, who apparently is so busy that he can't spare the time to travel with her—at least on unimportant family visits—so with all that success behind her, maybe I won't be such a source of embarrassment anymore."

"Well, I don't think you were exactly *that*. Merrie just always had some jumped-up ideas about everything. She was a city girl at heart."

"Reckon so."

"But I'll tell you what—you got the pick of the litter when you married Trish. Not saying any of the girls are dogs, but you know what I mean. She's the best."

"Can't help agreeing there," he grinned. "I just hope she feels okay about how things have turned out."

"Are you kidding? I only wish I felt about Dugan the way she feels about you. You guys have something special."

"Well, thanks, Muzzie. But aren't you and Dugan okay?"

"We are, I reckon. He's a good dad to the kids, and I don't have any real complaints. It's just—well, marriage ain't exactly the stuff of my teenage dreams, know what I mean? Dugie and I just sort of get along, and do our own thing most of the time. Hum-drum, I s'pose, is how you'd describe our marriage. We must be getting old!" She laughed, but it was a sad laugh, not the kind he would expect from Muzzie Evans Winston, the scintillating, flirtatious vamp of his high school days.

She had married Dugan Winston when she was a year out of high school and Dugie had just come home with his bachelor's degree from Auburn. It had been a celebrated wedding, with as much splash and style as Fairhaven could muster, and the pair had gone off to graduate school at the University of Florida, moving back home two years later with gorgeous tans, another degree under Dugan's belt, and a baby boy. They purchased a new house in an up-and-coming suburb, and Dugan had taken his place in his uncle's business, handling the paperwork and promotional side of selling RVs and boats, leaving his uncle to do what he loved—the demonstrating and selling. Muzzie had always seemed as dazzling as ever, and he was surprised to hear that things were not what she had hoped and dreamed. He wondered if Trish knew.

"Well, gotta hurry," Muzzie was saying. "I'm picking Chloe and Marie up from school today. They have ballet, and it's their turn to bring cookies. See ya, Jim! Hang in there."

"Sure, Muzzie. You do the same." *Marie*, he thought. That

was Muzzie's real name, which she had given to one of her daughters. "Muzzie" must have been a younger sibling's attempt to say Marie, and it had stuck. That happened. He knew several "Bubbas" whose nicknames had come from babyish attempts to say "Brother." He wondered why people felt obliged to allow the childish titles to hang on forever.

He drove home in a contemplative mood, pondering relationships. Roscoe and Hilda had managed to keep their shine, all their lives, despite having very little of this world's goods and despite the disappointment of having only one child and then losing her too soon. Muzzie and Dugan had apparently lost some of the shine with which they had begun life together, despite having three beautiful children and plenty of material goods. If they had experienced some adversity together, early on, might it have strengthened them as a couple, or would they have dissolved into an early divorce? Or if everything had come up roses for Roscoe and Hilda, would they have appreciated each other less? One obvious difference, it seemed to him, was that Roscoe and Hilda had the advantage of the fullness of the gospel, including the concept of eternal families, whereas Muzzie and Dugan did not.

But then there were the Padgetts. Melody and Jack were members of the Church, and supposedly working toward having their family sealed in the temple for time and all eternity—and yet he perceived trouble there. And trouble of varying kinds and degrees, he was becoming aware, afflicted many of the families of his ward. He was not naive enough to suppose that merely knowing the basics of the restored gospel of Christ was enough to keep families happy and strong. The tenets had to be practiced, love strengthened, forgiveness readily given, priesthood used to bless and not to subdue or control.

And how were he and Trish doing? From Muzzie's point of

view, very well, he supposed. But what did the Lord think of them? He had allowed them to serve in this calling, and President Walker had heartily concurred with that choice. No small part of that, he was sure, was due to Trish herself—her faithfulness, her testimony, her willingness to support him. But suppose he and Trish had encountered opposition and disappointment early in their marriage—how would they have performed? He hoped they would have come through with flying colors. He knew their love was genuine and felt it was strong—but had it been tested?

"Not that I'm asking for a test," he muttered. "It's enough for me right now that I feel intimidated by my in-laws, which, as a problem, is probably as silly and small-minded as they get."

He pulled the truck into the garage and parked, wondering what was for dinner. A bank of dark blue clouds had moved in, cooling the air slightly, and a smell of promised rain hung in the air. He was glad it had waited until Roscoe was safely buried. Even the best of funerals were sad; funerals in the rain must be sadness squared.

"Hey, baby," he greeted, as Mallory flung herself at him on the back porch.

"Hey, Daddy. Where's my hot dog?"

"Hot dog. Oh, shoot, Mal—I forgot all about 'em. Let's say hi to Mom and the others, and then you and I can run back out and get them, okay?"

She turned and ran into the house. "Mom-mee! Daddy forgot to bring dinner!"

Trish was on her hands and knees on the kitchen floor, scrubbing with a brush and pail of soapy water the spots in corners and by the appliances where the mop didn't quite do the job. She sat back on her heels and regarded him, her face perspiring.

"I'm sorry, sweetheart," he said contritely. "I totally forgot the dogs and burgers. Mallory and I'll run right back out and get them."

"Oh, don't bother, it's okay. Besides, it's going to storm any minute. We'll just make something here."

"No, Mommy! I want my hot dog."

"Me, too," said Jamie, from his computer corner. "With chili and onions, remember?"

Trish frowned. "I don't have any hot dogs on hand. I have ground beef, but it's frozen. I could thaw some in the microwave, but I don't have buns. I could hurry and make spaghetti or chili, I guess. I just have so much to do that I didn't want to take the time to cook."

"Where's Tiff?"

"Baby-sitting for the Hallmarks. It's their anniversary. They picked her up, and she's supposed to eat dinner with their kids."

"You look tired, babe. Why don't you put your feet up for a while? Come on, Mal—let's go for a ride. Want to go, Jamie?"

"Uh, no, I want to finish my game. I'm trying to beat my last score."

"Well, then help your Mom, okay? You could put out napkins and ketchup and stuff on the table."

"It's okay," Trish said wearily. "And all I want is a chili burger—no cheese or fries. And I'll drink water. I need to lose a couple of pounds."

"Where from?" her husband asked, frowning. "I don't see any extra."

"You have my undying love for saying that, but I know exactly where they are. And so will Meredith. I'll never hear the end of it."

The bishop compressed his lips. Such comments did nothing to endear his youngest sister-in-law to him.

"Aunt Merrie's coming, Aunt Merrie's coming," chanted Mallory as he seatbelted her into the backseat of the car, which he deemed safer than the truck to transport small children.

"And Nana and Papa, too," he reminded her.

"I know! They'll be here when I get home from school on Monday, Mom says."

"Monday. Wow. That's coming right up."

"Yep!"

"How come you like Aunt Merrie so much?"

"Tiff says she's fun, and she brings us neat presents, and takes us places."

"I guess you don't remember her much yourself, do you?"

"Just kinda. I think she has blonde hair, like me."

"M-hmm, last time I looked, she did. So what are you having tonight, Mal?"

"A hot dog, just plain, like I said. And fries and onion rings and a drink and a big ice cream cone and—"

"Whoa! All that, for such a little girl?" He peered at her in the rearview mirror.

"What are you having, Daddy?"

"A chili cheeseburger with fries and onion rings and a drink and a big ice cream cone to share with my little girl."

She giggled.

Y

It was Sunday evening. Dinner was long since over and cleaned up, and the familiar place mats replaced with new finery—eggshell lace over a dusty rose cloth. A crystal vase held place of pride in the center, waiting to be filled the next day with fresh-cut flowers from the yard. The table typified what had gone on in the rest of the house—things were picked up, polished, buffed, steam-cleaned, or brand new. The bath that served the guest room had its new matching towels and rugs, and the guest room itself was prepared and inviting with its new sage-green paper and collection of birdhouses. The pink, ruffly thing on the bed had been replaced by a tailored beige spread with coordinated plaid skirt and what his mother would have called pillow slips, but which Trish called shams. Mallory's room had undergone less of a change, since she was moving back into it after a week, but it had grown up somewhat under Trish's determined hand, and now sported a cluster of scented candles and several of the latest books on Mal's erstwhile toy shelves.

Normally, by this time on the Sabbath day, all cooking efforts would have ceased, all necessary meetings would have been attended, and if he and Trish were lucky, they would be strolling hand-in-hand around their neighborhood, speaking to this person or that, visiting with each other about family concerns, and refreshing their souls with the peace of it all. Not so on this evening, however. Mingled aromas of spice cake baking and chicken breasts simmering to become tomorrow's salad emanated from the kitchen, where Trish was kneading a soft dough for croissants.

"Want to take a break, go for a walk?" he asked, lounging in the doorway.

She looked up and used her forearm to brush a strand of hair from her eyes, leaving a streak of flour on her face. "There's no way," she told him. "I've got enough stuff still to do to take all night."

"Is it all necessary, babe? I mean, maybe bakery croissants would have been okay, don't you reckon? You're knocking yourself out."

"Jim, I'm fine. I just want things to be nice for my family. I mean, for the part of my family that's visiting. Is that a problem?"

"Only because I'm afraid you'll be too wiped out to enjoy their visit. How can I help?"

"You don't need to do anything. You've had a busy day, too. Why don't you just relax, or go for a walk yourself? Maybe one of the kids will go with you."

"Get out of your hair, in other words."

"I didn't say that! But I can't just run off and relax, even though I might like to, with cake in the oven and chicken cooking and dough to tend."

"'A man may work from dawn to dusk, but woman's work is never done?'"

"Something like that. Except that saying never made sense to me. Dawn to dusk is pretty much the same thing as never done, isn't it?"

"Maybe that's the point. There's work enough to do for everybody to keep us busy all the time. But, honey, if you've got an ox to pull out of the ditch, I don't want to go off and leave you to tackle him alone. There must be something I can do."

"Well, Tiff said she finished dusting, but you could look around and follow up on that if you want, and maybe check outside to be sure things are okay—no debris or toys on the lawn, no flowers that need deadheading."

"Busy work," her husband muttered as he went to do her bidding. There were times when it was wise for a man to stay out of the kitchen.

Y

Twenty minutes later, he ventured back. Trish was rolling triangles of dough into curved shapes on a baking pan, her lips compressed and her cheeks pink from the heat of the oven. He sat down at the table and watched.

"Don't say it," she warned.

"Say what?"

"That this is too much work, and unnecessary. This is something I *want* to do."

"Okay. All I was going to say is I forgot to tell you there's a new family moving into the ward."

"Oh?"

"Yeah. The Case family. I believe the husband's name is Court, and his wife's called Jewel. They've got a girl and a boy, Charity and Justin." He paused and looked at his wife.

"Uh-huh?" she murmured absently, rolling another sheet of stretchy dough.

"I'm told they're bringing along a couple of dogs, too—one's called Hopeless, and the other one's name is Brief. He's a dachsund, and really short."

She smiled slightly. "Brief. That's cute. How old are the kids?"

"Trish."

"What?" She looked up, confused and a little annoyed at the interruption. He raised his eyebrows and spread his hands in a gesture of silent appeal. She frowned, and then he could see her reprocessing what had just been said. Light dawned.

"Oh, my gosh! Oh, that's funny. Justin Case, Charity Case . . ." She began to laugh, a girlish, high-pitched giggle he hadn't heard for a long while. She came around the table to shake and then hug him with her floury hands and arms. He didn't care. He wasn't even too surprised when her giggles suddenly turned to tears, and she collapsed onto his lap and sobbed against his shoulder.

"I'm sorry," she squeaked between sobs. "I've just been so tense, so uptight."

"I know, it's okay," he told her, rocking her slightly in his arms as he would Mallory. "Is it Meredith? Because, babe—you don't have anything to prove to her."

"But I do! I want her—I want all of them—to see how perfect our life is, here in Fairhaven."

"If it's so perfect, how come it needs all fancying up?"

"I just want—I just—Oh, I don't know."

"Honey, don't worry. Nobody's life is perfect all the time. Nobody's house never gets dusty or shabby. Nobody never gets mad or sad or bored or worried. Nobody's kids are perfect all the time, and nobody married a perfect guy."

Her crying had tapered off into little hiccups, and she managed a small chuckle. "Nobody sounds like a lucky woman. Either that, or you just used more double negatives than the language can bear." She got off his lap and reached for a tissue to blow her nose. "Brief Case," she murmured, and giggled again. "Hopeless Case."

He grinned. "Speaking of me, or the dog?" He sent a small prayer of relief and gratitude heavenward. His wife was back.

CHAPTER TWELVE

Y

" . . . TEACH US TOLERANCE AND LOVE"

Trish fell asleep that night as soon as her head touched the pillow, or so it seemed to her husband, who couldn't, despite his own weariness, seem to do the same. Maybe it was because when he had knelt to have his personal prayer, all the people and events of the weekend had come parading back before him, and now he couldn't seem to banish them. He had prayed for Hilda and for the Rexfords and for Muzzie and Dugan Winston, asking that all might be blessed according to their needs. For his in-laws, that they might travel safely. For himself and Trish, that they would be able to endure and even enjoy their visit. He had even remembered his friend Peter MacDonald and asked that he be blessed with wisdom in making decisions with his family. He thought back over the ward social and prayed that Mrs. Martha Ruckman, who had accompanied her granddaughter Tashia Jones to the party, would continue to have a warm feeling about the people in the ward and continue to allow Tashia to attend and eventually to be baptized. She had seemed to be enjoying herself, daintily spooning up gumbo and greeting various former students whom she recognized. She had spent some time getting acquainted with Joe and Camelia Arnaud, presently the only African-American family in the ward. He hoped they gave her a good report on the suitability of the Church as a place for Tashia to worship and to flourish. Tashia had talked and giggled happily with Tamika Arnaud, who was close to her age, and he hoped the association would blossom—that Tashia would feel comfortable enough to sit with the Arnauds at services, instead of by herself as she usually did.

He had prayed for the Padgetts—not, by any means, for the first time—conspicuous in their absence from the social, but there on Sunday morning in their usual spot toward the rear of the chapel. Melody had brushed by him after sacrament meeting, on her way to Primary, and he had stuck out a hand for her to shake.

"Hi, Bishop," she had said, smiling as usual.

"How's everything, Sister Melody?"

"Oh, just fine!" (Had he expected any other answer?)

"Hey, Andrea. How are you today?"

"Good," the little girl chirped, her small hand swallowed in his. She was hardly any bigger than Mallory, though a year or so older.

"Well, you ladies have a great time in Primary, okay?"

"We will," Melody promised, tugging her daughter along, smiling. He had looked up to see Jack Padgett's eyes boring into him from across the chapel. The bishop nodded and raised a hand in greeting but felt that his smile had turned sickly.

"Father, forgive me for my feelings toward this brother," he had pleaded this night, on his knees. "I don't know for sure that he's being abusive, and I shouldn't assume such a thing, when his wife hasn't even complained or accused him. On the other hand, if this feeling I have is a prompting of the Spirit, I don't want to be guilty of ignoring it. If any real harm came to Melody or Andrea, I wouldn't want it to be because I wasn't vigilant or responsive. Please help me sort out my thoughts, Father, and be fair. And please protect them in any needful way."

He sighed wearily, his eyes wide open in the relative darkness of the bedroom. He had prayed, too, for the ability to be gracious to Trish's family—to make them welcome and to truly love them as he should. They were great people; it shouldn't be difficult to do that, he reasoned. What *was* his problem?

He flopped over on his side, closing his eyes determinedly. Losing sleep would only make things worse.

He left for the store a bit early the next morning, promising Trish that if at all possible he would be home for lunch to greet her family. He examined the calendar in his office, half hoping there would be a forgotten luncheon meeting of the Kiwanis or the Fairhaven Boosters filling in the square for June first, but that space was unmercifully blank. He went about his duties as usual, stopping now and then for brief visits with customers he knew. At ten-thirty he called Trish, who confirmed that her folks had indeed landed on time in Birmingham and were on their way to Fairhaven in their rented car.

"You're coming home for lunch, aren't you?" she queried anxiously.

"Looks like I will be," he said.

"Jamie'll be here, too—they only go half a day today."

"That's right—school's out, isn't it?" He was happy for that; the kids might provide a chatty, distracting buffer.

"Tiff doesn't get out until two-thirty, but I can't wait lunch that long, and she'll probably have eaten something at school, anyway."

"So you're all ready, hon? I mean, you ought to be, with all the preparations you made."

"I think so. I'm feeling better today. Just excited."

"That's great. That's how it should be."

"Right. Well—gotta run. I'm setting the table before they come, so we can just visit and eat whenever they're ready."

"Want to give me a call, or should I just show up?"

"They should be here by twelve or twelve-fifteen. Come when you can."

"See you then, babe."

"Oh, Jim—um—don't call me 'babe' around my mom, okay? I like it, but she thinks names like that are demeaning to women."

"Oh. Okay. Sorry." He hung up, feeling more the clueless, country bumpkin son-in-law than ever. What other faux pas might he commit, in all innocence, that would offend Trish's parents and sister? How often did they roll their eyes at each other behind his back? And *was* "babe" a demeaning nickname for him to call his wife? He had certainly never intended it to be anything other than an endearment. But, obviously, what did he know? He looked across the office at Mary Lynn, busily occupied with the computer.

"Hey, Mary Lynn—can I ask you a dumb question?"

She sat back in her chair and flipped a handful of long brown hair over her shoulder. Her bangs were so long that the tips of them could be seen behind her glasses. He wondered why she didn't trim her hair.

"What dumb question would that be?" she asked warily.

"Well, if your husband called you 'babe,' would you be offended? Would you think it was demeaning?"

She looked at him steadily. "I don't have a husband."

"Oh, I know that. But if you did, do you think you would take offense?"

"Let me put it this way: if I was married to a good, faithful man, he could call 'Soo-eee, pig, pig, pig' if he wanted, and I'd come running. Assuming, of course, he didn't intend it to be demeaning."

He couldn't see how it could fail to be, but he took her point.

She still watched him. "Trish is offended by 'babe,' is she?"

"Nah, I don't think so," he replied. "It's her mother."

"You call her mother 'babe?'"

He chuckled at the idea. "Not likely."

"Well, good, because that would definitely rank as pretty cheeky. But to call your wife 'babe'—I think it's kinda sweet. Don't worry about her mother, if Trish doesn't object."

"But she just did—I mean, she asked me not to call her that in front of her mother, because her mother finds it demeaning to women—which is something that never remotely entered my mind. Now I've gotta wonder how Trish really feels about all my silly nicknames for her."

"Huh. Mama must be some kind of feminist."

He frowned. "I don't think so. She's just—uh—cultured, I reckon. Refined, and so on."

"Well, personally, I think she ought to be glad and grateful to have a son-in-law who loves her daughter enough to call her sweet nothings. I mean, think what some women get called."

Unbidden, he wondered what Jack Padgett called Melody. He didn't think it was "babe."

"You're right, Mary Lynn, and I'm sure I'm bothered about

nothing. I just always feel like such a hick around Trish's family."

"Well, you're not," Mary Lynn said loyally. "I grew up with the biggest, crudest bunch of redneck, hick-from-the-sticks brothers you ever saw, and believe me, I know one when I see him—and you're not one."

"Thanks. But don't you think it's probably all relative? I mean, to Trish's parents, I'm probably pretty red under the collar."

"Big-city folk, are they?"

"Well—more military. They've been around. And they're educated."

"Uh-huh. Well, so're you. You've been to college."

He shrugged. "Two years. Hardly anything to brag about."

"I expect the training your daddy gave you here in the store was worth another couple of years, wasn't it?"

"Practically speaking, it has been, all right."

"Well, see? If that doesn't count with them, then they're the ones who're ignorant."

"That's one way of looking at it, I reckon." He regarded his office girl curiously. How old was Mary Lynn? Thirty-two or so? Not a teeny-bopper, that was certain, but not middle-aged, either. Maybe older than she looked, though, hiding behind all that hair. He took her for granted, he realized. This was probably the longest and most personal conversation the two of them had ever had, although she had worked for him for over ten years, and their relationship was relaxed and comfortable. She ran a tight ship, and he depended on her to relieve him of a number of annoying details—such as working with the computer.

"How come you've never married, Mary Lynn? Nice, sharp girl like you can't be going unnoticed."

"Now, Jim, you know you never ask a lady her age or weight or her real hair color or why she isn't married," she scolded, but her lips turned up at the corners and her cheeks reddened before she flipped her hair to the front again and ducked her head toward her work.

"Sorry," he said, grinning. "Told you I was ignorant."

"Well, be good, or I'll tell Mama-in-law. Now, quit stewing about things and run along. I've got work to do. My boss might get mad."

Y

He drove home slowly at about twelve-fifteen, and sure enough, there was an unfamiliar car, new and shiny, parked in a patch of shade in front of his home. He pulled into the driveway and got out.

"Daddee! They're here, they're here!" squealed Mallory, launching herself at him from the edge of the back porch. He caught her in mid-air and carried her into the dining room, where Jamie, Trish, and her family were just sitting down to lunch. Larry Langham, Trish's dad, pushed back his chair and stood to come and shake Jim's hand.

"Jim! Good to see you, man—how's our bishop?" Larry was tall, tanned, and youthful-looking under his white hair. He patted Jim's shoulder as they shook hands.

Ivy Langham, whose dark hair was turning a pretty silver, also rose and hugged her son-in-law. "Hi, Jim. You're looking good—being bishop must agree with you."

"Oh, I think it's Trish's cooking that agrees with me," he

said, kissing Ivy's cheek. "You look wonderful yourself." He straightened and caught the eye of his sister-in-law, Meredith, across the table. She was flanked by Mallory and Jamie, and made no effort to get up, but smiled. He reached across the table and shook her hand.

"Meredith, how are you?" he asked. "Looking lovely as ever, of course. Good to see you. Sorry Dirk couldn't make it."

"It's okay. This is my special time with my family," she said, winking at Jamie, who grinned foolishly up at her. Was she warning him off? Jim wondered. In a subtle, lighthearted way, was she requesting that he, too, not interfere with her special family time? Well, he would do his level best not to, he decided. He dropped a kiss on Trish's cheek and took his place at the head of the table. He offered a brief prayer, giving thanks for the safe arrival of their loved ones, and only a small dart of guilt for hypocrisy troubled his petition. As Trish started the croissants and chicken salad around, he examined his feelings. *What*, he asked himself—*would you rather they had met with an accident along the way, or been detained by bad weather—or simply not have wanted to come? No*, he was honestly able to answer himself. In a very real way, he was glad they had come—glad it was important enough for them to spend the time and money necessary to travel across the country and be with them. Especially for Trish's sake, and for the sake of the kids, so that they could know their mother's side of the family, he was glad. He would just have to deal with his own nasty little demons of insecurity and inadequacy that seemed to pop up whenever he was around the Langhams.

How, he wondered, had he ever dared to propose to their daughter? It must have been the folly and bravado of youth. He glanced at her, his gaze softening as he acknowledged that it had also been because he had truly loved this girl—and still did—and because he had received confirmation of the rightness of the decision as answer to prayer. So, why, if the Lord in heaven approved the match, did he still feel ignorant and clumsy around these people?

"Who is it who wants you to feel that way?" asked a small voice from deep inside. "Do Trish's parents want you to? Do they criticize you, put you down, embarrass you?" He knew the answer was no—they had never been anything but gracious and kind to him. It was just his own recognition of the differences between their lifestyle and his own—their knowledge of things that had never been a part of his life, such as travel, art, a certain elegance of style, and the confidence of being fourth- or fifth-generation Latter-day Saints, descendants of valiant pioneers. And he knew it was the fact that Trish's younger sister, Meredith, had also recognized the gap between his qualifications and theirs that had made her less than accepting of him as a proper brother-in-law. But she had been young then, and supercritical of practically everybody. In recent years, he had to admit, she seemed to have mellowed considerably, and she loved his and Trish's kids, he had no doubt of that.

Okay, Bishop, he told himself silently. *Time to get over yourself.*

He tuned back in to the conversation at the table. Mallory was directing Meredith as to the disposition of melon balls to her plate. "Two red, two green, and that orange one," she said, and Meredith carefully complied. Meredith seemed to enjoy children so much; he wondered why she and Dirk had none, as yet.

"How are things at the store, Jim?" Larry asked.

"Doing well, thanks," he replied, on safe, familiar footing

here. He went on to discuss the impact that had been anticipated by the building of a large Albertson's store across town
and the measures Jim had taken to maintain his customer base.
He and Larry spoke of how the fluctuation in gasoline prices
affected the cost of produce that had to be trucked in and of
how fortunate they were to live in a climate that allowed for the
nearby production of many fruits and vegetables. Then Ivy
inquired about the ward, recalling members they had known
and catching up on the recent changes. The conversation was
easy and genial, and he wondered why he had stressed. They
spoke of going together to the Birmingham Temple, and of
Mallory's fifth birthday, which was imminent, and of Jamie's
plans for summer sports. In all, the lunchtime reunion proved a
pleasant interlude in his day, and he went back to the store
a much relieved and relaxed man.

That evening they enjoyed a brief home evening lesson
given by Tiffani, then played board games, with Aunt Merrie
taking turns playing whatever game suited each of the children.
Jim smiled, watching them. Meredith's hair was a streaky
blonde, with some of Mallory's platinum and some of Tiffani's
antique gold in the mix. He had no clue whether the streaking
had been done by the Arizona sun that had tanned her skin,
nor, with Mary Lynn's warning under his belt, did he dare ask—
at least until he and Trish were alone in their room, preparing
for bed.

"Today went well, I thought," he said, peeling off his socks.

"M-hmm. Did you think it wouldn't?"

"Um—no, not really. It's just—you know—Meredith.
Sometimes she hasn't exactly approved of me, and I wondered
how things would go this time."

"Oh, she's over all that nonsense. She's grown up now."

"Ah-h. Glad to hear it. Why d'you reckon she and Dirk don't have any kids yet—has she said?"

Trish gave him a raised-eyebrow smile. "She hasn't, and I'm not asking. Not my business. Merrie's always been very private about things."

"If it's not your business, it sure as heck isn't any of mine. I just wondered, because she's so good with our kids and seems crazy about them."

"They adore her, too. I could probably get jealous. If she were around all the time, I'd be constantly upstaged."

"If she were always available, she'd probably lose some of her appeal. I mean, it's one thing to swoop in occasionally and spoil everybody for a few days, but that'd be a hard act to maintain full-time."

"I expect that's true."

He got into bed, and Trish sat on her side, rubbing some lotion onto her legs.

"Did I do okay with your mom and dad? No embarrassing nicknames or anything?"

Trish turned toward him. "Jimmy, I could have bit my tongue soon as I'd said that to you on the phone. I'm so sorry, honey. I love it when you call me 'babe,' and I don't know why I was worried what my mom would think. I guess I was just a little nervous about how things would go, too—though I don't know why."

He pulled her to him and spoke against her fragrant hair. "Your folks are terrific people. Maybe they're so wonderful that they seem a little—well, hard to live up to."

"They wouldn't mean to seem that way."

"Nope. They wouldn't. They're just striving toward perfection like the rest of us—only they're probably a lot closer than most, and it's intimidating—at least to galoots like me."

"I love galoots like you."

"Oh, yeah? Who are these galoots? I'll beat 'em up."

"You're my one and only galoot."

"Okay, then. So, does Meredith color her hair, or are her streaks natural?"

Trish pulled back and looked at him quizzically.

He shrugged and grinned. "Just wondered. It was something Mary Lynn said, about never asking a lady her real hair color."

"To tell you the truth, I don't really know. She says she plays a lot of golf and tennis, so all that sun could have an effect. She always had the lightest hair of all of us. It was almost like Mallory's when she was little. She takes after Dad."

"Mm. Well, I'm glad you took after your mom that way. I love your shiny dark hair. Wouldn't trade it."

"So not all gentlemen prefer blondes?"

"I ain't no gentleman. I'm a galoot. And the only blondes I prefer are my daughters."

"I guess I'll share you with them. But not right now. Let's get some rest."

CHAPTER THIRTEEN

Y

" . . . AND SO MY NEEDS ARE GREAT"

It was Tuesday evening, and the bishop was in his office, as was his custom. He could have opted out this week, he admitted, with Trish's folks in town, but he told himself that this was a chance for them to visit as a family without the constraining presence of a son- and brother-in-law. They could talk freely about whatever they wanted. They could talk about— well, about him, if they chose. Trish would be loyal and take up for him if need be.

"So, are you self-centered enough to think you'd be their topic of choice, or just insecure?" he muttered to himself, reaching for the evening's schedule of appointments prepared by Brother McMillan. Lisa Lou Pope was first. "Bringing dinner" was printed neatly beside her name. Apparently it was Sister Pope's turn to furnish dinner for the bishopric, and she was sending it along with her daughter, whose follow-up appointment was at 5:30. At 6:15, Brother McMillan had listed Buddy Osborne, a fifteen-year-old who had spent his life bouncing back and forth between his divorced parents and their various relatives. And at 6:45, Rand Rivenbark was scheduled. He had never met Rand, a young man who was just home from his first year at the University of Alabama. At 7:30, Sister Reams had claim on fifteen minutes of his time, and after her, Sister Glenna Darke was listed for a temple recommend interview. There was a break from 8:00 to 8:30, and then he would meet with the Young Women presidency to discuss some concerns about Girls Camp. He sighed. Maybe dinner with the Langham in-laws would have been preferable after all.

Y

"Hello there, Sister Lisa Lou. How've you been?"

"Just fine, Bishop, and Mama says she hopes ya'll like chicken and rice bake. She fretted over whether to put pine-apple and bananas in her cabbage salad or to make it with horseradish and cream like slaw, but she figured that'd go better with fried fish and hushpuppies than chicken, so she did the pineapple."

"Um—I'm sure whatever your mother sent will be absolutely delicious. Please tell her we're very grateful. Don't know what we brethren would do without the Relief Society to take such good care of us."

Lisa Lou flounced a little in her chair, settling herself as if she wore a ruffled dress instead of the jeans and T-shirt that seemed to be regulation uniform for the girls these days as well as the boys. "Well, like Daddy says, reckon ya'll would just call out for pizza or send out for hamburgers, but Mama said you work hard and need a good home-cooked meal. 'Course, if it was me, I'd rather have the pizza than chicken-rice bake."

He chuckled. "I expect my kids would agree with you."

She nodded. "Your daughter Tiffani's getting real cute. All the guys are noticing her."

"They are?"

"When she gets her braces off, she'll be a hottie."

"Hmm—thanks." He wondered if the orthodontist could be bribed to leave the hardware on for a while—say ten years or so.

"So okay, Bishop, I tried to do what you said," Lisa Lou continued. "You know, like you told me to find out about Ricky Smedley and all? So I go up and ask him all about what he wants out of life, and he looks at me funny and he's all, 'How come you want to know?' and of course I can't say it's because I *like* him! I mean, I'd die—so I say it's for an assignment for church, which it is, right? So then I reckon he thinks we're going to spotlight him at some youth activity or something, 'cause he makes up some dumb answers, like his fondest dream is to catch the biggest catfish in the river and barbecue it over hot coals and eat it all himself. So then I try to get him to be serious, and I'm like, 'Where do you want to go on your mission?' and he goes, 'Disneyland.' And I go, 'Well, what do you want to do for your career?' and you know what he says? 'I want to be on the pit crew for a Nascar driver. Maybe Mark Martin.'"

The bishop nodded. That ambition had occasionally crossed his mind, too. "So you don't feel he took your questions very seriously?"

"Oh, please. As if! But you know what, Bishop? It really doesn't matter, because now I know I wasn't really in love with Ricky."

"Is that right?"

"He's just way too immature, and you know they say girls grow up a lot faster than guys, so I figure it'd like take him forever to catch up with me, you know what I mean? So I thought about it, and I decided I should look at guys who are older'n me, because then we'd be more—you know—matched?"

"Ahh. I see. And have you found an older man?"

"Well, for a while I had the biggest crush on Elder Kornegay—you know the missionary with the red hair? He's such a hottie—I mean, he would be, if missionaries *could* be—but you know how Sister Castleberry goes around whispering real loud, 'Arm's length, girls, arm's length' any time we try to talk to the missionaries. It's so embarrassing!"

Good for Sister Castleberry, he thought, smiling inwardly.

"So one day, she snuck up and whispered that at us, and he like backed off and cut off our talk we were having, and the next week I heard he'd been transferred. It about broke my heart. The elder who took his place is nowhere near as cute."

"It must be hard for you girls to have these fine young men come into the ward and not be able to socialize with them the way you'd like—and probably the way they'd like, too. But we've got to realize that this is a dedicated time in their lives—they're not their own—they belong to the Lord for these two years, and we all need to be supportive of that."

She sighed, ducking her head. "I know. That's why I'm not going to like any more missionaries. Besides, I've already started liking someone else."

His eyebrows raised. Dare he ask?

She looked up, and her expression grew beatific but solemn. For some reason, he thought of Joan of Arc.

"It's Rand Rivenbark," she said softly, as if she were uttering a prayer.

"I haven't met Rand yet," he commented. "But as a matter of fact, I'm seeing him later tonight."

"Are you? Wow. He's like totally cool. He's so . . . noble."

"Noble. Really."

She nodded. "He's way intelligent, and mature. And so cool-looking. He really is, in spite of . . . everything."

"Everything?"

"Well, you know. His handicap."

"Ah." He wanted to ask what kind of handicap, but somehow felt it unfair to the young man to be discussing his problems with Lisa Lou before even meeting him.

"Well, Lisa Lou—it—um—seems that you've been doing some growing toward maturity, all right. Now, let's talk for a minute about what you've discovered about yourself. What do you see yourself doing two years from now?"

She closed her eyes. "Getting ready to go to the temple with Rand. Picking out my wedding dress."

"And in five years?"

"Being Rand's wife. Devoting myself to his care."

"Hmm. And in twenty years?"

"The same. We'll get old together, reading and listening to music and all the stuff he likes."

"What about the things you like?"

"I'm willing to sacrifice them for him. He's worth it."

"Okay, just for a moment, let's leave Rand out of the picture, all right? Let's just say that for some reason you and he decide not to get married. Let's say it's five or six years from now and you're not married to anyone."

He almost laughed at the look of horror in her eyes, but controlled himself with an effort. "You'll be what—twenty-one, twenty-two? What do you see yourself doing then, if you're not married?"

She shook her head slowly. "I just . . . can't imagine it."

He clasped his hands on his desk. "Lisa Lou, I'm going to

tell you something straight. It's very important, and I want you to listen carefully, and remember it, all right?"

She nodded again, looking scared.

"It's true that marriage is a wonderful thing, and worth striving for. It's part of our eternal plan, and necessary for exaltation in the highest degree of the celestial kingdom. But . . . how can I put this? You're a daughter of God, a real person, all by yourself. You do not need a husband or a boyfriend to make you a real or valid or valuable and happy person. What you do need is to develop yourself into a young lady with her own interests and accomplishments, her own relationship with the Lord, and her own strong testimony of the gospel, so that when you do meet a fine, righteous young man who's right for you, you'll have something to bring to the marriage."

Warming to his topic, he leaned forward. "You know, in olden days, girls were expected to have a dowry to bring to a marriage—money or property or household goods to make them more attractive as marriage partners, sort of like a business partner. Today, a girl may have a hope chest, or a car, or a few belongings to bring to the marriage, but it's more important that she have some real preparation to be an interesting companion, a knowledgeable homemaker, a good mother, and a valuable servant in the Lord's kingdom. A woman needs these things in her own right—she can't just depend on her husband to know everything and be everything and do everything." He studied the girl's face. She looked confused and on the verge of tears. "Do you understand what I'm trying to say?" he asked gently.

"I reckon you're just saying I'm not fit to be a good wife."

He sighed. "I think one day you'll make somebody a fine wife. But certainly right now, I don't think you are ready to consider marriage—and not just you, but any other young lady your age who I know. I think you'll meet and be attracted to lots of different young men before you're ready to settle down—and if you're careful, you can have a lot of fun along the way and learn a lot about getting along with people. But all I'm saying, Lisa Lou, is don't try to skip the preparation stage. Be working on you—creating the best Lisa Lou there could possibly be! Learn skills, work hard in school, learn to love and understand the scriptures, be healthy and strong, give service to others whenever you have the chance. Then when the time comes, the guys'll be beating the door down, because you'll not only be pretty enough to stop 'em in their tracks, but you'll have a wonderful dowry to offer, as well."

It was her turn to sigh. "Okay. Reckon I'll try. What do I do first?"

"Why don't you look in your Personal Progress book and set some goals with your Young Women leaders? Next time we visit, bring that book with you, and we'll go over some things together. Okay?"

She looked dubious, but she agreed, leaving his office considerably more subdued than when she came in. He closed his eyes and rested his head on his hands, going over their conversation. Had she understood what he'd tried to convey? He prayed that she would be able to comprehend what was needed. She scared him.

The chicken and rice bake was excellent, its delicate flavor putting him in mind of a similar dish of his mother's that he had loved, growing up. She had always taken it to potluck suppers. He could even picture the blue pottery baking dish she used, and how she would tape waxed paper over it for a cover, because the lid had fallen in their driveway one day and broken. *Funny,* he thought, *how flavors and fragrances can trigger memories so suddenly and strongly. Must be why women like to wear perfume.* He set his plate aside, wiped his hands and mouth, took a long swig of ice water from the mug he always brought with him to the office, and went to open the door to Buddy Osborne.

Buddy, a small, slender boy with dark hair and prominent blue eyes, looked worried.

"Hi, Buddy. How're you doing?" he asked, shaking the slim, cold hand and motioning the boy to a chair. He seated himself casually nearby, rather than behind the desk.

"Fine," came the inevitable answer. The voice was low—had apparently already changed—and seemed bigger than its owner.

"What's been happening? I haven't seen you around much, since they put me in this position."

"Yeah, I been with my mom for the last nine months or so, and she don't come to church much. She's got a new, uh, boyfriend, and he likes to go and do other stuff on Sunday."

"I see. And they like you to go with them?"

"Well, no—but I don't have a ride when I'm over there, and it's fourteen miles. But now I'm back with my dad for the summer, so I'll prob'ly come more. He's okay with me coming, and I can ride my bike."

"Got any fun plans for summer?"

Buddy shrugged. "Deddy wants to go up in the mountains, camp, do some fishing. Stuff like that."

"You enjoy that kind of thing?" He tried to remember if Buddy had ever gone on any Scout camp-outs a few years earlier, when he had been assistant Scoutmaster. He didn't think so.

Buddy shrugged again. "Not 'specially. S'okay."

"What would you rather do?"

"What difference does it make?"

He looked at the boy closely. No, he wasn't being rude. He truly felt it made no difference what he wanted to do with his summer. Maybe it didn't.

"Well, if you had your druthers, what would you like to do?"

Buddy considered for a long time. "I'd like to see the Southwest, where the Indians lived—Mesa Verde, places like that. Find some petroglyphs. Maybe paint some pictures of places there. See the Painted Desert. Petrified Forest. Stuff like that. I like rocks, and I like to paint."

"*Do* you? That's really cool. I'd like to see your paintings sometime."

Buddy shrugged again. "I don't really paint much."

"What else do you do, in your spare time?"

"Watch TV. Do stuff on the computer, when I'm at my dad's. Mom don't have one."

"I see. Man, I've gotta tell you, I don't understand much about computers."

Buddy shrugged. "They're easy."

"Well, maybe you can show me how to use mine sometime."

"Guess I could."

"We'll plan on it. Let's see now—you're a deacon, aren't you, Buddy?"

"Yessir."

"Would you like to be ordained a teacher?"

"What would I have to do?"

The bishop leaned forward and outlined the requirements and duties of a teacher in the Aaronic Priesthood. Buddy considered for a moment.

"Be okay, I reckon. Long as I can get it done before I go back with my mom, in September."

"I believe we can do that, if you'll come to church and quorum meeting every Sunday you're in town this summer."

Buddy nodded. He didn't look overly enthusiastic, but his bishop had begun to wonder if anything at all could elicit enthusiasm from this boy. He seemed defeated, even when talking about his desires to paint and visit the Southwest. Perhaps he saw no hope in any avenue of his life. The indifferent shrug that preceded so many of his answers seemed a telltale sign.

"And I'll tell you what—my wife's family is visiting us right now, so I'm pretty tied up—but soon as they leave, I'll give you a call about our computer lesson, okay?"

A small nod.

The bishop rose and shook Buddy's hand, patting his shoulder as he saw him out. Buddy looked very alone as he got on his old bike and rode away.

"Depression," muttered the bishop. "Bet you anything that kid is seriously depressed—and probably with good reason." He made a mental note to learn more about Buddy Osborne and his family.

"I wouldn't be a teenager again for anything in the world," he told himself as he waited for Rand Rivenbark to arrive. Rand, he assumed, probably still fell into that category, too, having had just one year of college. Probably about nineteen. He checked the ward directory. He was wrong. Rand had turned twenty-one on the third of April. He had two younger sisters, and his parents, Collier and Pauline, lived in a very nice part of town, an area on the north side that had fallen into the former Second Ward. He had shaken their hands a couple of times at church—

a tall, dark-haired couple—but they were among those he had yet to get to know.

He opened the door to the clerk's office, where Dan McMillan, Sam Wright, and Joseph Perkins were chowing down on the chicken-rice bake and cabbage salad.

"What can ya'll tell me about this Rivenbark boy?" he asked, stealing another biscuit and spreading peach preserves on it. "I understand he has some kind of handicap?"

His ward clerk looked up and nodded. "Fine young man. Known the family since they came here from Georgia a couple of years ago. I believe the story goes that Rand was out for a drive with some older cousins while they were at a family reunion, and the kids hit a bridge abutment and flipped the car. It caught on fire. Couple of 'em died, and the others were pretty badly burned. Rand's legs got the worst of it—almost lost both of 'em, I'm told. Tell you the truth, it might've gone easier for him if they had amputated. Had a bunch of surgeries, but he still can't straighten his knees very well, and his feet are real bad. He gets around a little on crutches, but it's painful, so most of the time he uses a chair. Tough thing, for a young guy like that."

"Wow." The bishop wrapped the biscuit in a napkin and laid it on the counter. "I'll say it's tough. I'm meeting with him in just a few minutes."

"You'll like him, Bishop—he's a good kid. I don't think he spends much time feeling sorry for himself."

"Well, that's commendable. Remarkable, in fact. Thanks for the heads-up."

He went back into his office and opened the door to the hallway. He bowed his head for a quick prayer and then stepped outside to watch for Rand. It wasn't long before an SUV with a wheelchair mounted on the back turned into the parking lot and pulled into a handicap-designated spot. The driver put two metal crutches out first, then turned himself carefully and used them to lower himself to his feet. Ignoring the chair, he laboriously made his way up the ramp to the door, which the bishop held open for him.

"Come in, come in—you must be Rand."

"Hi, Bishop." Rand paused, balancing on one crutch, and held out his hand. "It's good to meet you."

The young man's hand was callused and his grip was firm. He preceded the bishop into the office and settled himself in a chair facing the desk.

"Good to meet you, too, brother," responded the bishop. "Just home from school, I understand?"

"Yessir. One year down, several more to go."

"So how was it—a successful year for you?"

"It was pretty good. Took some adjusting, getting to class on time and so forth, but I worked it out."

"I expect that would be a challenge. Decided on a major yet?"

Rand shrugged slightly and smiled. He had what the bishop imagined the girls would deem a cute smile—or was it a *killer* smile? He also had deep-set, hazel eyes with dark lashes to match his hair. Yes, he could see why Lisa Lou Pope thought him good-looking. He was. A puckered scar ran up the side of his neck to just under his right ear, and there was considerable scarring on the underside of his right arm, as well. It had been a blessing that the fire hadn't damaged his face, which the bishop liked for reasons other than the pleasing symmetry of its features. It was an open face, honest and guileless.

"Not entirely sure what I want to major in," the boy was saying. "I like math and physics and computers. I also like music, but I don't have any great talent there. I read a lot and kind of like English lit, but I don't really want to teach or write. Might enjoy editing. Maybe someday I could edit a scientific journal, something like that. What do you do, Bishop?"

"Me? Oh, I run a grocery store—a business that I inherited from my dad. It's been good, but I sort of fell into it by default. That's what happens when you only finish two years of college." He grinned. "It trims your options."

Rand grinned back. "I don't have a long list of options, any-way. I'd better stay in school. But that's what I wanted to talk to you about. I'm a couple of years behind, because of being in the hospital so much, but I want to start the process of applying to go on my mission."

"Really? That's great. You know what, I'm so new that I haven't gone through that procedure before—you'll be my first. Didn't serve a mission, myself, which I've always regretted. I wanted to, but it didn't work out for my family, at the time."

"I see. You're probably wondering how I'd get along as a mis-sionary—I mean physically. I wonder myself—but I've read of other guys with serious disabilities serving, and I figure if they can do it, so can I. I really don't require a lot of help. I'm pretty independent."

"That's good. I hear missions can be pretty rigorous, but I expect there are some places that are less so than others."

"I've heard that some guys are allowed to take their own cars along. I'd be real popular as a companion if I had my own car, don't you think?" He chuckled softly.

"Especially if you were in a walking or bike-riding area," the bishop agreed. "Guys would be finding all kinds of reasons to ask to be assigned as your companion." He didn't know exactly how to frame his next question. "Do you—are you expecting to need any surgical or other treatment in the next few years? Anything that would interrupt your missionary service?"

"Well, you know, my disabilities aren't permanent. They're just temporary."

The bishop felt a leap of hope. "Is that so?"

Rand grinned. "Sure—they're just for this life."

"Oh." He didn't know whether to laugh or cry. He did neither, just returned the boy's smile.

"Eternal perspective, Bishop. I had to learn about it early." He looked down. "Truth is, I am going to need several more surgeries. But I'm at a stage where I can decide when, on those— it's not like they're urgent. I'd like to get my mission behind me first of all. I know I have a mission to serve, Bishop Shepherd. My patriarchal blessing stresses that, and I've had other experiences that confirm it to me." He looked up, his expression serious. "I have a strong testimony of the Savior, Jesus Christ—and his gospel. I honestly believe I'll have something to offer in the mission field."

The bishop believed he would, too. The word that Lisa Lou had used to refer to Rand Rivenbark echoed in his mind. *Noble*, she had called him. He liked the word. Maybe Lisa Lou had more discernment than she sometimes demonstrated.

CHAPTER FOURTEEN

Y

"WITH HIM WE WALK IN WHITE . . ."

His last three appointments had been much less wearing than the first three. He administered his first temple recommend interview to Sister Glenna Darke, a faithful lady whom he had known since boyhood. She was confident in her responses to the list of questions, and it was both humbling and satisfying to sign his name to the slip of paper that would, with the stake presidency's approval, allow her entrance to the house of the Lord. His interview with Ida Lou Reams was short—she was reporting on a few sisters he had asked her to look out for, and the only troubling thing was that Lula Rexford seemed worn down with the care of her mother and the financial stresses of the family. Tom, her husband, didn't appear to be actively looking for work, according to Ida Lou. The Young Women leaders were making final preparations for Girls Camp and wanted his approval on them. They also extended an invitation to him and his counselors to come to camp for a special dinner and testimony meeting on the last evening.

"You know, when I was a boy, I always wanted an excuse to sneak off to Girls Camp," he told them, which elicited a laugh. "Now when I finally have the opportunity, here I am the bishop, and expected to set a good example! Can't even throw rubber snakes into cabins or stomp around pretending to be Bigfoot. No fair!"

"I don't know—the girls'd probably love it if you did," said Jenny Gurganus.

"Yeah, but Tiffani'd give me away. She knows my style."

"She's a nice girl, Bishop," commented Eliza Suggs, the Young Women president. "You and Trish can be proud of her. Well, not proud, I guess—we're not supposed to be prideful, are we? Let's say you can be grateful for her."

He nodded. "We are that," he agreed. "And probably proud, too."

It was full dark by the time he reached home, but the family was still out in the yard, relaxing in lawn chairs in the fragrant, warm evening air. Trish had lighted a couple of mosquito-repellent candles, and he caught a pungent whiff of citronella. Samantha the kitten romped happily about the lawn, apparently leaping into the air for moths, but he suspected her of performing for the entertainment of the human audience.

"Well, there's the working man," hailed Larry Langham. "How's it going, Bishop?"

"Going like gangbusters. I never totally appreciated bishops, until I became one."

Larry chuckled. "Sort of like the girl who said, 'I used to couldn't spell *secatary*, and now I are one'?"

His son-in-law smiled in return. "A whole lot like that, I'm afraid. I learn new things every day, but I don't know when I'll ever feel comfortable and competent in this calling." He sank into the vacant chair, depositing his briefcase in the grass beside him.

"You begin to feel comfortable about a year or so after you're released, wouldn't you say, Lar?" asked Ivy, Trish's mother.

"Sounds about right," her husband agreed.

"Did you get dinner, honey?" Trish asked. "There are left-overs, if you didn't."

"Chicken and rice bake, care of Sister Pope. It was fine. So what have I missed, besides dinner with you folks?"

"Just a lot of idle chat. Mom and Dad have been asking about some of the members they knew way back when. Do you know whatever happened to the Gilleys?"

"Wow. Marv and Mary Gilley—haven't thought about them for years. Didn't they move down to Pensacola?"

"I think they did, you're right. They were nice people."

"What about Terence Busbee?" asked Meredith from across the circle. Mallory, snuggled in her lap, appeared to be nearly asleep.

The bishop responded. "Terry went to BYU for a couple of years—maybe longer. After his mom died, he never came home, that I know of. At least, I never saw him again at church."

"I ran into him once at the Y," Trish said. "Seems like he was engaged at the time, to a girl from California. Let's see— you had something of a crush on him at one time, didn't you, Merrie?"

"Oh, not really—he was several years older than I was."

"Well," said her mother brightly, "so is Dirk, isn't he? Of

course, once you get into your twenties, a few years difference doesn't matter as much as it did when you were younger."

"I guess that's true," Meredith agreed. "In most cases anyway."

"Oh, by the way, Jim—we were trying to decide on a temple day," Trish said. "When can you go?"

"I'll try to get away whenever it's convenient for all of you."

"You're the only one with commitments," she reminded him, smiling.

"Yeah, the rest of us are lazy, vacationing bums," her father added.

"How about Thursday or Friday, then? Saturday's always pretty crowded."

"Friday's good," Trish agreed. "I can let Mal play with little Marina Hawks. We tended her when her folks went last month, so Mal has a standing invitation. I'll check with Sarah Hawks, and then call the temple for an appointment."

"I'd be glad to stay with the kids while you all go," suggested Meredith.

"Yes! Yay!" approved Mallory, but her grandmother had other ideas.

"I'd really like us all to be together in the temple," Ivy said. "We have so few chances to do that. Plus, Meredith, it's a good chance to experience one of the new smaller temples. You did bring your own temple clothes, didn't you? Remember, I told you that they don't rent clothing at the Birmingham Temple."

Meredith nodded. "I remembered."

"I reckon I could tend," Tiffani offered halfheartedly.

"You could," her mother agreed, "but we'll be gone most of the day, and I think it will be better if you all split up and spend the day with friends."

"All right!" said Jamie. "I'll go over to Randy and Billy's."

"We'll see about that," his mother responded. "I'll have to talk to Sandra first." She turned to her husband. "Anything new in the ward that I should know about?"

"Mmm—I don't think so. Tiff, it looks like Girls Camp is shaping up to be fun."

"I hope we get cabins this year and not tents," Tiffani said. "I hate putting up tents, and they get so hot during the day that your lipstick and candy and stuff all melt."

"Why would you need lipstick at Girls Camp?" asked her brother derisively. "Ooh, we've got to look good for the skunks and raccoons!" She didn't favor him with an answer.

"When we used to go to camp, I preferred the tents," Ivy Langham said. "The cabins we had were already inhabited with mice and chipmunks and spiders, and I got the feeling they didn't appreciate our presence."

Mallory piped up sleepily. "How come you gave 'em presents, Nana?"

Ivy snapped her fingers. "That was our problem! We forgot to bring hostess gifts."

Amid the laughter, Trish went to gather Mallory from Meredith's lap. "Time for sleep, little one."

"No, I want to sleep with Aunt Merrie!"

"That wouldn't be very comfy for Aunt Merrie, love—your bed's too small for two people. But Tiff's bed is big enough for you."

"But Aunt Merrie's got my bed—and it is, too, big enough for me and her! I'm just little."

Meredith hugged her niece. "We could snuggle up tight for just one night, couldn't we, Mommy?" she asked, smiling up at her sister.

"She kicks and flops around, Aunt Merrie," warned Tiffani.

"I can take it," Meredith insisted. "And then Tiff can get a good night's sleep, too."

"Are you sure?" Trish asked. "Don't feel obligated—"

"I don't. I'd really like to have a sleep-over with my little niece."

"Okay—but if things get too wild, feel free to sneak in and bunk with Tiffani."

"No problem. Shall we go up now, chickadee?"

The bishop smiled to himself. *Chickadee* was a nickname Trish herself often used for the children. He now suspected it was one Ivy had used with her girls. Funny, the little things that got carried over in a family through generations. He hadn't thought of it for years, but his father's nickname for him as a child had been *little buddy*. The memory caused an unexpected tightness at the back of his throat. He wished his dad could have lived to see and enjoy his grandchildren. Did he know them? He wondered. What kind of "visitation rights" did heaven allow? Were there interactions between those spirits who were yet to be embodied and those who had finished their mortal lives? He had heard stories of children who claimed to have known deceased grandparents before they were born and to have been prepared by them for their experience in mortality. But what if the grandparent hadn't accepted the gospel on earth? He and his mother had seen to it that his dad's temple work had been taken care of a year after his passing—but had his father accepted it? There were things he wished he knew.

Meredith made the rounds, holding Mallory like a little airplane in her arms and zooming her in, giggling, to parents and grandparents for her goodnight kisses. He watched as Meredith bore the child off to the house, wondering again that she and Dirk had no children.

The conversation continued for a while, until they all began to yawn and long for their beds. They finally agreed that the next day was bound to come and they needed to be ready for it. After he saw that the house was locked and the lights out, the bishop was the last one up the stairs to bed. Samantha sat in the hallway beside the door to Mallory's room.

Now? she asked, brushing significantly against the closed door.

"No, not now," he replied softly. "Sorry, but they don't need another warm little body on that bed tonight." Encouraged by his voice, she wound around his ankle and followed him to his and Trish's room.

"I think not, my friend," he told her, holding her off with his toe as he closed the door. "Go chase yourself."

"Meow," she said sadly.

Y

The temple excursion to Birmingham worked out well. The day was warm and breezy with a few puffy clouds to set off the blue of the June sky. It was still a particularly poignant thrill for him and for Trish to be able to travel only a little over an hour to a temple—to see that spire rising against an Alabama sky—a phenomenon that only a few years earlier had seemed an impossible dream. The white marble structure was actually located in the northern Birmingham suburb of Gardendale, for which he was especially grateful, since it meant he could avoid downtown traffic and congestion. As a small-town boy, he had no particular love for the rigors of city driving.

It was good, as his mother-in-law had anticipated, to be together as a family in the temple. He felt strength from Larry, seated next to him, and it was good to look across the small endowment room and see Trish seated between her mother and her sister. The three Langham women were an attractive group, all dressed in white. He wished his own mother had been able to join them. She had looked forward to this temple, but her stroke had occurred just prior to its dedication, so she hadn't yet been able to attend. He bowed his head, silently praying that she would recover sufficiently to be able to come with them one day. It wasn't a prayer that he had a great deal of confidence would be answered affirmatively, but he had placed his mother's name on the temple prayer roll, and he believed in miracles. At least his mother had been able to make a few earlier excursions to the Atlanta Temple, where she had been sealed to his father, and he, the son, sealed to them. For that he was profoundly grateful.

After the endowment session, they were invited to participate with another couple from their stake in some family sealings. That was another special privilege, to kneel at the altar again with Trish and look into her eyes as the vows and promises were repeated for deceased couples—the same vows and promises he and Trish had participated in nearly seventeen years earlier. He gave her hand a little squeeze and smiled at her, hoping she would get the message that he would do it all again—and that he wanted their marriage, their family, to be truly eternal. She smiled back—a small, serene smile that reassured him.

As they stood to allow the other couple to take their places at the altar, his glance happened to fall on Meredith, seated against the mirrored wall waiting her turn to act as a proxy daughter or wife. She ducked her head quickly, but not before he noticed that her cheeks were wet with tears. Her mother, sitting beside her, had noticed, too—and silently pulled a tissue from her dress pocket and put it in her hand. She slipped an arm around her younger daughter's shoulders for a brief hug and a pat. He wondered what had occasioned those tears.

Was Meredith missing Dirk, remembering their own vows, or was she just touched, as often happened in these circumstances, by the Spirit bearing witness of the validity of these ordinances? Trish often shed tears in the temple, and he had been known to choke up a bit himself. It was not unusual—it was just unusual for him to witness such feeling in Merrie. He chided himself for having kept her, in his opinion, relegated to the past, still the teenaged Meredith, who had looked upon him as less-than-worthy to marry her big sister. For that matter, he conceded, she had probably been right. He fully realized that he was lucky—no, blessed—that Trish had agreed to take him on. In this sacred setting, seeing her in her white temple clothing, even a glimpse of the magnitude of that blessing was almost overwhelming.

Y

Of late he had developed the habit of keeping a couple of appointment times open on Sunday, either during the auxiliary meeting times or after the block. He had found that as he sat on the stand during sacrament meeting and prayerfully glanced around the congregation, the Spirit would often prompt him to call in certain people for a visit. Sometimes he knew why—often he did not. Frequently the reason would become obvious during the course of the visit. When he received no prompting, sometimes he would simply leave the door to his office open as an invitation for anyone who wanted a word with him. On this particular Sunday, with Trish's family present, greeting people they remembered from twenty or so years ago, he wondered if he ought to schedule anything more than absolutely necessary after meetings. He knew Trish had a pot roast simmering at home and fully expected him not to be late for this last family dinner before her parents and sister left to meet their flights for home the next morning. Also, later that afternoon, Larry and Ivy wanted to go with him and Trish to visit his mother, while Meredith held down the fort with the children at home.

He allowed his gaze to move from one person to another, trying to be open to the Spirit as he looked on each face. It startled him how beloved they were becoming, how much he cared about their individual circumstances and needs. He saw Hilda Bainbridge, stalwart as always, sitting beside Ida Lou Reams. He knew Hilda couldn't see him looking at her and saw her gently wave away the hymnbook Ida Lou offered to share with her. She couldn't see to use that, either. *I hope we're taking good enough care of her, Roscoe,* he thought. He saw Rand Rivenbark come in with his family—this time, in his chair—and noticed the greetings he received from his peers—lifted hands from the boys and little waves and smiles from the girls. Rand, he realized, had the power to influence a lot of the kids for good—and probably many adults, too—just by being himself and doing what he could to progress and live as normal a life as possible, despite his painful affliction.

His gaze fell upon Thomas Rexford, who was sitting in one of the folding chairs in the overflow at the back of the chapel, even though the pews were nowhere near full. T-Rex leaned forward, his elbows resting on his knees, as he rocked slightly back and forth, his eyes searching the air above the congregation for . . . what? Inspiration? Escape?

How would you react, T-Rex, if what happened to Rand happened to you? the bishop's internal dialogue continued. *What would you do if you suddenly found yourself—the admired, sought-after athlete—barely able to get out of a wheelchair because of painful limitations? And would the girls still be attracted to you, as they seem to be to Rand?*

That likely was not a fair question, the bishop conceded. Rand's test was probably tailor-made for him, and not more than he could bear, with the Lord's help—while T-Rex's test might be in the form of popularity and temptation, suited to his own spiritual growth-needs. He hoped it wouldn't be a harder test than he could handle, especially since he doubted that T-Rex had so far felt all that much need for the Lord's help. He glanced around. The Rexford parents had not yet made their appearance. He hoped that didn't indicate any new problems for the family.

He noted that the former First and Second Ward members still sat in pretty much segregated groups. Maybe that was normal—just human nature to migrate to those they knew best. The mixer social had been hailed as a great success by all, and still they sat in clumps. Probably it would just take time. The teenagers had fewer problems mixing than anyone else—they had already been together in school and in early-morning seminary and were just delighted to be together on Sundays as well, though in sacrament meeting they usually sat with their families, as the Church had requested. They were few enough in number in their high school that they were, by and large, fairly close and supportive of each other.

Ralph and Linda Jernigan sat on the last pew, by the door. Ralph sat turned sideways, his back against the wall, his eyes, like the bishop's, scanning the congregation, though for different reasons. Ralph, he knew, was looking for signs of danger. Linda, beside him, also glanced around nervously from time to time.

The Ernie and Nettie Birdwhistle family—all fourteen of them—filed into and filled up an entire pew. He was glad they were all here. With so many children, it was seldom that everybody was well enough to come together from their home thirty or so miles away, up in the hills.

Nettie was a large woman with a cheerful, florid face and an affectionate but no-nonsense approach to parenting. The children were remarkably well-behaved, with the exception of occasional squabbles between Limhi and Lehi, the nine-year-old twins. They usually ended up sitting on either side of their father, a short, rounded fellow who had little to say, but whose occasional word was law. The twins would lean forward when they were feuding, sending each other malevolent glances around their father's bulk, but remaining silent. When the twins weren't squabbling, they often went everywhere together, with their arms companionably over each other's shoulders. The bishop, who had never had a brother, wondered what it might be like, not only to have six brothers, but to have one who was exactly like oneself.

In their remote log home, the Birdwhistle children relied primarily on each other for company. Their mother home-schooled them because of the distance to school—and, he suspected, because of the expenses involved in dressing and providing school fees and transportation for all twelve. He wondered how difficult it might be, one day, for Limhi and Lehi to establish separate lives. He smiled to himself, envisioning them at age sixty, still alternately arguing or going around arm-in-arm.

His gaze fell upon Jack and Melody Padgett, and a small, nagging worry began to nudge him. It was familiar, that worry— it had been edging around the corners of his consciousness for several weeks, like heat-lightning on the horizon with far-off grumbles of thunder that never really materialized into a storm, but always threatened. *What should I do, Lord?* he prayed silently, and the answer came, unmistakably: *Talk to her.*

He took a deep breath. *All right,* he agreed, and he realized that the perfect—probably indeed, the only possible—time to talk to Melody alone was during Primary, when Jack would presumably be in priesthood meeting.

Accordingly, he acted on the prompting, asking the Primary president if one of the counselors could sit with Melody's class for a few minutes while they visited. She agreed, and he beckoned, smiling, to Melody as the counselor went to take her place. Melody smiled, too, but her expression was quizzical as he asked if he might have a few words with her in his office. They moved silently through the building, cutting through the empty chapel to avoid going by the room where the elders quorum met.

Melody sat in one of the chairs across the desk from him and folded her hands in her lap.

"What can I do for you, Bishop?" she asked.

He drew a deep breath. "Melody, I'll be honest with you. Something keeps troubling me, and I feel prompted to ask you about it. Please be honest with me, all right?"

"Of course."

"Is Jack abusive to you—or to your daughter—in any way?"

Melody's eyebrows rose slightly, and there was the slightest hesitation before she said, "Of course not, Bishop. He isn't. He's crazy about Andi. He wouldn't hurt her. And I'm fine."

"Then why do I keep getting this prompting?"

Her gaze fell to her hands. "I sure don't know. I mean, it's true that Jack has a temper, but no worse than most other guys I know."

"How does he express his temper?"

"Well, he raises his voice sometimes."

"Does he hit you, or abuse you physically in any way?"

She hesitated, then said, "Um—well, he's grabbed my arm a time or two. It's not like he beats me up, or anything. He was a Marine, you know—and they're taught to be pretty tough."

"Not with their wives, I'll bet."

"Of course not, but—you know—the training kind of comes back to them when they're under stress, and they just sort of react."

"Is Jack under a lot of stress?"

"He is, what with trying to establish his business, and all. It's growing really fast, which is good, but it means he has a lot of people to keep an eye on, to keep things running the way they should. Then we're just finishing up our house. We've been building a new one, you know, and that can be really stressful, especially if you're your own contractor, which Jack was. People just don't always show up and get things done when they say they will, and that drives Jack nuts."

"They're not as disciplined as the Marines."

"Well—no. They're not, that's for sure."

"So Jack brings home a lot of his stress, does he?"

"I try to help him relax when he gets home. I figure that's part of my job. I try my best to keep a clean house, and have dinner ready just when he wants it, and Andi on her best behavior. It seems to help if everything's in order at home, even if it isn't in the rest of his world. Don't you think a man likes to come home to a clean, orderly house and a good meal?"

The bishop smiled. "I sure do. But sometimes that just isn't possible. How does Jack react if you've had a bad day, and dinner isn't on time, and Andi's on a tear?"

"Well, I don't have to work outside the home, and Andi goes to a nice day-care every afternoon so she can get all her playing and wiggles out. So I have plenty of time to make sure things are nice and dinner is ready."

The bishop persisted. "But if it weren't ready—say the washing machine leaked all over the floor, and you had the flu, and the steak got overdone because you were chasing the neighbor's dog out of the petunias he was digging up that you and Jack had just planted—what would Jack do?"

She shrugged, and smiled weakly. "I guess the Marine might come out and start yelling. But I would deserve it, wouldn't I, if I didn't have more control over things than that?"

"Would you deserve it, really?"

"Now, Bishop, don't you ever yell at your wife when she doesn't do things right?"

"Heaven help me, Melody, I have sometimes raised my voice and criticized the way things were going—but not often. And I've never hurt Trish physically. The very thought of it makes me sick. I try hard, but I'm not a perfect man, a perfect husband, or a perfect bishop. But this isn't about me. I'm concerned for you. I keep feeling that Jack is very controlling of you and Andi, and that he is either harming you in some way, or coming close to it. And that feeling comes from the Holy Ghost, Melody. He knows all things. He knows exactly what goes on in your home."

Melody's face paled slightly. "I'm not complaining about

anything Jack has done," she said staunchly. "He's a good dad and a good provider, and I'm lucky to be married to him."

"I saw bruises on your face, when you and Jack were in my office a few weeks ago."

"There are lots of ways people get bruises."

"And one of them is getting hit by an angry spouse, who lost control long enough to do damage where it showed."

"I never said so. I told you, Bishop, I have no complaints."

"That's your story and you're sticking to it, is that it, Melody?"

"That's about it."

"Well, I admire your love and loyalty for Jack—if that's what it is. But if it's fear of retaliation, my dear sister—that's a different story. You know, there are anger-management classes, therapists who can help people overcome the tendency to abuse others. Maybe Jack would benefit by something like that. Maybe he wants to do better but doesn't know how."

Melody's laugh was brief and humorless. "He'd never— ever—go to anything like that."

"Well, then other measures may need to be taken."

Her eyes widened. "Bishop, you wouldn't—you're not going to call the police, are you?"

"I don't know. You see, the thing is, I have to do what the Spirit directs and what the law requires."

"Have you spoken to Jack about this?"

"Not yet."

"Please don't. Please, please don't. Let me deal with it, Bishop, all right? I promise I'll come to you if anything really bad happens. But I really don't think it will. He just has a little temper, is all. He's not a bad person."

The bishop looked searchingly at Melody. Her smile, for

once, was gone, replaced by pleading and stark panic. Her hands were visibly trembling.

"You know, Melody," he said gently, "just looking at you convinces me that my fears are based on fact. You're always smiling and appearing calm and confident, but I see through that facade. I see a lady who is scared to death, the way you look right now. Whatever's going on, please realize that you don't deserve any kind of abuse—not physical, verbal, emotional, or sexual. And neither does Andi. Jack obviously has trouble managing his temper and his need to control you. As your bishop and friend, I can't just stand by and ignore the symptoms I see. Tell me this much—are things getting worse? Is the problem escalating?"

"I—I don't think so. As long as I do my part, everything's okay. Most days are just fine."

"But you never know when the volcano's going to erupt, do you? Or what's going to set it off."

She shook her head slowly, her eyes on the floor. "If I could just learn to anticipate everything that might go wrong, and head it off, then—"

"But how could you do that? How could anyone? This is not your fault, Melody. I can't say that often enough, or strongly enough. You do not deserve any of these eruptions. Jack just plain needs help."

She looked up, her eyes pleading. "But he won't—he doesn't—please don't say anything yet, Bishop, I'm begging you. Please let me handle it."

He sighed. "I don't know how long I can. I'll try to be sensitive. But I'm really worried for you, and I'd be criminally liable if I knew something was going on and didn't report it. Not to mention feeling that I had totally let you and Andi down, as your bishop."

"But we're okay. If you did report it, I'd just deny it. But then he'd think I'd complained to somebody—and I haven't. Please give us a while? I'll do better. I can improve things, I know I can."

He sighed deeply. "I'll try, but I can't make any promises, Melody. I'm afraid in cases like Jack's, better is never going to be good enough."

CHAPTER FIFTEEN

" . . . WITH A LOAD OF CARE"

hen Melody had composed herself and fled back to
the sanctuary of Primary, the bishop left the door to
his office open while he reviewed a pamphlet on
spousal abuse passed on to him by one of the former bishops.
The statistics and outlook for men who committed such offenses
were not comforting. He knew he would have to confront Jack
Padgett. That knowledge was of no great comfort, either.

"Hey, Bish!" Thomas Rexford put his head in at the door
and grinned. "How ya hangin'?"

Hanging. A good term, the bishop reflected, for how he felt
just now. "I'm okay, Thomas, how are you? Come in and visit
for a minute."

"Aw, I cain't stay. Gotta go spell Mom off, watchin' Grandma.
She was up with her all night, but she wanted me to come to
church at least for part of the time, so she's still over there.
Figgered I'd better go take over for a while."

"Your grandma's worse, is she?"

"Yessir, she is. I used to like bein' with Grandma, but man, it's kinda spooky, now. I mean, I used to could kid with her and tease her, but now she just stares at me without blinkin', and her head kinda wobbles, and she—you know—drools, and all."

The bishop nodded. He knew. "It's tough, watching loved ones get old and sick."

"It's the pits, man! She puts me in mind of one of them little bobble-head dolls. Tell you the truth, I don't think she's real sure who I am. It plumb creeps me out."

"And yet you're willing to go help. That says a whole lot for your character, Thomas."

"Nah-h. I just worry about Mom."

"How about your dad? Does he help out, too?"

"He does, but he's worse'n I am. He can't only take but about an hour at a time, and we get there, we find him sweatin' and pacin' the floor."

"Now, I told your folks, and I'm telling you the same—our Relief Society sisters could help out, when your mom needs a break. It's too much for just one person, especially with her working part time, as well."

"Aw, you know how it goes—we take care of our own. Besides, I reckon you know Grandma's not a member of the Church."

"That doesn't matter. It's your mom who would benefit the most, and she's a good member."

"I'll remind her," T-Rex said, nodding. "Better run now."

"Sure—and just keep in mind, Thomas, that once your grandma's gone, you'll never be sorry for any kindness you show her now."

"Reckon that's so. See ya, Bish!"

The boy was gone. The bishop had wanted to ask if his dad had any leads on a job, but he hadn't wanted to embarrass

T-Rex. At least the young man was showing some responsibility and concern for his mother, who, by anybody's standards, was presently hoeing a pretty tough row.

He sat for a few minutes, gazing at a wall calendar from Busbee's Mortuary, pondering how to help the Rexfords and the Padgetts. He heard the cheerful swell of voices as the women moved out of Relief Society, the men out of their priesthood quorums, and the children out of Primary, gathering toward the doors and the trip home.

"Hi, Jim—you're looking mighty official and serious," his sister-in-law Meredith said brightly. "Are you really busy right now?"

"Never too busy for you, Merrie, come on in." He tried to keep the surprise from his voice and let it be just cordial and casual, like her own, but he stood and gestured Meredith toward one of the more comfortable chairs. "Have you seen very many people you remember from way back when?"

"Not so many. Brother and Sister Mobley, and Sister Bainbridge, of course—and Terri Ann Compton, now Strickland, all grown up and married."

"Like yourself."

"Right. Um—Jim—do you mind if I close the door for a few minutes? And are you sure you don't have an appointment right away?"

"I'll get the door—and no, I don't, honestly. What's on your mind?"

She crossed her legs and rested her head on one hand, allowing her blonde hair to swing forward and partially hide her face. It was a defensive gesture he had seen her use before—and somehow it reminded him of Lisa Lou.

"Well, the thing is," she said, "I really didn't especially want to go to the temple with you guys the other day. In fact, I had mixed feelings about coming on this trip at all."

"Is that right? I'm sorry if you got talked into doing something you'd rather not have done."

"It isn't that I didn't want to see everybody. That's why I did end up coming."

"Uh-huh. But . . . ?"

She sighed. "But it's hard. It's just really, really hard."

He waited, casting about in his mind to see if he could discover where she was going. He couldn't. "What is it that's hard, Meredith?"

"I haven't said anything to Mom and Dad or Trish. Or anyone else, for that matter. But you being a bishop, and being who you are—I thought maybe I could talk to you, see what you think I should do."

He was surprised, and he thought he had just been complimented, but he wasn't sure.

"Well, sure, you can talk to me. I'm not only a bishop, but I'm your brother-in-law. Of course, as brothers-in-law go, I know I probably don't rank up there with Jerry and Wendyl, but hey—I'm available."

"Oh, Jim . . ." She pushed her hair aside for a moment and gave him a glance of mixed reproach and amusement. "Don't you know you're my favorite brother-in-law? Jerry and Wendyl are both great guys, but they're so much older than I am that they seem almost like uncles, or something. And I know I gave you and Trish a hard time, when I was a bratty little know-it-all, but believe me, I have done some growing up since then. I see you very clearly now—have for years—and I like what I see. You're perfect for Trish. She could always see it, of course, but I was just too dumb, for a while, to open my eyes to the truth. But anyway, the thing is—what you and Trish have . . . it's really special. And Dirk and I—well, we don't have it."

Ahh—there was the problem. She was comparing her marriage to his and Trish's, and it came out unfavorably. How unfavorably, and in what way—that would be the question.

"Just what is it," he prodded gently, "that you see in us that you and Dirk don't have?"

She glanced toward the window, and her eyes were bleak—possibly beginning to fill.

"You name it," she said. "Oh, we have a nice, new home—four bedrooms plus a den and office and family room and laundry and sewing room and formal living and dining areas and a sun room next to the patio, ya-da, ya-da, and a gorgeous yard, if I do say so—and so what? That's the house. Who lives in it? Who enjoys it? I bounce around it for a while in the morning, doing whatever little cleaning and dusting it may need—which isn't much, because it basically hasn't been touched since the last time I cleaned—and then I go out and jog or play golf or tennis at the country club, or shop for things I don't need, and then I go back and maybe work in the yard, and plan dinner, which I'll probably end up eating by myself, because Dirk is usually late, and will have had a sandwich or whatever, that they ordered in for their meeting. So I read, and I take care of my Mia Maid calling—in fact, that's a high spot in my week, being with the girls—but the rest of the time, Jim, I'm just so lonely I could die."

"Mmm. Are weekends any better?"

"Some. At least, Dirk's usually home on Sundays. We go to church and go home and have dinner, and then he's so worn out he just sleeps the afternoon away—and sometimes through the night, for that matter. I don't blame him. I know he's exhausted, with the pace he keeps—but sometimes I'm just as lonesome when he's home as when he's gone. I can see why women have affairs, I honestly can! Not that I'm contemplating that. But I need something to change, or I don't know what I'll do." The tears did fall, then, and he handed her a tissue, then waited awkwardly for her to compose herself.

"Does Dirk want children?" he asked after a while, when she seemed to be regaining control.

She shrugged. "He always said so, but it sure doesn't seem to be a very high priority with him, now. I mean, it's pretty hard to have a baby when you never—at least rarely—you know what I mean. There's just never time, or energy—to try."

"He's totally involved with his work."

"He loves it. Eats and breathes his job."

"Does his job—his career—demand these hours of him? Are they necessary?"

"He seems to think so, but I suspect they're voluntary. At least most of the extra ones."

"I reckon you've mentioned these things to him."

"Many times. He just looks kind of hurt and bewildered, and gestures around at our nice place, like what else could I possibly want, and he's providing it all for me." She cleared her throat and tried to smile. "I keep going back over when we were dating and engaged, trying to figure out if I gave him the idea that I was totally materialistic and didn't care about anything else. I don't think I did—I didn't mean to. I remember thinking it was a good sign that he was ambitious and hard-working, because he'd be a good, responsible provider for our family. But—what family? When does the family come? It's been six years, Jim! I've tried to be patient. I knew at first that he wanted to build up his business, and be secure as possible in it—but how secure do you have to be, to have a child or two?"

"Do you feel like he loves you?"

She shrugged again. "He says he does. I always get flowers and gifts on special occasions—though I suspect his secretary takes care of that for him. But he isn't very demonstrative. He hardly ever just hugs me, for no reason. Well, never, okay? And he acts really surprised if I hug him, though he responds. He keeps saying we'll take a vacation soon—to Hawaii or the Bahamas—but I'll bet he'd be bored silly after the first day. Or I can picture his whole office going, together, so there won't be a moment wasted while they lie in the sun! He doesn't know how to relax and have fun anymore. If he ever did."

He pondered a moment. "I'd imagine his work is probably so absorbing to him that it fills any need for recreation that he has. I know a couple of guys like that."

"I think you're right. He does exercise, but only because they have a gym in his building, and all the guys are expected to use it three or four times a week. Otherwise, I don't think he'd bother. And it's not like he's ever mean to me, Jim, so I feel disloyal even telling you these things! But—do you see what I mean? The other day I came in your house from outside, and Trish was sitting on your lap, and you guys were smooching, and I just started to bawl. You're so lucky—and so is she!"

He nodded. "We are lucky, I know that. Blessed." He tried to think how to counsel her. He sent up a silent prayer for guidance. The phrase benign neglect came to mind. There were more forms of spousal abuse than physical or verbal, and he could picture Dirk Hammond's astonishment if he became aware that anyone was even connecting him with the idea of abusing his sleek, well-kept wife. He had met Dirk only once, on the day of his and Meredith's wedding, and he had seemed a pleasant enough fellow, if quiet. He tried to remember Dirk's family, but he couldn't even picture them.

"What kind of relationship do Dirk's parents seem to have?" he asked.

Meredith frowned. "Well, they're nice. They're very low-key, fairly well-to-do, retired, involved in several charities in Minneapolis, where they live. Actually, we don't hear from them very often, but when we do, they're always—um—friendly. It's not like with Mom and Dad. I hear from them at least once a week—oftener if there's news to share, and they like to get together with all of us girls whenever they can, even though they stay busy with their own lives. I know Mom and Dad are always wondering why we don't have kids yet—but Dirk's folks, far as I know, have never brought it up."

"Does he have brothers or sisters?"

"One sister, Katrina. She has two little girls, but they live in Florida. We only hear from her at Christmas, and Dirk gets a birthday card."

"Uh-huh. So not a very close, demonstrative family all around?"

"Right. I don't feel like I really know them very well."

"Exactly. People like that are hard to know. But I'll betcha Dirk's probably just behaving like the people he grew up with. He likely has no clue that anything more is expected of him. I suspect you're going to have to teach him, Merrie."

"How? I'm all wailing and raging inside, but there's something about Dirk's assumption that all is well that just puts me off trying to explain it to him."

"Boy, oh boy." He rubbed his forehead with one hand, concentrating, trying to listen to the Spirit. "I think the man needs a wake-up call. You're going to have to make an appointment with him, if need be, to get his full attention, and lay it on the line. He's a businessman, he understands bargaining and ultimatums and deadlines, and I suspect you might need to use them all. I'm not normally real big on ultimatums in relationships, though, so start out kindly and patiently, okay? Realize that he's going to be bowled over by the depth of your feelings."

"But what should I say? Jim, I'm so scared I'll just let it all come blasting out and destroy any affection he has for me. I do still love the guy, you know? I just need him to be there. I don't want to be the widow of a living man!"

"You may have to tell him just that. Let him know you appreciate everything he's done for you materially, but tell him it's time to have kids, and spell out what needs to change to make that happen. Tell him what you need and what you expect, both before and after children arrive. Explain how lonely you are—and that you're lonely for him, not for women friends or business associates or even family or ward members. And realize, Merrie, that all the stuff he provides is probably how he expresses his love for you—by giving you anything you could ever need. He probably doesn't know how to begin to do anything else. You'll have to teach him—coax him—bargain with him, whatever it takes. And be patient. He won't change all at once. He may not change much at all—but any little improvement will be worth it, won't it? And most of all, pray about it, and listen to the Spirit."

She was sniffling. She nodded. "I will try. I've got to, or this marriage will just die of its own weight in boredom and gloom. And I know that isn't how he sees it—he probably thinks we're perfectly happy, and that's my fault. I just expected . . .

something different. Something more like what you and Trish enjoy. I see you with your kids—I know you're crazy about them, and you and Trish are so spontaneous with each other. I've got to do something, or I'll go crazy."

"You guys probably need a good marriage counselor, too. If it costs Dirk a little time and money, he might pay more attention. Try, if possible, to find one who's LDS, or at least, a person of faith."

She nodded. "Thank you, Jim." She leaned back and drew a deep, shaky breath. "I feel so much better, just telling you. Like maybe I'm not totally crazy and unappreciative."

"Nope—I don't think you're either." He grinned. "And thanks to you, Merrie, for trusting me with this."

The next morning, as he stood out front with Trish and Tiffani seeing the family off, he found himself regretful to see them go. He returned their hugs enthusiastically, feeling— perhaps for the first time—a real part of the family. Or that they were a real part of his; it didn't matter which. There were a few tears amid the smiles. He sought his sister-in-law's eyes and gave her a thumbs-up sign of encouragement, and she nodded, trying to look hopeful.

As the rented car disappeared down the shady street, and Tiffani, still in her nightgown, padded sleepily back toward the house, he pulled Trish to him and let her cry for a moment against his chest.

"Why was I scared to have them come?" she asked shakily. "I love them all so much."

"I don't know. Maybe that's why. You wanted everything to be perfect—and far as I can tell, it was."

"It was a nice visit, wasn't it?"

"M-hmm."

"Merrie sure seems to have grown up, or changed, don't you think? She didn't once make me feel fat or unsophisticated or anything, like she used to."

"Reckon it's called maturity. Plus, I think sometimes we don't let people change. In our minds, I mean. We keep them the way we remember them, even though in reality, they've grown way past that stage."

"D'you think that's what I've done with Merrie?"

He grinned. "I know for sure it's what I've done, but she taught me better. She's turned into a very nice woman. Almost as nice as her sister."

He looked around him. Steam was rising from the sidewalk, where the early sun was making quick work of the heavy dew. Everything was still, the trees and grass of a green so intense it was almost unnatural. Trish's formal English garden in the front yard was a riot of color, from roses to daisies to numberless other blossoms that he couldn't begin to name, but which he was sure she knew off the top of her head. He leaned over and kissed the shiny dark hair on that head, which felt hot to his lips from the sun.

"Thank you," he whispered, knowing that he thanked both his wife and his Father in Heaven for the glories of life.

$$\Upsilon$$

Partway through the afternoon he recalled his promise to Buddy Osborne. Things were relatively slow at the store, so he hunted up the copy of the ward list he kept in the office and called the number listed for Gerald Osborne, Buddy's father, who, as far as the bishop knew, hadn't darkened the church doors since his baptism at age eight. Buddy answered, his voice low and guarded.

"Buddy? This is Bishop Shepherd. How're you doing?"

"Um—okay."

"I just wondered if you might have an hour this afternoon to show me around your computer. I've got a little time around three or four."

"Uh—well—okay, I reckon."

"What time is good?"

"I don't care. I'll be here."

"Say three-fifteen, then?" he asked.

"Reckon."

"Great! Thanks—I'll see you then."

He replaced the receiver, wishing he really wanted to learn about the computer, wishing he really wanted to spend time with Buddy instead of just going on home and spending the time with his own children. *Help me, Father, remember that Buddy is thy son, too,* he prayed silently, gazing past Mary Lynn's bent head. Mary Lynn could teach him all he needed to know about computers. So could Trish, Tiffani, or Jamie, for that matter. But he knew Buddy needed him—and had that need confirmed to him by the Spirit even as he sat there, half-dreading the visit.

CHAPTER SIXTEEN

"... BLESS OUR
EFFORTS DAY BY DAY"

The Osborne home was a narrow frame house of what was known as "shotgun" construction, supposedly from the notion that a person could open the front and back doors and shoot a shotgun clear through from front to back without hitting any walls. The siding was green—a faded shade that managed to clash with the riotous greenery of the surrounding trees. There was no lawn to speak of—just patches of weeds of varying heights. A truck with no rear tires sat on concrete blocks toward the small, detached garage at the back of the lot. Buddy's bike was tethered to a two-by-four that served as a support for the small overhang—too small to be called a porch—that covered the front steps.

The bishop grabbed the sack of goodies he had brought from the store, hoping that Buddy liked corn chips and salsa and chocolate and vanilla sandwich cookies and root beer. He knocked on the frame of the tattered screened door. A couple of holes in the screen were filled with cotton balls. He smiled, remembering the old belief that cotton would deter flies. At least they wouldn't find entry in those two spots.

Buddy came to the door and pushed it open.

"Hey there, Buddy, how you doing?" the bishop asked.

"All right."

"I brought us some stuff to snack on. Don't know about you, but I get kinda hungry about this time of day."

"Okay. You want it now?"

"Up to you, my friend. Whenever. Here you go." He handed the sack over to the boy, who took it without any apparent curiosity.

"Computer's in here," he said, making a sort of gesture with his free hand that the bishop interpreted to mean "follow me." He stepped across the miniature living room with its much-used looking sofa that faced a television on a metal stand. Another chair slouched in a corner. There was little of cheer or color in the room—no pillows, books, plants, or pictures—not even curtains or drapes at the windows—just bent, aluminum-slatted blinds that were closed to keep out the light but raised at the bottom to let in some air. The next room was a dining room, with an enameled metal table to the right that served as the dining table, or so he deduced from the salt and pepper shakers, the jar of hot peppers in vinegar, the box of saltines, and squeeze bottle of ketchup that stood against the wall. Across the room a card table sagged under the computer components. One chair was pulled up to the monitor and keyboard, and the bishop appropriated another from the dining table.

"Why don't you open up that root beer, Buddy? I hope it's still cold—it's been chilling in the cooler, but it was pretty hot in my car. You like root beer?"

"Reckon. Be right back."

He returned shortly with two open cans and set them on the card table, then tore open the bag of chips and twisted the lid off the salsa. "You want cookies now, too?"

"Hey, friend—it's all for you as much as for me. Just dig in to whatever you like."

"I'll go get some money then."

"Buddy! No way—just call it payment for the lesson you're about to give me."

"Deddy don't like us to be beholden . . ."

"Don't worry, you're not. We're just bartering here. Stuff from my store for stuff from your brain. Deal?"

"Reckon. So—what do you wanna know?"

"Son, I don't even know enough to ask questions. Start with turning it on."

"Booting it up? Right here—this green button."

"Just lead me through it."

For the next hour, the bishop concentrated on the unfamiliar terms and procedures, and found Buddy to be knowledgeable, if less than forthcoming as a teacher. He learned to find his way around the desktop and how to use the basics of a word-processing program. "It's for, like, if you have to write an important letter or something for school," Buddy explained. The bishop also learned to play a couple of games, which he enjoyed so much it surprised him.

"Man, it's a good thing we didn't have computers and games like this when I was in school," he said at last, leaning back and finishing the last of his tepid root beer. "I'm afraid I'd never have got around to graduating."

Buddy grinned slightly. "I'm only allowed an hour a day during the school year," he said.

"'Course, Monday to Friday, I'm with my mama, and like I

said, she don't have a computer. So they ain't much problem there."

"But then you don't have it available to help with home-work, either, do you?"

Buddy shrugged. "I use one at school, when I can. We didn't get into the Internet. Did you want to see about that now, or another time?"

"My old brain couldn't handle one more thing today. How about next week—same time?"

"I reckon, if you want to."

"I do, and I'm surprised to say that, because I've kept myself computer-free all this time. I figured it'd be just one more thing to take my time and complicate my life, but I can see the appeal now. I had fun, Buddy! Thank you. You're a great teacher."

Buddy shrugged again, but there was a touch of color in his cheeks. "Ain't nothin' to it."

"Now, don't tell me that, 'cause I feel like I made great strides today. You taught me a lot."

"You done fine."

"Thanks. You just keep the rest of the goodies for today's pay—you and your dad enjoy them. What's your favorite snack? I'll bring that next time."

Buddy considered the question seriously. "You wouldn't want to eat my favorite thing."

"Try me."

Shyly, the boy named a fruit-flavored dry cereal that was a favorite with Jamie as well.

"Heck, yeah, I eat that," the bishop assured him. "I'll bring a big bag of it and a gallon of milk to wash it down. How's that?"

"That's cool. Deddy, he don't like to buy it—says it's junk, and too expensive. He makes hot oatmeal most ever' morning, even in the summer." Buddy's expression showed what he thought of that.

The bishop laughed. "Oatmeal's good for you, sure enough," he said. "But we'll have a junk cereal feast next week, okay?"

"Sounds okay to me."

Y

A few evenings later, he and Trish lounged lazily in their chairs after the children had left the dinner table to enjoy the last of the evening light.

"So," Trish said, as she collected the empty plates he handed her, "I went visiting teaching today—my first visit to Melody Padgett."

"How was she?"

"She seemed okay. Maybe a little nervous. Her house is gorgeous. All brand new and beautifully decorated. She showed us through. I think she's really proud of it."

"I don't reckon there would've been any whips or instruments of torture in evidence."

"Jim!" Trish stopped wiping the plates with napkins to frown at him.

"Well, I wouldn't be surprised," he said darkly. "I just can't bring myself to trust that fellow."

"You're probably right."

"Did you see little Andi?"

"No, we didn't. She was playing at a friend's house."

"Um."

"I invited Andi to Mallory's birthday party. I figured they're close enough in age to get along, and Mal knows her a little bit from Primary."

"That's cool. Did Melody agree?"

"She said Andi could probably come. Then I asked her if she could possibly stay and help me with games for the kids, thinking that it'd give me a chance to get to know her better, but she said she'd be busy that day. I suppose I was asking a bit much, since I don't know her all that well. She did sound really sorry to say no, though."

"She seems good with kids—I expect she'd be a big help. Too bad."

"Well, I can get Muzzie to help—her girls are invited, too."

"When's the party?"

"Two-thirty next Wednesday. Can you make it?"

"Should be able to. Remind me, though, okay? You know how I am these days."

"The absent-minded bishop? Not surprising, given everything on your plate."

"What're we giving Mal?"

"I've got that Barbie house she's been yearning for, and some summer play clothes and cute hair things and a couple of new books. And I thought she could join a little dance class that Sister Strickland is starting. She's always twirling around and trying to be a ballerina. Jamie's building her a version of those little Philippine stick houses she saw at the ward social, and I don't know what Tiffani has in mind. Oh, and Merrie left a wrapped present for her—it's in the top of our closet. I suspect it's a new Sunday outfit."

"What a lucky little girl."

"I just want her to know she's cherished. All our kids, for that matter."

"I'll bet they know."

"Do you think? Or do they just take it all for granted, as

their due? I've always thought that there's so much meanness and violence in the world that if I could do anything as a mom, it would be to make sure that my kids know there's also love and kindness and decency. But I don't know if they're getting the message. Maybe I'm just making them materialistic."

"Well, it's not as though you give them material gifts instead of love and discipline and good teachings," he comforted. "That's how they learn that there's goodness and love in the world. They see and feel it from you."

"I hope so. And from you, Daddy dear. But sometimes I think Tiff's getting pretty high-maintenance in her wants and wishes. She can think of more videos and CDs and shoes and clothes that she just has to have than you can imagine."

"Yeah, she's getting to that age—when her wants are becoming adult-sized and adult-priced. I remember my sisters constantly wanting new clothes and new record albums and makeup and so forth. I thought I was pretty low-maintenance. All I wanted was a basketball, and later an old truck to work on. And I earned the parts for that."

His wife nodded. "I remember that old truck," she said with a smile. "And so far, Jamie's pretty reasonable, too. He loves his electronic games, but he doesn't seem to want new ones all the time. He's such a good kid. I hope he stays reasonable!"

"Oh boy, so do I. And I hope he doesn't discover girls till he's through college."

Trish chuckled. "'Fraid that's not likely. And Tiff's already well aware that boys exist and are interesting. In fact, I think Mallory knows that, too. She's always saying she's going to marry somebody named Nickleby, who's really cute."

"Oh, yeah? Well, Nickleby'd better be a darn fine fellow!"

"I'm sure he is. I suspect he lives in her own sweet little mind, so he must be nice."

"Trish—d'you ever wish you could just . . . infuse the kids with testimony of the truth and love for the Lord? I know it isn't right, but sometimes I wish we could sort of bypass all this free agency business and guarantee that they'll be good and happy."

"Now, now, Bishop—whose plan was that?"

"I know, I know. But sometimes it seems to have a little merit."

"I'll betcha we've only begun to deal with the free agency issues."

That wasn't a bet he cared to take up.

Y

"Brethren," he told his counselors and clerks at their Tuesday evening meeting, "we've got the ward pretty well organized for the moment, and I've been feeling lately that we need to make more of an effort to get out of the office and into people's homes. There are still lots of folks I don't know as well as I'd like, and there's that whole list of less-active people that none of us seems to know much at all. I think we need to reach out and be a little more proactive."

"Would you like me to make a list and set up appointments?" asked Dan McMillan, readying a sheet of paper on his clipboard.

The bishop smiled. "You bet, Dan, thanks. Now, we don't want to neglect the active folks, and assume all's well just because they show up every Sunday, so I've been thinking and praying about the matter, and what I'd like to have happen is for us to kind of rotate as to who visits who—or is it whom? What I mean is, sometimes I'll take Brother Bob with me to see a couple of families, and another evening, I'll take Sam. I'd like us to visit the members who are less active, or experiencing some obvious difficulties. Then, on other occasions, I might want Bob and Sam each to pair off with our clerk and executive secretary, if you brethren don't mind being pressed into service in this way, to visit our more active families and be my eyes and ears there. We can be flexible, according to your schedules and the members'—but eventually I'd like for all the ward families, active and less-active, to have received a visit. Then, on a need basis, we'll start over and rotate who goes to the same homes. Some, I expect, I'll need to see by myself, though I'd prefer to have one of you along." He passed a list across to his executive secretary. "Dan, this is a list of the folks I want to see—and this first time, I believe I'd prefer to drop in unannounced on those with asterisks. I'm afraid if we call for an appointment, they'll turn us down flat. But the others, I'd appreciate if you'd set up appointments for us—two per evening, and on Wednesday or Thursday if possible, according to everybody's schedules. If necessary, I could go on a Sunday evening."

"Yessir. I'll get right to work on it."

"Thanks, Dan. When you call, don't make it sound too formal or intimidating. Just tell folks we're trying to get around to visit everyone in the ward and that we'd sure appreciate the chance to see them when it's convenient. Okay?"

"Yessir, understood."

"Sam and Bob, is this going to be too great a burden on your time?"

"No indeedy, Bishop, there's nothin' I love better than a good visit with the Saints," Sam agreed.

Bob Patrenko nodded. "Count me in, Bishop. My time is yours."

"Well, I'll try not to presume too much on that. Gotta be careful myself, or Trish and the kids'll feel abandoned, too, and we don't want that in any of our families. But I do feel strongly that we can't serve people we don't know, and who don't know and trust us. So, thank you, Brethren, for your support. This Church couldn't operate without all of us doing our parts, and I sure do appreciate and love you men for your willingness to do yours."

He stood on the patio in the shade of the house and watched eleven small girls being shepherded through lawn games of various kinds, squabbling over whose turn it was and whether it was fair that someone won a prize. Mallory was beside herself with excitement, spinning from friend to friend and activity to activity, being silly and loud and thrilled to be five. Her father watched her fondly, enjoying the gleam of sun on her platinum hair, hoping Trish had remembered to slather sunblock on her fair skin. Muzzie and her two daughters, Chloe and Marie, helped Trish and Tiff with crowd control. His job was to monitor the ice cream machine, which was making the groaning noises that indicated the process was coming to its conclusion. Trish had made peach, and he could hardly wait for the first creamy, fruity taste of it. She had also borrowed Muzzie's machine, which had already produced a container of chocolate, now waiting in the freezer. Mallory's cake, an elaborate concoction that acted as the skirt for a new Barbie doll, held the place of pride on a paper-covered picnic table. He had also been instructed to guard it from little fingers or curious kittens. Samantha, in her usual sociable way, was springing and bounding among the little girls, absolutely certain of her invitation to this party—and probably, he thought, assuming it was being given for her pleasure.

He looked over the company—there were eight girls from Primary, and the rest were neighborhood playmates. Little Andi Padgett squealed and dived for an oversized beach ball that they were supposed to keep from touching the ground. She seemed happy and not at all shy around the other children, which was encouraging. He had greeted her when Trish showed her into the backyard and had said, "Hi, Andi! Welcome to Mallory's party. Too bad your Mommy couldn't come, too."

"Yeah," she had responded, matter of factly. "She couldn't come, 'cause Daddy had to go back to work."

"I see," he had said. But he hadn't seen at all. He was still working on what she had meant when he reached over to flip the switch on the ice cream maker and put it out of its misery. He knew Melody Padgett drove, and he knew the family had two cars. Why would Melody need to stay home from the party, just because Jack had to go back to work? Was there, perhaps, some appointment—someone coming to the house? A repairman, maybe, that someone needed to be there for? It was the only thing that made sense to him. Whatever, he decided, he wouldn't ask little Andi about it. She was their invited guest and not here to be pumped for information—no matter how tempting it might be to get a child's-eye view of the Padgett family life.

He signaled to Trish that the ice cream was done, and she passed the word to her helpers that after the current game was finished, it would be time for refreshments. Things were a little hectic for a while after that, and he was kept busy pouring lemonade, wiping up spilled ice cream from the flagstones (with the help of Samantha's eager pink tongue), and manning the video camera to record this event for posterity. But nothing kept him from reveling in his first taste of Trish's fresh peach ice cream.

That evening, with the festivities over, he wouldn't allow Trish to prepare supper. The children each had their choice of a place to go out to eat on their birthdays, or a special food to request at home, and on this occasion, Mallory declared that she was much more interested in staying home and playing with her new presents than going to a silly old restaurant. In the end, he took Trish out for a hamburger, and they ordered three more sandwiches to take home when they were done. They ate at the Dairy Kreme, and, it being Wednesday, Lisa Lou Pope was on duty, looking flushed and harried, but cheerful.

"Hey, there, Bishop! Hey, Sister Shepherd. What can I do for y'all this evening?" she asked.

"Hey, Lisa Lou," he greeted, grinning at her. "You look mighty busy and official."

"She's just faking," put in a teenage boy behind the counter, nudging Lisa Lou as he passed behind her. Lisa Lou blushed even more as she turned to swat at him.

"You hush, Tommy G.," she told him. "This here's my bishop."

"What's a bishop?" he asked.

"Like a preacher, only better," she told him.

"That right?" The boy flashed a grin at the customers. "Looks to me like Mr. Shepherd, that runs Shepherd's Food Mart."

"Yep, he does that, too. Now, make him one of your real good strawberry-banana malts, Tommy."

"No, no," protested the bishop and grocer. "I'm full-up on ice cream, from our little girl's birthday party. I'll have a large fresh lime and a double bacon cheeseburger. How about you, hon?"

"You're living dangerously," Trish told him, snuggling against his arm. "Lisa Lou, I'd like a grilled chicken sandwich with all the trimmings, and just a little mayo. And a small fresh lime."

"How about some fries or onion rings with that?"

"No," said Trish.

"Both," said her husband.

Trish overruled. "He's got enough fat and cholesterol in that burger, thank you anyway. I have to keep an eye on him, you know. We all need him."

"Well, we sure do. Sorry, Bishop. Maybe another time." Lisa Lou grinned at him.

"But, hey—I love fried food! I can't help it; I'm a true son of the South," the bishop protested.

"Too many sons of the South die early from heart attacks," Trish told him. "You're not allowed to do that."

"I'll be back," he promised Lisa Lou, as his pretty wife steered him away from the counter. "You're bossy, sometimes," he groused with a fake frown.

"I know," she agreed, "but you love it."

He regarded her. She was right; he did love it when she took care of him—even when it meant he was deprived of favorite foods.

"I'm a conquered man," he told her, and kissed the tip of her nose.

CHAPTER SEVENTEEN

" . . . BE WITH US IN OUR HOMES, WE PRAY"

Riding in Bob's Honda, Bishop Shepherd and his coun-selor Bob Patrenko bumped along the dirt lane that led to the Ralph and Linda Jernigan home, ignoring the "Posted—Keep Out" and "Private Property—No Trespassing" signs that adorned practically every fence post they passed.

"It isn't that Ralph and Linda mind having visitors from the Church," Bob explained. "You just kind of have to go about it their way. Call ahead of time, let them know exactly when to expect you, and whatever you do, be prompt."

"What's made these people so paranoid, Bob?"

Bob shook his head. "Darned if I know. They don't talk much about themselves—not so you could really get to know them. They'll talk about their garden, and their food storage, and his guns, and the threats to the government, and perceived threats to the Church, even—but hardly a word about where they came from or why they feel the way they do. Very close-mouthed folks, and yet—I dunno, Bishop—I do feel they're goodhearted, if a bit wacky. They give generously to the Scouts and to other good causes. They're even helping to support Donnie Smedley on his mission, though that's privileged info. They don't want it known."

"I didn't even know that. Brother Smedley never mentioned it."

"No—that's just their way. He's been their home teacher ever since they moved here about eight years ago, and they think a lot of him, but even he can't get real close. Poor folks— it's kind of sad the way they isolate themselves."

The house, a small frame rambler, sat in the middle of a fenced area, with no trees or shrubs to give it shade from the sun. All the windows looked dark, as if they were hung with black drapes. Linda had planted a few zinnias around the porch, and the grass, though spotty, was green and trimmed. The fence was chain-link, topped with three rows of barbed wire.

Bob pulled his truck up to the driveway gate, which rolled smoothly back on it wheels to allow them entrance, then closed behind them with a clang. The bishop shivered. The word *compound* came to mind.

"Now we wait," Bob instructed. "Watch for the dogs."

"Dogs?"

"You'd better believe, dogs. Here they come."

In silence, three large animals rounded the corner of the house in tandem and swarmed around Bob's car, sniffing at the tires and undercarriage, the hood and trunk. One, with a wolfish look about it, raised slightly on its hind legs and gazed briefly into the bishop's eyes, its nostrils working overtime. The bishop was startled by the intelligence that met his own in the encounter.

"What are they doing, checking our blood types?" he asked, only half-kidding.

"I think they're trained to sniff out explosives."

"Sure glad I didn't bring any firecrackers. Why don't they bark?"

"I s'pose that'd mean they'd found something suspicious."

Finally satisfied, the dogs went to sit by the porch steps. Ralph Jernigan came out the front door and tossed some kind of tidbit to each of them, after which, the bishop thought, they finally began to act like real dogs, vying for Ralph's attention, whining and wagging their tails and thrusting their heads against his hands for a caress as he came down the steps. He beckoned his visitors forward. Cautiously the two men climbed out of the car.

"How do you like my troops?" Ralph asked, fondling each animal's head in turn.

"They're not going to have us for dinner, are they?" the bishop called.

"No, sir, they're good soldiers."

The dog who had examined the bishop through the car window now wagged its way toward him, a silly doggy grin on its face instead of the feral but savvy expression it had exhibited before.

"At ease, Corporal," Ralph said, and the dog turned aside to flop in a patch of shade by the steps. "He tends to fraternize a little too much," Ralph explained. "You brethren come on in. I figure the wife's got something cold to drink for you."

"Thanks for letting us come see you folks, Ralph," the bishop said, extending his hand. "Sorry it's taken me so long to get out here. I'm trying to repent and get around to see all the members, now that things are a little more organized."

"Good to have you, Bishop. Brother Patrenko."

"How's it going, Ralph?" Bob asked.

"Things're stable on our four acres. Garden's growing. Not much enemy activity of late—at least that I've been aware of. Middle East's a mess, of course."

"Isn't it always," the bishop murmured, wondering if the man referred to enemy activity on a national, international, or local level—or if he differentiated.

Ralph showed them into a small living room with a picture window that gave a slightly grayed view of the front yard. The bishop realized the glass was covered with a film that allowed them to see out but prevented anyone outside from seeing in— hence the black drape effect. An oscillating floor fan stirred the air, which otherwise seemed close and warm. The walls were lined with stacks of boxes and large food-storage cans. Linda had made an effort to soften the effect with tablecloths and houseplants. A photograph of a small blonde girl stood beside a lamp on a makeshift table that was actually four cases of powdered milk covered with a crocheted doily.

Linda served them tall glasses of limeade and passed around a plate of sugar cookies, then perched on the edge of a chair, her lips pursed, her eyes large and watchful, as if it were a matter of national security to be sure their glasses were refilled and the cookies handed around again. Except for her initial greeting, she didn't say a word.

Ralph did the talking. As the bishop had been warned, he steered the conversational ship, speaking of things he had read or heard pertaining to arms shipments to Cuba or Central America or Afghanistan, and a new and desolating strain of virus that he feared the Iraqis were about to unleash upon the world. He voiced his opinions that the international banking community exercised far too much power in world affairs, and he didn't like the cutbacks to the military that had taken place during the last administration. Finally he stood, obviously showing his visitors to the door, and spoke in a lower tone to the bishop.

"Concerning what we talked about in your office, Bishop—things are fairly quiet right now, but I expect they'll heat up a little later in the summer. I'll keep you posted."

"Um—thanks, Ralph. Appreciate your concern. Say—who's the cute little girl in that picture?"

"Relative. Thank you, Brethren, for coming to see us. Let us know if we can be of any help to you. Don't worry about the dogs, and I'll open the gate for you. Good day, now."

The bishop didn't say a word all the way back down the bumpy drive to the farm road. Finally, when they were on state pavement again, he looked at his counselor.

"I'm speechless."

Bob Patrenko nodded. "Has that effect, doesn't it?"

Y

Mrs. Martha Ruckman's neat white bungalow with dark green shutters was apparently an inspiration to her neighbors, Bishop Shepherd observed as Bob Patrenko eased to a stop at the edge of the road. Those houses closest to hers were neat, with cared-for yards and gardens. The farther afield he looked, the untidier the places became. Mrs. Ruckman's front yard reminded him of his own, except that he could see that the flowers were mixed with vegetables. Pole beans on a trellis formed a backdrop for rose bushes, and collard greens nestled among orange nasturtiums. Lush tomato plants, heavy with red and green fruit, shared space with what appeared to be pumpkin or melon vines.

"Think the car's okay out here?" Bob asked uneasily, looking around the neighborhood.

"Trust me, nobody's going to bother any car parked at Miz Ruckman's house," the bishop assured him. "She's a force to be reckoned with. Got your storm gear on?"

Bob chuckled. "That's right—she was your teacher, wasn't she? What grade?"

"Fifth. She was a great teacher—she took no nonsense whatever, from black kids or white. We were all scared silly of her. I still am," he admitted with a laugh. "But I respect her now even more than I did then."

"She seems to be doing a great job, raising Tashia."

"Well, she's a lady who takes her responsibilities very seriously."

They knocked at the green-painted screened door. A delicious aroma of frying onions and peppers emanated from the back of the house, just tickling their nostrils and reminding them of their own suppers waiting at home. Mrs. Ruckman appeared, wiping her hands on a kitchen towel.

"Welcome, gentlemen, to my home, and Tashia's," she said warmly, unlatching the screen to admit them. "Come on in and be comfortable, and I'll get her for you."

The bishop smiled. "Thank you, Miz Ruckman. We'd be delighted if you'd sit in on the visit, too, if you have time."

"I'm preparing dinner, but I'll join you if I have a chance. And I'll listen in from the kitchen, in any case."

"Um—of course, certainly. And this is my counselor, Brother Robert Patrenko. Miz Martha Ruckman, Tashia's grandmother."

Mrs. Ruckman shook Bob's hand politely. "Counselor? You brought your attorney? My, my, James—you don't expect that much trouble from me, do you?" Her smile was serene, but he detected a bit of a challenge in it.

"My counselor in the bishopric," he explained. "My assistant. My right-hand man."

"I see." She went to the kitchen doorway. "Tashia! Your guests are here."

"Your yard is wonderful, Mrs. Ruckman," Bob ventured. "I like the way you've mixed vegetables and flowers."

"I thank you. They seem to enjoy it that way, too. I like to combine beauty and utility in my surroundings. Sit down, if you will. Tashia will be right in."

They sat, the bishop swallowing an impulse to say, "Yes, ma'am," as he'd been required to do at age ten. Mrs. Ruckman had combined beauty and utility in her home as well as her yard, he noted, looking around at the decorative plants, the crocheted afghans and hooked rugs that gave color to the small living room with its white walls and gleaming hardwood floor. One wall was covered with well-stocked bookcases, except for two long windows, draped with sheer white curtains. He saw two sets of encyclopedias, a large dictionary, a set of children's classics and numerous other interesting-looking volumes. It was a room that invited serenity and study. He stood, moving to examine an intriguing watercolor print above the white leather sofa, turning when Tashia came into the room, her dazzling smile in place, her head bent slightly as both hands busily finished braiding a pigtail and tying it off with an elastic.

"Hey there, Tashia," he said, going forward to shake her hand. "How are you this evening? You know Brother Patrenko?"

"I'm fine, thank you, Mr.—um, Bishop—Shepherd. Hey, Brother Patrenko. Ya'll sit down."

They sank back onto the sofa, and Tashia curled her feet

under her in a rocking chair by a window. She made a picture that the bishop wished he could somehow capture and take home to Trish.

"So, how's your summer going, so far?" he asked.

"It's good," she said shyly. "Grandma keeps me busy."

"That right? What's she got you busy doing?"

"Well—I'm learning how to crochet, and how to put up fruit and veg'ables—and I help out in the yard, and I read a lot. And she's teaching me Bible stories." She indicated a large white family Bible on a side table.

"Now, that's great, isn't it, Bob?"

Bob nodded. "Wish I knew that my kids were having that productive a summer. I'm afraid they're swimming and watching TV and playing with the neighbor kids."

"Oh, I watch some TV, too, and Grandma and I play on the Internet some, and look up fun stuff. And we play games. She's so good at chess and checkers I don't know if I'll ever get to win. And I've been over to the Arnauds's a couple of times, to play with Angeline and Tamika."

"I saw you sitting with them at church," the bishop remarked.

"Yessir. They're real nice. And I have a couple of other friends that I get to play with, once in a while. I just wish't they lived closer."

"Nobody right around here, to play with?" Bob asked.

Tashia shook her head. "Well—there's lots of kids, but Grandma won't allow me to play with them, much."

"I expect your Grandma knows best," the bishop assured her. "Did you know she was my fifth-grade teacher?"

He enjoyed her wide-eyed, surprised grin. "No! Grandma, you didn't tell me that!"

Mrs. Ruckman put her head around the door. "I taught hundreds of students over the years," she commented, smiling. "But, yes, I remember James Shepherd well enough. You liked history, as I recall."

"Yes, ma'am, that's true. I'm amazed you remember that."

"I remember a great many things."

"Uh-oh," he said, winking at Tashia, who laughed in delight.

"Mrs. Ruckman," Bob called, "how many years did you teach?"

She came a few steps into the room. "Thirty-two," she replied. "I started in a little country school out by Boaz. One room—all black children then, of course. Segregation ended after my twenty-first year, so for the last eleven years of my career I had more-or-less mixed groups."

"It must have been a challenge, making that adjustment," the bishop suggested.

She smiled serenely. "I believe it was as much an adjustment for my colleagues and the administrators as it was in the actual classroom. Most of the children took it in stride. For me, it was a pleasure to have access to newer and better materials to work with. I don't care how much they said about 'separate but equal,' there was a whole lot more separate than equal going on in the school system in those days."

"I'm not surprised," the bishop said. "But I know one thing—and that is that we were mighty fortunate to have you come and teach in our school." He smiled at her. "In fact, I wish my children could each spend a year in your classroom."

"Now, James, you're flattering an old lady, and that's not fair. Tell me about your children. You have three, I believe?"

"I do indeed. Tiffani is fifteen, Jamie's nine, and Mallory just turned five. They're good kids, Miz Ruckman, but I believe they'd benefit by your no-nonsense, no-excuses approach to schoolwork."

Mrs. Ruckman gazed out into the still-bright evening. "Was I too strict, James? From your grown-up point of view?"

"No, ma'am! You were fair, and we always knew exactly where we stood. Well, to tell you the truth, we were all shaking in our shoes when we found out we were going to be in your class, but before long, we were proud to be there. You gave us something—I don't know—a sense of honor, maybe. We all felt like it mattered to you, personally, whether we mastered fractions or diagramming sentences or whatever." He looked at his hands. "I'm not saying this very well, but you were a great teacher."

"M-mm, you're kind. But I've always wondered—did the children know, did they ever suspect—how much I loved them?"

"Um—well, I reckon we'd have been a little surprised at the time to think of it that way—but we knew you cared about our progress."

"And isn't that love, James? Isn't that how you feel about your children? Don't you care about their progress, how they grow, how and what they learn, what kind of character they develop along the way?"

He nodded. "That's exactly how I feel." He looked up and smiled. "And you know what? I believe that's exactly how our Father in Heaven feels about all of us, as his children."

"So do I, James. So do I."

He looked at her granddaughter. "And how about you, Tashia? Do you feel Heavenly Father's love for you?"

The young girl beamed shyly. "Yessir. And if he loves me as much as my grandma does, that's good enough for me."

"Oh, child, he loves you so much more than I can, because he's God, and he's love itself. He loved us all enough to suffer and die for us. Your church teaches that, doesn't it, James?"

"Yes, ma'am. It certainly does."

"Tell me how you see it."

He swallowed. "Well, we believe in the great atoning sacrifice of the Lord Jesus Christ—that he took upon himself our sins and transgressions, and also our sorrows and pains—and that's why he can succor us in times of need. We teach that he provided immortality and a literal resurrection for all of us, and the opportunity to gain eternal life with our Father in Heaven."

"By grace or works?" she asked sharply, frowning at him.

"Both, actually," he replied. "We believe that the Lord expects us to do certain things in the way of ordinances, such as baptism, as well as good works, such as kindness to our fellow man—but we also believe that it is by grace that we are saved, after all we can do."

She nodded. "Second Nephi." She pronounced it "Neffy," and the bishop didn't dare smile. He was astounded that she knew the reference, but with his next thought he wondered why he should be. Of course she would read anything her beloved granddaughter brought home.

"Grandma, that's Nee-fie," Tashia stage-whispered.

"Thank you, Miss Lady. In any case, I believe that's what the Bible teaches, if you take it all together, and don't try to pull it apart like some folks. Now, James, would you give us a prayer, before you go?"

Obviously, the meeting was being adjourned. He wasn't certain whether to stand, kneel, or sit forward, but Tashia and her grandmother answered his dilemma by getting to their knees on the braided carpet. He and Bob Patrenko did the same. He prayed sincerely, asking the Lord's blessings of protection and wisdom and bounty on this good home and its inhabitants. Grandmother and granddaughter echoed the amen, so he hoped the prayer was acceptable, both to the Lord and to them.

"Tashia, run around back and fetch both these gentlemen one of our good muskmelons," Mrs. Ruckman directed. While the girl was gone, Mrs. Ruckman looked searchingly up at her former student. "Well, James, you don't do too badly for a lay minister. In my mind, the jury's still out on your beliefs, but I feel your heart's in the right place. Tashia seems happy worshipping with you, and so far, I'm still all right with her doing so." She smiled and reached out to tap his arm. "But you can rest assured I'll continue to monitor the situation."

He nodded. He was certain she would.

Y

He was starving by the time Bob dropped him off at home, and he bounded into the house like a teenager, sniffing the air eagerly to see what Trish had prepared for dinner. He hoped it was something with onions and peppers. He was in luck—she had made steak kabobs, with chunks of not only onions and peppers, but zucchini and yellow squash on the skewers. She served them on a bed of rice pilaf, with a salad of spinach, fresh mushrooms, and some kind of sweet dressing. It wasn't a meal his mother would ever have prepared, but he had to admit that Trish's innovations were mighty tasty. The children had already eaten, but Trish had waited for him, and they ate on the patio, watching Jamie and Mallory play with a lightweight plastic ball and bat.

"Mallory said something kind of disturbing today," Trish remarked, refilling his glass of ice water.

"What was that?"

"She asked me if I'm ever naughty, and if you give me spankings."

"Oh? Where'd she get such an idea? I don't even give her spankings."

"I tried to inquire, tactfully, and I guess it was from something little Andi Padgett said when she was here for Mal's party."

"Uh-oh."

"Right. Andi reportedly said that sometimes her mommy was so naughty that her daddy had to spank her all over."

He put down a kabob, suddenly less hungry than he had been. "I'm going to have to do something, aren't I?" he said. "I just don't know what's best. I spoke with President Walker about it, and he said to let the Spirit guide me, and to be mindful of the state laws on family violence."

"Then just keep praying, sweetheart. I'm sure it'll come to you."

"I think I'll fast about it tomorrow. That's all I know to do at this point."

Trish smiled at him, her eyes warm and sympathetic. "I can't think of anything better."

CHAPTER EIGHTEEN

" . . . FOR THE INJURED INTERCEDING"

The owner of Shepherd's Quality Food Mart arrived at work early and went into his office. Mary Lynn wasn't due in for another hour and a half, and he locked the door, leaving the light off, hoping his arrival had gone unnoticed by anyone who might come knocking. Plenty of summer morning light filtered in through the high, dusty, barred window, but no one could see in through that unless they had a ladder. He knelt beside the old oak swivel chair with the leather seat and back. It had been his dad's chair, and he wouldn't have traded it for the newest, most ergonomically correct office chair on the market. He folded his hands on the worn seat and bowed his head.

"Heavenly Father," he said aloud, and then didn't know how to continue. For several long moments, he just let his thoughts and feelings flow heavenward, then finally began again. "Lord, you know—that is, thou knowest—how weak and confused I feel. How concerned I am for Sister Melody Padgett and her little girl, how certain and afraid I am that Brother Jack

Padgett is abusing his wife, though she refuses to say so, and begs me not to do anything. I feel I've got to do something, Heavenly Father, but this is such a delicate matter that I don't know how to go about it. It won't do any good if I frighten them away from church. And I've got to acknowledge before thee, Father, that my feelings toward Brother Padgett are not as loving right now as they probably ought to be. The man just rubs me the wrong way, and I know it's my own weakness that makes it hard to be his bishop. Even though I suspect him of ugliness and meanness, I know I need to approach him with a desire in my heart to help him overcome his problems, not with the same kind of anger that causes him to strike out at his family.

"Lord, I don't know what's happened to him in his life to bring him to this kind of behavior, and I need a spirit of love and compassion to replace my anger and disgust, or I don't think I can minister to his needs or his family's. So it's for this cause—for wisdom and love—that I submit myself to thee this day in fasting and prayer. There are other problems in our ward, too, and I know thou art aware of each of them—far more than I am—and I pray thy tender watchcare to be with each family, each individual, according to their various needs. But for right now, I plead with thee for help in dealing with the Padgetts."

He closed his prayer in the name of the Savior and stayed where he was, on his knees, thinking and mulling over the situation, mentally listing his options, and trying to be open to any inspiration the Lord might see fit to send him. After a while, his knees began to complain, and he pushed himself up into the chair and leaned forward, burying his head in his arms on the desk.

He woke to the sound of Mary Lynn's key in the lock and

lifted his head, momentarily confused to find himself in his office. He had thought he was tramping the green hills of Shepherd's Pass.

"Jim! What the heck're you doing locked up in here? You don't look so good. You okay?"

"Good morning, Mary Lynn, and I'm fine. Just doing some thinking, and you know that's hard on an old man like me. I fell asleep working at it."

"Old man!" she chided. "Not likely. Just a worried man, from the looks of you. Everything okay at home?"

"Oh, yeah. Home's fine, work's fine. It's just my other life that isn't always so great. Well, no, that's not exactly right, either. Let's just say *I'm* not always so great—at figuring people out, and knowing how to help them."

"Oh—you mean your job as bishop, or whatever?"

"That's it."

"Can I help?"

"Probably not, but thanks."

She shrugged and flipped her long brown hair over her shoulder. "Don't reckon I even know anybody in your church, so feel free to run it by me if you want."

"Well, just tell me this—why would a woman deny that her husband physically abuses her, when it's evident he does? Why would she beg me not to do anything about it? Wouldn't she want him to stop?"

"Oh, boy. Well, my cousin Selma was in a situation like that. Her husband beat her every week or so, but she defended him to everybody, even the law. Her mama asked her how come she did that, and she just said, 'He's all I've got. At least I know what to expect outa him.' So maybe she's scared of what changes it'd bring, other than him stopping the beatings."

"Interesting. But this woman's young, good-looking, and smart—has everything going for her—and I can't, for the life of me, see why she'd think she needs to put up with such mistreatment. This guy strikes me—no pun intended—as a grown-up playground bully."

"Into controlling everybody and everything, is he?"

The bishop nodded. "Sure looks that way."

Mary Lynn considered the ends of a long strand of hair. "Fear," she said succinctly.

"Well, yeah, I'm sure she's afraid of him—"

"No, I mean him. He's full of fear. At least, most bullies are. I think of my brother Dwight, when he was in grade school, you know? He was the worst bully you ever saw. But alls it was, was that he thought if he didn't control everything and everybody in his life, it'd all come tumbling down like one of those card houses kids try to build, you know what I mean? See, the thing was, right then Mama and Daddy was all concerned about my other little brother, Casey, who was in the hospital down at Birmingham with this real rare blood disease, and he like to've died of it. Poor old Dwight didn't see our folks for days at a time, and he wasn't allowed to go see Casey, and things just weren't the same at home, with all us older kids bossin' him, so he just plain took it all out on the kids at school. They were the onliest people on earth he could exert any control over, 'cause he sure as heck didn't have no control over any part of his own life, and he got to feelin' like as long as he kept them kids in line, ever'thing might turn out all right."

"What happened?"

"Well, the teacher and the principal couldn't let the bullyin' go on, and kids' parents were starting to complain, so they sent Dwight home with a note saying he was suspended till his folks could come to school and straighten things out. He was home for quite a spell, 'cause Mama and Daddy just couldn't leave Casey long enough to tend to it, and in fact, we didn't even tell them about it till later. Then, one day I was home, too, not feelin' so good, and first thing I know, Dwight's outside yellin' at our old dog, and goin' after her with sticks and rocks. I went out and grabbed him and asked him what in creation he thought he was doing, 'cause I'd always figured he loved old Maisie. And that poor youngun' just broke down and cried like a baby, and it all come out, how scared he was that Casey would die, and our family'd never be the same again, and maybe he'd get the same disease, but nobody'd care if he died, 'cause he was so mean and ornery." She sighed and leaned back in her chair, her eyes looking beyond him as if the past were being portrayed on the office wall.

"Mercy," the bishop murmured.

"So—fear was what it was. The little old kid was scared plumb to death."

"How'd things turn out?"

"Well, I tried my best to comfort him, which maybe helped some, and then finally, Casey got better, and they all come home, and I told Mama all about it. She cried, and said poor little Dwight, he'd been caught in the middle in all this, and she and Daddy went to school and tried to explain things, and they understood, and I think Dwight was just so glad to have everybody home, and to be back in school, that he didn't feel the need to try to control everybody any more. But it was a rough patch."

"Must have been. But now, I'm trying to apply that to these people. What would a big, strong husband and father—a former Marine, mind you, and a good provider—have to fear from a slender young wife?"

Mary Lynn shrugged again. "That she'd leave him?"

The bishop spread his hands. "So he thinks hitting her will make her want to stay?"

"I know. Sounds crazy, huh? But see, I don't reckon he's real concerned right now with how she feels and what she wants—just with keeping her under his thumb, like Dwight with his schoolmates."

"Okay. But why would she beg me not to talk to him, and not to turn him in to the authorities? Her own fear?"

"Like as not. Do they have kids? Does he abuse them?"

"They've got one, and offhand, I'd guess he doesn't. At least, not yet."

"Well, see—she may be scared that he'd start in on the kid, if she rebelled, or left."

"Or, like you said earlier—she may dread the unknown—the changes that might occur, if he's caught."

"Could be. 'Course, I don't know, those're just my home-spun reckonin's. Maybe you oughta talk to a psychologist, or a marriage counselor or the like."

He smiled at his bookkeeper. "I probably should, but don't knock your insights, friend. I thought they were pretty profound."

She ducked her head, but he saw her pleased little smile before her hair swung forward to cover it. He suspected she had received far too few compliments in her life.

The image from his dream of Shepherd's Pass kept intruding on his thoughts, and by noon he was on the phone with his cousin Spurling Deal, who lived there.

"Hey, Spurl? Jim. Doing great, how're you folks? Super. Hey, listen—do ya'll care if I come up and hike around the hills a little bit this afternoon? I just want to get out in the sunshine, but I don't feel sociable enough to go play golf, you know? Thanks. Just give the guys the word not to shoot if they see me, okay? I won't be rustling cattle or sheep. I'll probably hike up to the falls. Thanks, Spurl, I owe you one."

He told Mary Lynn he'd be unavailable for the afternoon, called Trish and advised her of his plan, and set his truck in motion. He felt just a little guilty, like a kid playing hooky from school, but he craved silence and solitude and the peace of the sunlit hills. As his truck headed into those hills, he wondered if there was a prettier place on earth than northern Alabama, with its many waterways and foothills and gorges, all green in the glory of June, with wild blackberries and roses climbing on fence posts and rocky outcroppings. At one of his favorite spots along the way, huge trees formed a canopy of deep shade over the road for at least half a mile, providing a tunnel of natural air-conditioning that he slowed down to enjoy.

Since he was fasting, it wasn't a day for serious hiking. He just rambled slowly along a sheep path after he left his truck, stopping whenever he wanted to gaze out over a meadow, which was still veined with silver streamlets from the spring rains and runoff, though by now they had dwindled to a trickle. In late February and early March, the whole meadow would have been wet. A few of his cousin's small band of sheep grazed peacefully on the sloping ground, their bells tinkling faintly when they moved. A couple of lambs cavorted playfully for a few moments, then returned to their mothers. He knew the fields of the Holy Land were probably far dryer and the forage much more sparse for those Biblical sheep, yet in this setting he could imagine the

Savior teaching about the ninety and nine and the importance of the one that was lost.

He had a sheep in his flock in danger of being lost, did he not? Wasn't Jack Padgett spiritually headed out into the desert?

"Stupid, stubborn ram," he muttered, and then remembered Mary Lynn's story of her frightened little brother, Dwight. "Okay," he amended. "Make that a frightened ram, butting against the very sheep he should be protecting, trying to ignore the calls of his shepherd, insisting on doing things his own way."

But did that fit with his image of Jack? He thought of Jack's face and the expressions of stubbornness and annoyance he had seen there. He imagined Jack backhanding Melody, knocking her against a wall of their beautiful new house, or grasping her upper arms so tightly they bruised. "I don't see fear, there, Lord," he whispered. "I see anger. So much anger, and I don't understand why. Does Melody have a knack for setting him off, somehow? How can it be anything kin to fear that he's feeling?"

He sat in a patch of shade and bowed his head, trying to clear his mind and open it to promptings of the Spirit. But his mind, stubborn thing that it was, insisted on intruding with random thoughts of this and that, unrelated memories and bits of trivia.

"Sorry, Heavenly Father. Reckon I need more practice in meditating. Or maybe I have an attention deficit problem. Please bear with me, and bless me with the wisdom I need."

He stood again and plodded slowly upward, hand-vaulting over a fence post and entering a wooded area where the mingled fragrances of sun-warmed pine and wild flowers acted as a relaxant, calming his mind. He climbed to the spot the family called "the falls," which was perhaps a glorified name for an area where a small stream came to about a three- or four-foot drop off, then spilled over some rocks to puddle in a small pond before meandering on its way. It was little more than the sort of thing many backyard gardeners constructed to provide the soothing sound of water, but it was private, the woods surrounding it were shady and fragrant, and it was a place where generations of Shepherds (and Carsons and Deals) had come to picnic, or to think, relax, and possibly commune with their Maker. At this time of year, the volume of the stream was negligible, but he'd been here before in early spring or anytime after a good rain, and he knew how it could increase.

He sat on a primitive bench—actually a weathered log that someone had stripped the bark from and set in a low cradle formed by notching two sections of split logs and fitting them together in X-shapes, and binding them with leather thongs for extra stability. Who? He wondered. Which of his ancestors had provided this simple seating, and how long ago? The bench creaked as it took his weight, but it held. He looked around, enjoying the pattern of the sunlight as it filtered through leaves and needles high overhead. It caught and sparkled now and then on facets of the water, which here flowed reddish-brown from the color of the soil. So much of Alabama's soil was red clay, which, he reflected, was the slipperiest dang stuff on the planet when it was wet, but which also, in his opinion, provided a pretty contrast with the green things that grew so readily from it. He remembered how, as a boy, his socks and sneakers—and, indeed, the rest of him—usually had a rusty cast that his mother despaired of getting white again. Now Trish fretted over Jamie's socks and shoes and the knees of his jeans. He smiled.

It was good to relax. Good to feel the worry, the edginess, ease out of him. He sat still, listening to the subtle sounds around him—faint rustlings of small animals in the underbrush, sporadic calls of birds, or the faint whir of their wings as they made brief flights from limb to limb. It was a relatively quiet time of day for birds. An occasional mosquito hovered, whining, by his ear, and he stirred to bat it away.

He felt prayed out. He had petitioned the Lord, who knew what troubled him, what his needs were. Now he simply murmured, "In thine own good time, Lord," and allowed the peace of the place to minister to his soul.

How long he stayed, he wasn't sure, but the sun had moved a ways across the sky when he stood, in response to a sudden thought that it was time to go, now, and began to make his way back to his truck. He felt comfortable, his limbs free, his neck and shoulders relaxed in a way he hadn't realized they needed to be. Best of all, his mind was at ease. He still hadn't received an answer to his prayers, not that he could recognize, anyway, but somehow he was at peace. Perhaps that was the answer.

He wasn't too sorry to leave the falls; the constant splashing of the stream had begun to make him thirsty—that and the fact that he hadn't had a sip of water for approximately twenty hours. Fasting from food had never been a particularly hard thing for him to do, but he craved water like a man on a raft by the time the twenty-four hours were up, and usually drank most of his first meal to break the fast.

It was funny, he reflected, how fasting worked. How it made a man realize his dependence on regular supplies of food and water to be able to function, and how it humbled him, and made him realize, as well, his dependence on God and the things of God for spiritual nourishment. Interesting, too, how the experience could soften a person's heart, allowing him access to those deeper feelings he might at other times ignore or not even recognize. No wonder tears flowed so readily at fast and testimony meeting.

$$\Upsilon$$

As he turned his truck back toward Fairhaven, he switched on the radio as an automatic response, wincing as a blare of music jarred his senses. He punched the button for another preset, a talk station he sometimes enjoyed.

"You're listening to 'Family Spotlight,' with Dr. Randall Deems," a woman's voice informed him. "Today's topic is anger on the home front and how to deal with it."

"Huh!" the bishop said with a chuckle, and turned up the volume.

"Dr. Deems, in our last segment, you said that anger is a secondary emotion, rather than a primary one. Could you explain that a little more?"

"Yes, Virginia," came the familiar, friendly voice of the family therapist and radio personality. "You see, what happens, especially with men, is that when something occurs that causes us hurt, for example—or frustration or fear—we very quickly gloss over those emotions, which are the primary ones, and move right into anger, which is a secondary response. If we felt comfortable and free to feel and acknowledge the fear, or hurt, or frustration for what they are, we might not be so quick to become angry. This happens with women, too, of course, but we find that it's far more common with men—probably because we guys feel society's pressure to be strong and in charge—macho, if you will. Anger, in our society, is a more acceptable feeling for a man to express than hurt, frustration, or fear, which might make him appear weak, or not so much in control of himself."

"So, you're saying that when we feel angry, we should look back to see what the very first emotion was that we felt—what, in effect, *made* us angry?"

"Absolutely. Sometimes it's hard, because the anger comes so quickly. But with practice, we can identify what that primary emotion was, and learn to respond to it appropriately, rather than unleashing anger all over the place. And I might add, Virginia, that anger is a choice. It's a momentary, split-second decision that we make, to choose anger over the emotion we regard as unacceptable, or too painful to acknowledge for what it is. Once we realize that, we can begin to learn to control that anger-response, and keep from saying and doing things we'll later regret."

"Now, let me get this straight—you're saying that nobody really *makes* us mad? That it's a choice we make, to get angry?"

"That's exactly it," he agreed with a chuckle. "Although we'd much prefer to blame the other person, wouldn't we? We like to say, 'Ooh, you make me so mad!' We don't want to say, 'Ooh, that remark hurt my feelings so much,' or 'Ooh, I'm so afraid I'm going to lose your love or respect.'"

"Well, that's a new perspective on anger for me. Thank you, Dr. Deems. When we come back, we'll discuss how to apply this knowledge to various family situations that come up."

As the station moved into the commercial break, the bishop thought about what he had heard. It was uncanny, really, how the explanation made sense, and how it dovetailed with the conversation he'd had earlier that day with Mary Lynn Connors. He thought about his own response to Jack Padgett— the anger he felt toward the man. What primary emotion had he skipped over—was it fear for Melody and Andi? Frustration that Melody wouldn't admit there was a problem that needed solving? Fear that he, as their bishop, might fail them? All the above? And what of Jack, himself? What fear or hurt or frustration was he masking with his angry, abusive ways?

He listened to the rest of the discussion to see if there were more insights to be gained, but only one statement stood out in his memory after the program ended: "In almost all cases, people who abuse their spouse eventually turn to abusing their children as well. If no one intervenes, the anger just spills over and wreaks havoc in all close personal relationships, especially with those younger or weaker than the abuser. That's why anger management is so very important in our lives."

"If no one intervenes," the bishop repeated to himself. "Well, Brother and Sister Padgett, somebody's going to intervene, before your little Andi gets physically hurt." The child was already obviously aware of what was going on between her parents, with her comment about Daddy spanking Mommy all over. In spite of Melody's pleas, he couldn't, in good conscience, let the matter go unchecked any longer.

Y

"Hey, there, you're home early," Trish greeted, coming to give him a hug. "How's your day been?"

"Very interesting. Enlightening, even. How's yours?"

"Good. Had a call from Meredith, and she sounded happy. She gave me a message for you. Let's see—'the method seems to be working,' I believe she said." Trish gave him a curious glance, but he just nodded, smiling a little.

"Good," he said. "That's great, I'm glad to hear it. Say, who's that out playing with Mallory?"

Trish frowned. "That's little Andi Padgett. It's kind of weird, actually. I got a call from Melody today, asking if I could pick Andi up from her day care and bring her here till Jack can pick her up after work. Melody said she hated to bother me, but she couldn't go get her, herself, and the day care lady said Andi had thrown up, and she was afraid she'd get the other kids sick, if she was coming down with something. It kind of ticked me off, you know? It was almost like, 'it's okay if your kids get sick from her, though, so take her to your house.' Andi seems okay, so far—no fever or anything, so I've let her play with Mal—but I don't understand why Melody couldn't take care of her, herself. She's not working, is she? And I know they have two cars. I'd certainly think she could cancel any plans she had, and stay home with a sick child. It's all just kind of strange."

The bishop gazed at his wife for a long moment, then looked out toward the backyard where Mallory and Andi squealed and ran from a playful cat.

"I think I'm going to break one of my own resolutions, and ask that little girl a question or two," he said.

Trish looked at him soberly. "You think maybe this has to do with what's going on in their marriage? You think Melody's been beaten up or something?"

"It's my first thought, but I could be wrong." He frowned. "Maybe I'd better call Melody first. S'cuse me, sweetheart."

He went up into their bedroom and dialed the Padgett's number. Melody answered after the fourth ring, her voice anxious.

"Hello? Sister Shepherd? Is Andi okay?"

"It's the bishop, Melody. Andi seems fine; she's out playing with Mallory. I'm just wondering if you're okay? Wondering why you didn't pick Andi up, or have Trish take her home to your house?"

There was a silence. "Oh. I'm just fine, Bishop. Truly, I am. It's just that—Jack and I have an arrangement, that only he can pick Andi up from day care, or somebody that he calls and okays to do it."

"Why can't that be you, Andi's mom? And why can't she come home to you?"

A longer silence ensued. Finally, reluctantly, her voice small and far away, Melody replied. "I'd rather not answer that, Bishop, if it's all right with you. It's just an arrangement—an agreement—that Jack and I have. I'm sorry if it put your wife out. We won't bother you again."

"Aw, Melody—Trish was glad to help. I just don't understand. It seems like Jack doesn't trust you to take care of Andi, or something."

"Well, I guess—yes, that's it. I guess he doesn't."

No, that wasn't it. She was too quick to jump on that explanation. He cast about in his mind for a better one. "Melody, Jack hasn't beat you up, incapacitated you somehow, has he? Broken your arm, or something?"

"No, honestly, Bishop. If you wanted, you could come look at me and see that I'm perfectly all right. Jack just . . . he just likes to supervise my mothering. He likes us to be a family together."

"Uh-huh, okay. Well, we'll be glad to keep Andi till he gets here. And we'll be glad to help with her, anytime. Please don't ever feel like you're imposing on us. She's a sweet little gal, and Mallory enjoys her. You take care, now."

He could hear her sigh of relief before she said good-bye. His own sigh, once the call was disconnected, was longer and more troubled. He had not yet arrived at the complete truth.

CHAPTER NINETEEN

Y

" . . . STILL IN ERROR'S GLOOMY WAYS"

Slowly the bishop descended the stairs to find his wife. She looked at him with a question in her eyes, and he shrugged.

"She insists she's fine. Says she and Jack have an arrangement that only he, or someone he okays, picks Andi up from day care. But she's not allowed to. She says he likes for them to be a family, together."

Trish frowned. "Meaning what? That she can't be alone with Andi, or drive her anywhere? Oh, of course, I'll bet that's it. Jim, remember when I asked Melody to help with Mal's birthday party, and she said she couldn't? I'll bet it's because if she came, Andi couldn't! Jack doesn't allow them to be alone together, does he? But why?"

Suddenly the bishop was certain. "Because he's scared to death she'll take Andi and run—leave him—if she's ever allowed to have any opportunity alone with her."

Trish stared out toward the backyard. "Jim, that is so sick.

And so sad. He's got them held captive, doesn't he, right in everybody's plain sight?"

"It's looking that way. Hon, do you happen to know the name or number of the day care lady where you picked Andi up?"

"I do. It's Mrs. Marshall. I don't know the number, but I remember the name of her day care, because I thought it was kind of cute—Kinder-Tenders. I'll see if it's in the phone book."

With grim determination the bishop punched in the number his wife showed him and asked for Mrs. Marshall. He explained that he was the Padgetts' clergyman, and that he was concerned that all might not be well in their home.

"Have you ever noticed anything unusual about the family, or how they do things?" he asked her. "Or has little Andi ever said anything to make you wonder if there was some kind of abuse going on in the home?"

The woman wasn't immediately willing to answer. "What did you say your name is?"

"I'm sorry. I guess I didn't. This is Bishop James Shepherd." He wondered if it would help if he said he was a representative of the Mormon Church, then decided against it. "I'm the family's . . . pastor, and I'm fearful that Andi might have some special needs."

"I see. Actually, I have wondered about the Padgetts, at times. Andrea's a sweet little girl, but every now and again she yells mean and abusive things at the other kids, and pretends to hit them with toys. It's kind of strange, because she just seems to do it in the course of play, not when she's angry or upset. It's like she's just acting out something she's seen, same as having a tea party, or playing with pots and pans. But if she's really upset about something, she tends to go off in a corner and huddle down and cry, real quiet. That, in itself, seems kind of strange to me, because most kids, when something or somebody bugs them, they really set it up and want justice done right now."

"Exactly—and that's very interesting. How about her mother? Does she come often to pick Andi up, or for any other reason?"

"You know, I've only seen Mrs. Padgett the one time, when the three of them first came to look at our center. I've assumed she doesn't drive, or have a car, because it's always Daddy that picks Andi up, or somebody that he calls ahead of time and authorizes, like today. Was that your wife?"

"It was. We've just gradually become aware that something might be amiss in the family, and I'm going to talk to Mr. Padgett and see if we can get them some help. Would you just kind of keep your eyes and ears open? I may get back to you about this, if you don't mind."

"Well, I'm glad you're checking into it, sir. And it just may be that the authorities need to know, too, if the little girl's in harm's way."

"It may come to that," he agreed. "I hope it won't have to. But thanks so much for your help."

He put down the phone and sat for some time with his eyes closed. He pictured Andrea Padgett, huddling in a far corner of her room, crying quietly as her mother was being bombarded with verbal and physical abuse. How long could it be until Andi herself was the recipient of such treatment—from her out-of-control father, or even, possibly, from a mistreated and over-wrought mother? He knew these things were sometimes passed along.

He stood and went into the kitchen, where mouth-watering smells were emanating from the oven and stovetop. His stomach reminded him, forcefully, that he hadn't fed it in some time—but he knew he couldn't eat. Not yet.

"Trish? babe, how would you like to put all this on hold, and take the Andi and the children away for a while? A park, a meal, a movie—whatever—to give me time to talk to Jack before he just grabs Andi and takes off. Could you do that?"

She switched off the stove and looked at her watch. "He's due here in less than an hour," she told him. "About five-thirty. But, Jim—I don't think you ought to be alone when you confront him. He's mean. Well, I guess that's obvious."

"I won't be alone." He smiled at her, and she understood.

She took a deep breath. "Okay," she replied and reached to kiss his cheek. "You be careful, though. Jamie's having a sleep-over at Dennis's house, and Tiff's tending the Arnaud kids till about eleven. What shall I do, timewise?"

"Give us at least until six-thirty or seven. Take the cell phone and call here anytime after that, and I'll tell you what to do about taking Andi home or bringing her back here for the night. I just don't know how things are going to play out."

"I hope Jack doesn't come out tracking down my car to get her."

"I don't think he will. If necessary, I'll tell him you took the kids down to the zoo at Birmingham. Um—you are considering the zoo, aren't you?" He prompted, grinning.

"Oh, absolutely. Either that or the new animated movie at the mall theaters. I'm not sure which, so neither are you."

"Right. I'm not. Thanks, babe. Will dinner be ruined?"

"No, actually it's about done. I'll just put it away for later."

"You're the best."

Y

When he was alone in the house, it seemed strangely quiet, and he thought how seldom he found himself alone there. Much as he valued his privacy and quiet times, he would hate being alone too much, especially here at home, where he was accustomed to the cheerful noise of three active youngsters and an almost equally active wife. He thought of his sister-in-law, Meredith, wandering around her large and lavish home by herself, and was glad, again, that there were apparently some hopeful signs of awakening in her work-bound husband. Then he thought of Jack Padgett. Was being alone in his new home what he feared most? If so, by binding his wife and daughter so smotheringly close to him, wasn't he putting himself in jeopardy of the ultimate loneliness of divorce?

He knelt beside his bed and gave himself up again to a time of prayer and meditation.

"This is it, Father," he prayed. "Be with me as I counsel with thy son Jack Padgett. Be with him, I ask thee, and soften his heart toward his wife and child—and toward me. Help him to see me as his friend, and help me to be his friend, in truth. Bless me with boldness, as it may be required, and with wisdom. And Lord, please grant me courage, because I confess I'm afraid, right now. Bless us both to hold our tempers."

When Jack's truck turned into the driveway, the bishop was walking around the yard, admiring Trish's flowers, deadheading a few spent roses she had missed. The sun was still high in the sky, but the trees in his and Mrs. Hestelle Pierce's backyards made those areas oases of deep shade. He moved to greet Jack Padgett.

"Hello, Jack," he said easily. "Come on back and have a glass of lemonade in the shade."

They shook hands.

"Thanks, Bishop, but no can do. Melody doesn't like me and Andi to be late for dinner. Where's Andi—inside? Is she feeling okay?"

"She seems to be doing just fine. No, I'll tell you—Trish took the little girls off somewhere with her, and they're not back yet, so you might as well relax a minute and cool off. I've been hoping for a chance to visit with you anyway, and this would seem to be a good time."

Jack frowned but followed him into the backyard and accepted a glass of iced lemonade. The bishop sat down in one of the white-painted lawn chairs, but Jack continued to stand, his feet apart, his expression wary.

"How's the Auto-Tec business doing?"

"Excellent. Very busy. Expanding."

"Lot of stress, opening and staffing new stores, keeping an eye on everything?"

"Goes with the territory." He finally sat, but ready for flight, on the edge of his chair.

"Seems like extra duty for you, having to do all the driving to take Andrea to day care and pick her up, doctor's visits, whatever. How come you don't let your wife help with the chauffeuring?"

"Well, to tell the truth, Bishop, Melody's not the safest driver in the world. A woman driver, you know what I mean? Talks with her hands, doesn't keep her eyes on the road. One time, with Andi aboard, she had to run off the road to keep from plowing into the car ahead of us. Right then, I decided that Andi rides only with me. Sorry if that seems strict, but Andi's too precious to risk losing her to Mel's carelessness."

The bishop looked at him searchingly. "I wonder what you're most afraid of, Jack?" he asked.

"Afraid? I'm not afraid of anything but Mel's driving. She's a nut behind the wheel, like I just said." He laughed nervously and drained his lemonade, dropping the tumbler on the soft grass.

The bishop took a deep breath and let it out slowly. "Brother Padgett, I'm not going to ask you if you abuse your wife—if you yell verbal abuse at her and hurt her physically and emotionally. I'm not asking, because I know you do. I know that happens. What we need to do is figure out where to go from here. How to get you the help you need to stop doing those unacceptable things. How to keep Melody safe—and ultimately, Andi, too."

He saw the fear, raw and stark in Jack's eyes for a moment, as his face paled noticeably, then the color rushed back from his neck to his cheeks and forehead, where a pulse beat rapidly.

Okay, he's angry, now, the bishop thought, surprised at how detached he felt in this moment, how his fear had left him as soon as the words he needed to say were out of his mouth. *It's true what I heard on that program, today,* he thought with interest. *I saw the fear and shock before the anger came.*

Eyes hard, Jack glared at him. "Melody tell you I hit her?" he asked.

The bishop shook his head. "No, in fact, she didn't. She's never lodged any kind of complaint against you. She's a remarkably loyal woman, all things considered."

"Then who? I'd like to know who's accusing me of this, if it's not too much trouble. And I'd like to know just how anybody thinks they know what goes on in our marriage, in the privacy of our home!"

"The signs aren't so hard for anybody to read. Bruises are visible, even under makeup. I've watched both of you avoid uncomfortable questions, and I've seen your need to control even what church calling Melody accepts. I'm aware of your decision not to allow her to be alone with Andi, in case she should take your daughter and escape—is that what you're most afraid of? And even little Andi has been noticed, acting out scenarios she's seen and heard at home, and talking about how Daddy spanks Mommy all over when she's naughty."

"All circumstantial nonsense," Jack objected, his hands clenched on the chair arms. "Mel bruises easy—she's got some confounded vitamin deficiency or other. And we horse around a lot, playing—wrestling, tickling, and so forth. Andi's just playing like that."

"Verbally abusing and hitting kids at her day care?"

"What—did that Marshall woman tell your wife that?"

"No, she told me."

"Well, she should've told me if my kid's misbehaving, not you! Where do you get off, anyway, coming at me with all this garbage? You say you're my friend? I don't think so, *Bishop!*" He gave the title an ugly emphasis. "I want you to stay out of our business—out of our lives. Do you understand me?"

"I understand you perfectly, but I can't do that. I'm Melody's and Andi's bishop, too—and I'm concerned for their safety and welfare. Now, I repeat, Melody has not asked me for help—has not complained—so there's no need to go home and punish her over this. But this is a serious matter, Jack, and the abuse has got to stop, one way or another. Either you actively seek help, which would be the best route, or the authorities will have to step in and do what they think best."

"You threatening me? You been in contact with the police or something?"

"No. I'm not threatening you. I'm just spelling out how things have to be. I'm bound by law and by conscience to report any spousal or parental abuse I know about."

Jack tried to laugh, but the sound was desperate and weak. "You know nothing! And if Mel doesn't file a complaint, they'll laugh at you. They'll throw the whole case out."

"I'm not the only one who knows. In fact, this first came to my attention because of observations by other ward members."

"Damn busybodies. They don't know anything, either. They don't know crap, and neither do you! Who told you this, and what did they say?"

"That's confidential, and so is this conversation. It's between us. I just needed to let you know that I'm aware of at least some of the things that are going on behind closed doors in your family, and that I want to help you get past this sickness in your life. It's a spiritual sickness, Jack, just like alcoholism and other kinds of addictions. It escalates, and it's tough to break out of, but for all your sakes, it needs to be done. I'm no expert, but there are family therapists around who are and who can help you."

"I don't need their help! Do I look like a guy who needs some kind of mealy-mouthed therapist to tell him how to take care of his own?"

"You don't look it, but, my brother, you surely do act like it. Look, I don't blame you for being defensive and upset at me. I wouldn't want to hear what you've just heard, either. In fact, I've dreaded this conversation myself and tried to find a way to squirm out of it, but the Lord wouldn't let me. I've spent this whole day in fasting and prayer about your situation, and I—"

"Oh, how touching. How sweet. Who the hell asked you to do that?" Jack's sneer was ugly.

The bishop was silent for a moment, then he said quietly, "You know what? You did. And Melody. And Andi. You all cried out for help, by your actions, by your very denials. You're all hurt and confused, but I know there's a way out of this, a way you can all be happier, with no hurting going on. You're hurting your daughter, Jack. Don't you see that?"

"I've never laid a hand on Andi! I'm crazy about that kid."

"Sooner or later, you probably will, whether you believe that now or not. But even now, the way you treat her mother is having a tremendous impact on her. Anybody can see that. And she'll carry it on—maybe she'll abuse her children someday, or never be able to trust a man. Now, maybe somebody abused you when you were too young to fight back. Maybe that's where all this started. You don't have to tell me, but you've got to get help somewhere, please. I'd suggest LDS Social Services as a good place to start. I can give you a family referral."

Jack flung himself back in his chair and stared across the yard, his mouth forming a hard line. "You're a stubborn cuss, aren't you? Not going to believe me, not going to give up, are you?"

"No, I'm not. Can't do that."

"So, are you so perfect? You, so holier than thou, never made a mistake in your life?"

"Don't even go there, Jack. This is about you, and your present needs."

Jack leaned forward, his eyes narrowing. He spoke softly.

"What I need, what I'd really, really like to do, Mister Mormon mighty judge in Israel, is to punch your lights out!"

The bishop nodded. "I don't blame you. I've had the same feeling toward you a few times, to be honest. But that's gone now. It's kind of strange, but all I feel toward you right now is compassion."

"Well, I don't need your stinking compassion! Where's my daughter? Where'd your wife take her? I have the right to my child!"

"I honestly don't know where they are, but I'm sure we'll hear from them soon. We're not kidnapping Andi from you. I might suggest to you, though, that it'd be a good idea to let her spend the night here with our little girl. That'd give you a chance to go talk to your wife and begin a healing process. Because I do believe that on some level, you and Melody care for each other, Jack."

Jack stared at him, frowning, but for the moment seemed at a loss for words.

The bishop went on. "I've probably said my piece in a pretty clumsy way, tonight. I'm not much on eloquence. I speak plainly. You're a Latter-day Saint. You're a priesthood holder. You know that abusive behavior toward your companion and your family is totally unacceptable to your Savior, your Heavenly Father, and your church. I don't have to tell you that. I'd imagine you're pretty torn up inside already, because of the conflict of your actions with your beliefs."

"I've got a little temper, but I'm not admitting to anything else. Maybe I have a gruff way about me, but hell, I'm a Marine! What're you gonna do, call a bishop's court, get me excommunicated for that?"

"Right now, that's the farthest thing from my mind. I'm

hoping for changes here. I'm hoping to see you break a cycle. I know you were a Marine, and I know you have to be pretty tough to be one. But the drill-sergeant routine doesn't go over so well with families, you know?

"My father-in-law was career military, but he didn't behave toward his wife and daughters the same way he did to his men—and for that matter, I don't believe he abused his men in any way. He led them by his example, is what I've heard. He's no patsy, but he's no bully, either."

Jack ducked his head. "I don't know how to be different," he muttered, in a voice the bishop barely heard. His heart leapt up in gratitude for what might be the first sign of humility.

"I know, I understand. It's not something we're just born knowing, and it's not something that all of us saw, growing up. But there are skills and techniques that we can learn, about managing anger and stress and fear. There are people who can teach us, coach us, till the skills become second nature to us. I've been learning some new concepts, just today."

He heard the phone ring in the kitchen. "Excuse me a minute," he said, and sprinted for the house, on legs that felt as if they were powered by Slinkies, ready to drop him in his tracks.

It was Melody Padgett.

"Bishop? Has Jack come by to pick up Andi yet? They're not home."

"Oh, hi, Melody. Yes, Jack's here. He and I have been visiting, waiting for Trish to come back. She's got the little girls out with her for a bit."

"Oh. I—see. Is Jack—okay?"

"Well, we've been having a very frank discussion. I'm hoping he'll be making some changes in the way he treats you."

"You've been talking to him about—about our marriage?"

"Been trying to."

"Oh, no. That'll make him so mad. That'll . . ."

"He's been yelling at me a little, and that's okay. I've made it clear that you haven't said a word against him—that I learned what was going on from other sources. By the way, I've suggested that he allow Andi to sleep over here, with Mallory, so the two of you can have a chance to talk things over tonight."

"Oh, no, Bishop—let her come home, please! He's a little better, when she's here, and—"

"I don't really think he'll be abusive tonight. Not now that he knows people are aware and watching him."

She sighed. "Well. Whatever he decides, then. I'll just wait."

"I'll keep in touch, Melody. You call me, anytime, if you need me, okay?"

"All right."

He disconnected with the feeling that she thought he had just condemned her to a traitor's death. He keyed in the numbers to Trish's cell phone. She answered on the third ring, with a background roar of noise that almost obscured her greeting.

"Trish? Where are you? Sounds like the circus."

"We're at Pizza Playground. The movie was sold out, so we've eaten, and I'm standing here watching the girls romp in the Ball Pen. Did Jack come?"

"He's out back. I think you can come home now."

"Oh, good!"

"I'm trying to persuade him to let Andi sleep over, so he and Melody can be undisturbed to talk things over. Is that okay with you?"

"Sure. We'll be there shortly. I've had about all the pizza and good cheer I can stand. Love you!"

"Love you," he replied softly, not knowing if she heard, but secure in the knowledge that she knew.

CHAPTER TWENTY

" . . . Lord, behold this congregation"

Jack agreed, spurred by his little daughter's pleadings, to allow her to sleep over with Mallory. He scooped her up into his arms and kissed her, then set her down to run after Mallory and Trish into the house.

"I know this has been hard, Jack," the bishop said, walking with him toward his truck. Jack's lips were set in a bitter line, but his anger and bravado seemed to have abated. He stared at the ground and didn't reply. "I know, too, that the Savior's atonement can cover anything you've done that you truly repent of. I'll work with you, but my best advice is to take it to the Lord. He already knows all your faults, all your strengths, all your hopes and fears. You can safely trust him, Jack. He'll be with you every step of the way if you ask him to. He'll help you lick this thing."

"Seems to me you oughta be telling Mel to pray for help, since you think she's the victim, here."

"I do counsel her to pray, of course. But somehow, I suspect you're as much of a victim as she is. Oh, not her victim, I don't mean that—but a victim of somebody, somewhere along the way. Somebody who left you so little power and control of your life that you learned to be a bully in response."

Jack looked taken aback. His gaze flickered quickly toward his bishop and away again.

Hit, thought the bishop. *Thank thee, Father, for a timely radio program, even if it was oversimplified pop psychology. It was exactly what I needed to hear today. As was Mary Lynn's story.*

He faced Jack as the man reached for the door of his truck. "I'm not your enemy," he said quietly, holding out his hand. Reluctantly, silently, Jack gave it a brief grasp. As the truck pulled away down the long-shadowed street, the bishop slumped against a wrought-iron patio support and closed his eyes. Suddenly, the accumulated weariness, hunger, thirst, and emotional stress of the day descended upon him, and he realized exactly how much support the Lord had been lending him to get him through the confrontation. Now, for the moment, he was on his own again and painfully aware of his weakness and mortality. He dragged himself into the kitchen and flopped into a chair. Trish, knowing his habits, placed a tall glass of water before him.

"Thanks, sweetheart. And thank you, Heavenly Father," he added, lifting the glass in tribute before he drank. He leaned back in his chair and smiled feebly at his wife. "Feed me," he entreated. "Just something simple."

She prepared a quick scrambled egg sandwich and placed it before him—just the way he liked it, with soft white bread and mayonnaise. Comfort food. She stirred a little chocolate syrup into a glass of milk, not too strong.

"Now you are spoiling me."

"Just carrying on what your mama started. You've taught me

well exactly what you like." She slipped behind his chair and gave him a hug and a kiss on the ear. "So, how'd it go, with Jack?"

"I don't even know. I'm not real sure, right now, what I even said. It must have been somewhat successful because I'm still breathing. But something like he's doing—I'm not naive enough to think it can be all solved and made better just because I let him know that I'm aware of it."

"We could only wish that's all it took," Trish agreed, sitting down opposite him. "How was Shepherd's Pass?"

He described his visit to that favorite place, the feelings of peace that had come, and then the program he happened to tune into on the way home.

"You didn't happen across that program, Jim," Trish told him, reaching across the table for his hand. "That was no accident."

"I know," he acknowledged. "I'm sure that was why I suddenly jumped up, ready to leave, when I'd been drowsing happily only the moment before. And let me tell you what Mary Lynn said this morning," he added, and proceeded to do so.

Trish shook her head. "It's amazing. Shouldn't be, maybe, because we'd prayed for help, especially you, but still—when help comes in such obvious ways, it's kind of a thrill, isn't it?"

"It is. But you know, I think both of those little incidents were more for my benefit than Jack's. I needed to find a way to think about him and his behavior with some kind of compassion and understanding rather than just anger and outrage, which is my natural reaction. Couldn't have done it on my own." He yawned. "I am so beat. Just wrap a sheet around me. I'll sleep right here."

"Come on," his wife urged. "You go tuck up in bed. I'll see to the little girls."

Y

On Sunday morning he looked out over the congregation, his gaze lingering here and there, looking at his own dear ones on the third row. Tashia Jones sitting with the Arnauds, sending a little wave and a big smile across the chapel to another girl in her Primary class, who smiled back. Lisa Lou Pope, resplendent in a fitted green skirt and a lacy white top, stealing glances toward the Rivenbarks across the aisle. Rand, in his wheelchair, unconcernedly thumbing through his scriptures.

The missionaries, Elders Topham and McCall, ushered a family of investigators toward a vacant pew. He didn't know the family, but he hoped he'd have the opportunity to get to know them well. They had a teenage son and daughter. Lisa Lou's attention suddenly turned to them. He wondered if she knew them.

Buddy Osborne slouched into a folding chair just inside the overflow area and stared at his printed program. Their last computer lesson, including the bishop's introduction to the Internet, had gone well, and he knew Buddy had enjoyed his feast of cold cereal, more because of the amount he had consumed than because he said so. *Such a shy, sad little guy,* the bishop thought. *Good for him, to make the effort to be here.*

He realized he was looking for the Padgetts. No sign of them as yet. He looked at Ida Lou Reams, chatting amiably with Hilda Bainbridge. Ralph and Linda Jernigan occupied their usual post by the door, and Junious and Nita Mobley shuffled in, supporting each other, smiling and greeting everyone they passed. Frankie Talbot slipped into the pew behind Trish, patting her shoulder and leaning over to whisper something to her as she herded her family of redheads into their places. No one sat on the front row; by mutual consent, that was left for the Birdwhistles, who had the farthest to come and the most children, so that they had to travel in two vehicles. They generally trooped in just as the meeting was starting—or just after.

He looked with compassion at the Parsons—the young couple whose baby girl had been found to be profoundly deaf. The baby was beautiful, with her crop of dark curls and big blue eyes. He wondered what the future would bring for her. Another young couple, the Wheelers, who were waiting to adopt a baby, sat down beside the Parsons, and Connie Wheeler asked to hold little Alyssa. Connie made exaggerated, smiling faces at the baby, delighted when Alyssa waved her little arms and smiled back. He hoped Connie wouldn't have to wait too much longer for one of her own.

Tom and Lula Rexford came in and sat on a back pew, followed by T-Rex. The parents looked weary, but the son, as usual, was the picture of bounding good health and high spirits. He wondered what the presence of the three of them, together, meant with regard to Lula's elderly mother, for whom they had been so constantly caring.

Harville and LaThea Winslow took up their usual pew just behind the deacons, nodding and smiling to people as they settled in. The bishop thought what creatures of habit people were. Maybe the old-time churches with their assigned or rented or owned pews weren't too off base.

He sent up a prayer for the Fairhaven Ward—those who were struggling, and those who, at the moment, seemed to be doing well. The faithful and the faithless, the strong and the weak. He was surprised to feel the sting of tears behind his eye-lids that accompanied the rush of love he felt for these people. He opened his notebook and looked down, shading his eyes in apparent concentration while he regained his composure.

Toward the end of the meeting, he saw Melody Padgett slip in and take a seat in the overflow. Neither Jack nor Andi accompanied her, and he wondered what that meant. He hadn't heard from either of them since Jack's visit. Melody kept her face down, possibly reviewing her Primary lesson, he thought, during the closing hymn. He determined to speak to her.

As he made his way off the stand after the closing prayer, which was always a slow process due to people handing him tithing envelopes or stopping to speak to him or ask questions, he became aware of a low, growling sound from the organ speak-ers. He glanced at Sister Margaret Tullis, the organist, whose face was flushed and determined as she simultaneously tried to keep the postlude going smoothly and to swat at T-Rex, who had migrated to the front of the chapel and was leaning non-chalantly over the side of the organ, one beefy finger planted firmly on a bass key.

"How ya doin', anyway, Sister Tullis?" he asked innocently. "I sure do like the way you play the organ. It always sounds so . . . oh, hey, Bish!" The bishop collared him and pulled him away from the instrument, and the deep growl stopped.

"Thomas, what're you up to, harassing this good lady?" the bishop inquired sternly.

T-Rex looked over his shoulder and grinned at Sister Tullis. "Aw, she knows I love her, don't you, Sister Tullis? Been one of my favorite ladies since she was my den mother in Cub Scouts."

"Haven't changed much since then, have you, Thomas?"

she asked, with asperity. There was, however, an upward tug at the corners of her mouth.

"Well, I'm a lot bigger," the boy responded. "Actually, Bishop, what I come up front here to say, is that they took my grandma to the hospital last night, and it's likely she won't make it for long. My mom asked me to tell you that. She and Daddy went home to take a little nap, and then they're heading over there to be with her."

The bishop nodded. "Good for them. I'll check on them later today. Or tell them to call me, or you call, if she passes away. I'll want to go be with them when that happens—see what I can do to help."

"Right. Thanks, Bish. Bye-bye, Sister Tullis—that's a real pretty piece."

The bishop and the organist exchanged wry smiles.

He was surprised at who tentatively knocked on the open door of his office during the Sunday School hour. He had just about decided that no one needed him, and it would be a good chance to slip into the Gospel Essentials class and see if he could meet the new investigators.

"Sister Linda! Come on in, good to see you." He stood up to greet her.

Linda Jernigan left the door open but came to stand in front of his desk, clutching her purse before her. She seemed agitated, her prominent blue eyes worried, her mouth tense.

"Sit down, won't you?" the bishop invited.

She shook her head briefly. "No, thanks. I just wanted to tell you something."

"Sure, what's that?"

"See—Ralph, he can't bring himself to talk about it, but— well, that little girl in the picture at our house? You know, you asked about who she was . . . ?"

"Right, I remember."

"Well, she was our daughter. Jodie Lee."

"Was—did something happen to her?"

Linda nodded and tensed even more, if that were possible. "Kidnapped."

In his shock, he hardly knew how to respond. "Linda—did they find her?" he asked softly. All kinds of things were beginning to click into place in his mind.

Linda shook her head again. "No trace."

"Where—where'd this happen?"

"Arkansas. Where we used to live. She was playing in our yard. I called her in for supper, and she—she was just gone. Taken."

"How long ago? How old was she?" He was trying, in his mind, to grapple with the magnitude of the shock, the sorrow. Thinking of his own children—what he and Trish would do, would feel, if one of them—but it didn't do, to go there.

"She was eleven. In that picture, she was almost ten. Her last school picture. She's—that is, she'd be—twenty-three now."

Twelve years. Twelve long years of not knowing.

"Linda, I am so sorry."

"I know. There's nothing to be done. We stayed there for about seven years, searching, waiting for her to come home. But—she didn't."

He nodded. "She would have, if it was possible."

"Yessir. She would. Anyways, I just wanted you to know, that's all. Thank you."

He stepped around his desk and escorted Linda to the door. "Thank you for sharing that with me."

She paused. "Just don't—please don't—bring it up to Ralph. He can't . . ."

"I understand. I won't. Would you rather I didn't mention it to my counselors?"

She considered. "I don't mind if Brother Patrenko knows. But he can't, either, you know . . . say anything to Ralph."

"Understood."

"And your wife? Can she keep secrets?"

"She can," he said, grateful for that fact.

"Then you can tell her, if you want. Just, you know—so she'll keep a close watch on your kids. You have really nice kids."

"Thank you. I'm sure your daughter was really nice, too. I'd like for you to tell me more about her, sometime, when you feel like it."

"I don't—we don't—talk about her. At home, I mean. It'd be nice to be able to do that. I haven't—you know—forgotten."

"Of course not. You never would."

"No. Thank you, Bishop. 'Bye."

He closed his door behind her and sank into the nearest chair. "Oh, Father," he prayed brokenly, "no wonder. No wonder poor Ralph's the way he is! And that dear mother, not even able to talk about her lost child. There's so much pain, Lord, so much responsibility. How can I help these people? Who am I, that thou hast called me to this position? I feel like such a flimsy instrument, even in thy hands! All these folks, surely they deserve better than I."

He sat pondering the various needs of his ward, praying for

this family and that, missing priesthood meeting and the lesson in the priests quorum, feeling guilty but trusting the advisor to handle things. Finally, he wiped his face and blew his nose, hoping he looked presentable enough to face people for after-church interviews and meetings. He strode down the hall toward the Primary area, watching for Melody Padgett. She emerged from a small classroom and headed for the library, carrying a chalk bag and some pictures to turn in. He waited for her to come out, but when she did, she brushed by him with her eyes averted, her lips pressed tightly together.

"Melody?" he said. She didn't turn. This was not good. "Melody! Could we visit a minute?"

She whirled. "I thought we could trust you!" she whispered fiercely. "Even after the other night, I thought you cared about our family!"

He took her elbow and steered her into a nearby classroom, partially closing the door.

"Let's sit down, shall we?" He opened two folding chairs and sat in one. "Tell me what you're talking about, would you? I'm lost."

She flung her Primary bag into her chair and chose to stand behind it, gripping the back with white-knuckled fingers. "They're both gone, thanks to you. The nice people from the child protection agency came this morning, before six o'clock, pounding and ringing the doorbell and waking us all up, and they took Andi away. Protective custody, they called it, until it can be determined if she's in danger in our home. She was crying and struggling, Bishop. Too bad you weren't there to see that. I couldn't do anything, not even pack her things or give her her teddy bear to take along. They said all her needs would be provided. What about her need for her mommy and daddy?

And right on their heels, came the police, and took my husband in for questioning. He hadn't come back, by the time I left. I don't know what's going to happen to either of them! But that doesn't matter, does it? I'm just the mother, just the wife, just the one everybody's trying to protect. What am I supposed to say to you, Bishop? Thank you? Is that what you want me to say?"

He sat in stunned silence, staring up at her furious white face, her eyes that he now saw were swollen from crying. There was no smile on her lips now, no pretense that all was well.

"I came to teach my little class one last time, because I love them, and because I didn't want to leave them without a teacher. But you can call somebody else for next week, Bishop, because I can't come back to a church that's out to destroy my family!"

He found his voice. "Melody, I don't know who contacted the authorities about your situation, but it wasn't me!"

"You expect me to believe that? After you told both me and Jack that you'd be obligated by law to contact them if you believed there was abuse going on? You just couldn't wait to exercise that obligation, could you?"

He shook his head over and over. "It was not me, nor anyone I know," he insisted. "I told Jack I wanted to refer your family to LDS Social Services for counseling. I know I mentioned that I might be forced to contact the authorities, but I wasn't ready to do that, and I promise you I did not. Please believe me, Melody! It must have come from somebody else who saw your situation. I've been awfully concerned for you, as you know, but I haven't believed that Andi was in any imminent physical danger from Jack."

Melody shook her head, tears beginning to form and run down her cheeks. "He's never hit her. Not ever."

"And I felt the other night that Jack and I were beginning to reach an understanding. I was hopeful, not desperate! I haven't even talked to my counselors about the situation. This didn't come from me, truly. As far as I know, it didn't come from anybody in the Church."

Who had it been? he wondered. *The day care lady? An observant neighbor?*

Melody's tears were falling fast, and she edged around the chair and sat down, pushing her bag to the floor. The bishop leaned forward and grasped her hands in his.

"I'm sorry this happened, Melody. So sorry."

"They didn't even let me give her her bear," she repeated, her voice squeaking with tearful indignation. "What harm could that do? I think *they* were abusive!"

He shook his head in confusion. "Hopefully she'll be home soon. I probably don't have any clout, but I'll look into the situation for you if you want. You do believe, now, don't you that I didn't call them in?"

"I guess. I don't know. What'll happen to Jack? What if his company hears about this?"

He shook his head. "I don't know, but I'll go to bat for him, too. I really do believe he can get past his problems. I think he just hasn't known how to stop. But I believe in repentance, and in change. I mean, what point would there be to the gospel of Christ, if people couldn't change, and improve? That's what the Atonement's all about."

Melody sniffed and nodded. "I hope he can. I hope they'll let him." Then a fresh flood of tears fell. "It's my fault, isn't it? I should've told somebody a long time ago, before things got to this point."

"I wish you had, just for your own safety and well-being, but listen—none of this is your fault. Nothing you did should have provoked Jack to the kind of behavior he's been spiraling into. The problem is within him, and it's something he needs help overcoming. It's not your fault at all."

"Are you—are you sure?"

"Sure as I can be."

"Bishop, I'm sorry. I felt so . . . so betrayed, when I thought you'd sent the law after us. I know Jack has a bad problem, a serious one—but he's not bad, clear through. There's a lot of good in him."

"I know there is."

"Then you'll still help us?"

"I'll do my best. And if we all do our best, the Lord will do the rest."

She stood up shakily. "I'm going home now, to see if Jack's back, or if anybody's called."

"Listen—why don't you come over and have dinner with us, about three?"

She shook her head. "Thanks, but I can't. I can't bear to look at happy people—families—right now."

"I understand. Call me, then, as soon as you hear anything."

"Okay."

"And, Melody? I'm not going to look for another Primary teacher."

She nodded, tears starting again as she picked up her bag and left.

Υ

He gripped Trish's hand in his and then tucked it into the crook of his arm so that she was even closer to him as they slowly paced the uneven sidewalks of their neighborhood that evening. Honeyed sunlight spilled along the streets, pouring between the trees and houses in sharp contrast to the deep patches of shade.

"Sunshine and shadows—that's life, I guess, isn't it?" Trish commented. "Trite, but true."

"M-hmm," he agreed, trying to live in the moment, trying not to think about anything except the warmth of the sun on his shoulders or the sweet smell of honeysuckle on a neighbor's fence. He'd had enough of shadows for one day. He hadn't yet told Trish about the Jernigans' little daughter, nor about Jack and Andi Padgett being taken into custody. He would—perhaps even later tonight—but for now he didn't want to add any shadows to her sunshine.

"Evening, Miz Hestelle," he said as they finished their rounds and neared their home again.

"Hello there, neighbors! How're you folks doin'?"

He felt Trish's hand tighten on his arm. "We're doing great," she answered, before he could say a word. "We're doing just fine, and how are you? You're looking good."

"Well, I . . ." Mrs. Hestelle Pierce put up a hand to smooth her graying hair back from her face. "I do believe I'm feeling as well as ever I have, now that you ask."

"That's wonderful. Have a good evening now," Trish said.

"Good night," the bishop added, as Trish pulled him firmly

toward their gate. She gave him a look that plainly said, "See? That's how you do it."

"Positive suggestion," he murmured.

"Exactly. Much better than negative."

"I'll have to keep that in mind. I love you, Mrs. Bishop Shepherd."

She wrinkled her nose at him. "I guess it's not so bad, being the bishop's wife."

He kissed her lightly. "Got to admit, there are times when it's not so bad, being the bishop."